MW00780574

Bluebonnet
Days

Ali Marie

Copyright © 2022 by Ali Marie

All rights reserved. No part of this publication may be reproduced, distributed, or transmitted in any form or by any means, including photocopying, recording, or other electronic or mechanical methods, without the prior written permission of the publisher, except in the case of brief quotations embodied in critical reviews and certain other noncommercial uses permitted by copyright law.

Book Design by HMDpublishing

This book is dedicated to all the moms that have a dream to be more. To the women who want it all and keep pushing forward.

To Love. May it always find away

Prologue

Since I can remember, he's always been by my side, picking me up when I fell and never allowing anyone—not even my own brother—to pick on me. He even went as my date to high school dances when I didn't have one. How could I not fall in love with the one constant in my life who always wanted me to just be myself and made me feel like the most beautiful girl in his world? How do you let memories and feelings like that go?

Now, here I am staring at this sunset painting as the blended colors of pink, orange, and red seem to reel me back in to that specific moment in time where everything changed. That moment, that whole summer, is forever embedded in my heart. I can still smell the field of flowers mixed with his musk while he gently caressed my skin, whispering in my ear how much he loved me as we made plans for the future.

It was a hot evening in May when I wandered through the field of bluebonnets, taking in the sunset behind the barn, and reflecting on another year over and how both my brother and my number-one crush would be heading off to college in a few months. I had another year left, but the feeling of everything about to change rushed over me like a cold wave. I hugged myself. It felt like the temperature had dropped twenty degrees, even though it was clearly still a hot, humid one hundred degrees outside.

"Hey there, beautiful!"

I spun around quickly, faced with my crush. "Oh, hi! What are you doing out here? Shouldn't you be in the barn partying over your new freedom?" Even though I'd grown up around him, it never failed that my heart would race and my body would heat up when he was near.

"Actually, I was coming to get you," he said. "To join in on the fun."

In my daze, he had moved even closer to me. He brought his hand up to my face and pushed strands of my hair back behind my ear.

"Oh, really? Me?" I swallowed hard and tried to look up, only to meet his gaze and then look down at my feet again.

He grabbed my chin and tilted my face up to look at his. "Samantha, I need you to look at me. I have something to say. First, I will admit that yes, I have been drinking, but only to get the liquid courage to say what I need to say to you. Please don't hold that against me, okay?" Holding out his hand, he made me old-school pinky swear.

"Um, the last time you made me pinky swear, you walked in on me in the shower and didn't want my brother to find out because he would've killed you." I laughed. "What did you do now?"

"Ha! I remember that. It was a very defining moment for me." Taking my hands in his, he took take a deep breath, "Samantha Jane, I love you . . . Before you panic, just know my heart has only ever belonged to you all these years. No girl I've dated could ever replace you."

"What?....Why are you telling me this now? Are you crazy? Wait, you are drunk, so never mind. I'm going to leave and forget we ever had this conversation. See you in the morning."

As I started to walk off, he grabbed my arm, pulling me back into his chest, and kissed me. Kissed me so passionately, I lost all my senses, melting into him. I had only dreamt of this my entire young adult existence. Needing air, my senses flood, and I pull back from him.

"Sam, that was incredible," he whispered with his forehead pressed against mine. "I've been wanting to do that for so long. Tell me you have no feelings for me, and I'll leave you alone. Tell me you love me, too, and I'll be with you and protect you always."

"You have to already know how I feel about you, so I don't understand why you've waited this long to say anything to me. This isn't fair. Everyone has always known how I feel about you. I've always been the sad, pathetic sister in love with her brother's best friend."

Thinking back, I still can't believe I let myself cry in front of him then. I wanted to run away so badly.

"Sam, you are far from sad and pathetic." He glided his hand against my cheek. "It may not be great timing, but I want to—I *need* to tell you now—so we can have the summer to be with each other before I leave. Plus, I promised your brother I wouldn't come for you until you'd graduated high school. But he knows I can't hold myself back from you any longer. So, we are here now, and it's you I want in every way. Please say yes, Sam."

"When have I ever been able to say no to you?" I wrapped my arms around him, and he picked me up and twirled me around. We soon found ourselves on the ground, rolling in the bluebonnets. The sun had completely disappeared, and we were surrounded by lightning bugs dancing around us.

We spent many summer evenings like that.

I place my fingers on my lips, and I can still feel and taste his mouth on mine.

A door slamming behind me brings me back to reality, and I shake my head. "Snap out of it, Sam," I tell myself. "He's gone, and you're on the other side of the world. You need to get a grip and move on. That's what this whole trip is for."

Walking out of the museum, I head to the airport to leave Spain and head on to my next destination.

Contents

Prologue...4

1. Home At Last..9
2. Why Is He Here? 11
3. Alter Ego 15
4. Beach Party 21
5. Give Thanks 27
6. Paris..29
7. Family Secrets 34
8. Workday 38
9. Guess Who 41
10. Day 2 43
11. Wednesday Blues 48
12. Family Dinner 51
13. Whiskey Girl 57
14. Confession...63
15. Forget-Me-Nots 71
16. Not a Date..76
17. Sneaky Man..81
18. The River..88
19. No Turning Back...94
20. The New Normal..97
21. Something New, Something Old 104
22. Not Giving Up 109
23. Not All News Is Good News 113
24. Men Hiding 124
25. Family Announcement 132
26. All in the News...137
27. Who Is He? 143
28. Not Meant to Be 148
29. Someone Needs to be Afraid 152

30. Why Not Be Irish 157

31. Many a New Day 163

32. Nightmare in Egypt 166

33. Getting Fancy 171

34. Respect 177

35. Let That Pony Run 182

36. The Gala 185

37. Texas Heat and Gatherings 190

38. An Old Flame 194

39. Track (Her) 198

40. Awaken 201

41. Ruined 206

42. Kissing You 213

43. Felt Too Real 220

44. To Do or Not to Do.. 224

45. Seriously, Again? 228

46. Rehearsal Dinner 235

47. The Dress.. 240

48. It Is Time 244

49. The Reception 248

50. A Perfect Day 254

51. Sunrise to Sunset.. 258

52. A Piece of Me 263

53. Catching Up.. 266

54. Welcome Home 270

55. Growing Pains... 274

56. Graduation 277

Epilogue: 281

CHAPTER 1:
Home At Last

*H*eading home. It had been about five years since I'd been back to the ranch, let alone stepped foot back in this state. I was blessed to be able to travel after I graduated high school, and I completed my studies abroad and online. My parents fortunately understood the need for me to get away when the last half of my senior year became a shattered mess due to a broken heart. Everyone seemed to understand that this wasn't an ordinary high school crush but heartbreak from the one guy it was least expected from. The closer I got to home, the more my anxiety increased, and I prayed I'd find the courage to push through what was ahead.

My phone rang, interrupting my thoughts. It was my best friend, Mia.

"Hello?"

"Sam, how much longer until you're here? I swear you're driving below the speed limit and taking your sweet-ass time."

"Funny, Mia. I'm about forty minutes out now and just enjoying the view. Bluebonnets are in full bloom. Are you at the house already?"

"Yes! Everyone's here, and there's a special surprise."

"Mia, you know I hate surprises. Can't you just tell me before I get there?"

"Absolutely not. Anyway, I know I've been fortunate to see you throughout the years, but everyone's excited to see you, so hurry up."

"All right, fine. See you in a bit."

I just loved that time of year growing up in Alice, Texas. When school was out, I'd run wild as a kid through the fields. My first kiss even happened in a field of bluebonnets and carried many memories in between—until my heart was broken by that same boy.

Weston Lancaster . . . my one and only love.

We had basically been around each other since the day I entered this world. He was two years older than me, and he was my brother's best friend. Our dads were business partners, and our moms were best friends. They owned the Heart of Kings Cattle Ranch, the lead producer of the best beef in the central through the southeast states. The ranch had been owned by my family, the Duponts, and the Lancasters for over eighty-six years. Our grandfathers created the ranch and passed it down to their sons with the hope that it would be passed on through generations. Though the Lancasters had Lans Enterprises, they still played a large role with the ranch. The ranch was truly my daddy's passion, as he never wanted to venture into any other business. Both of our family's homes were on this property, and they had several other properties that housed the cattle. The property also housed horses and top-breeding steers that kept the line strong and healthy.

As I pulled through the large, black iron gates, I made my way down the long shaded driveway, and the large white farmhouse peeked through the desert willow trees. I took in deep breaths. I had to come home because Daddy said he needed me for the business and that it was time for me to take my place there at the ranch. He wanted to secure the future of the place, of the legacy.

CHAPTER 2:
Why Is He Here?

Taking one last deep breath, I climbed out of my car and started to walk up the steps. As I was about to reach for the handle, the rustic, French-like doors burst open.

My mama squealed, "Samantha!"

I was greeted by my parents with warm hugs and kisses, making me realize how much I'd missed them over the years. Sure, I saw them a few times. Daddy visited me two years before in Wyoming for a rodeo, and Mama visited me while I was abroad in Europe, though nothing compared to being at home with them.

After letting them know I could no longer breathe, they finally let go of me, and I began taking in everyone around the room.

My brother, Jackson, ran to me and picked me up, twirling me around. He had grown up into a nice-looking, rugged cowboy, and his fiancée, Lucey, only complimented him even more with her soft face, dirty blonde hair, and blue eyes. I'd always liked her, so I was elated to hear the news that they were finally together, then engaged to be wed the following November.

Jackson went to the University of Texas to study agriculture, so he had basically taken over much of the workload from Daddy and Mr. Lancaster. In that day and age, being a ranch owner with cowboys, ranch hands, and cattle didn't promise security for the future, and they both wanted to make sure all of their kids were fully knowledgeable in ranch ownership.

Mia punched Jackson to put me down so she could wrap her arms around me. It had been over a year since I saw her in person, and she got more beautiful every time I saw her. She had haunting green eyes and shoulder-length, dark brown hair, and a uniquely seamless face, plus a body all the ladies envied. I could've hugged her forever.

Family and friends gathered around me, including my white lab, Maddox. He jumped up on me and covered me with slobbery kisses, then I rolled him over and rubbed his belly while I chatted with the others.

All of a sudden, a rushed voice called out. "I'm here! I'm here! Did I make it?" A girl about my age appeared in the doorway, and the house went quiet as everyone stared at her and her face flushed red.

Then, out of nowhere, *he* stepped out from the corner. My breath hitched. Five years later, I was standing in the same room as Weston. His head was down, and I thought he was walking towards me, but he grabbed the girl's arm and whispered something in her ear.

I saw Mia's face fall, and I was speechless.

Oh, no. Now he's walking towards me.

Weston was wearing clothes that fit nicely in all the right places: black slacks, a sky-blue button-up shirt, and he topped it off with a black cowboy hat—everything that complemented his dark features even more. And those intense ocean blue eyes that kept staring at me. The closer he got, the weaker I became, and the smell of his cologne flooded my brain with memories of our last summer together.

Girl, get it together, I thought.

And soon enough, he was standing right in front of me, leaning in to hug me tightly. He kissed me on the cheek, then whispered in my ear, "Look how grown up you are now. And even more beautiful. I've really missed you."

Oh, God. Not now.

I felt like I might fall over dead as heat coursed through my body, and I blushed in front of everyone. I closed my eyes and told myself again that now was not the time.

I opened my eyes and smiled. "I hope everything's been good for you over the years."

As we're standing awkwardly and staring at each other, we hear, "Mm-hmm."

The woman reaches out her hand. "Hi, I'm Laura Belle, Weston's girlfriend."

I felt like the whole room was holding their breath in unison and watching me to see what might happen next.

I shook her hand. "Pleased to meet you, Laura . . . Belle. I'm Samantha."

"Oh, yes! I've heard so much about you from Weston and the family. Seems like y'all are a tight-knit group. Practically brother and sister, right?"

Green jealousy showed in her brown eyes, and I was unsure if she was trying to convince herself of that or threatening me.

Through a smile, all I could spit out was, "Practically." I looked back at Weston in hopes that he couldn't read the disappointment in my eyes.

He smiled awkwardly and looked away.

Mia saved me by grabbing my hand and pulling me outside to the porch. "Surprise!"

I glared at her. "Dammit, Mia. I thought he was on a business trip and that I wouldn't have to deal with him head-on. And where was the fair warning about *her*?"

"I promise, Sam, I had no idea she would be here. I found out last night that Weston was staying in town to welcome you home and would be heading out on Monday. Miss Southern Belle was not supposed to be here, so I thought we had time for him or myself to prepare you about her. But lo and behold, here she is. They've only been dating for six months and have only been out here a handful of times. None of us like her any more than she likes being here. But she has her hooks in Weston somehow."

"Oh, Mia. Even after five years of not seeing or speaking to him, my heart still aches for him. I wasn't prepared to see him today, but it looks like he's moved on."

Unfortunately, moving on for me hadn't been easy. I dated a few men over the years during my travels, but at times it felt as though I only wanted a companion to share things with, or maybe I just needed to be wanted. First, I ended up in Spain with Marco for some Latin experience, then I was wooed by Esteban in Paris for about six months until I decided to move on across Europe.

Then there was Noah in Australia. He almost had me. Blond hair, blue eyes—the kind of guy you see in the surfing magazines. Well, maybe because he was in them since he was a competitive surfer. He also volunteered as a firefighter and at the animal refuge, *(awe, right?)* which is where we met. Outside of him traveling for competitions, we were inseparable. I knew he wasn't the one when I was asked to join Colonial Corp full time back in the States. I wasn't sad about leaving. Eight months in, I was ready for a change—ready to be Stateside. Noah even offered to follow me, but I convinced him that he needed to focus on his career and that we'd keep in touch.

In the end, though, none of them were Weston. I guess I'd been holding onto some hope he would show up where I was or call me to apologize, confessing his feelings for me. But over those last five years, all I received was a few texts asking how I was doing or financial questions related to the ranch.

Time really does not heal the heart.

CHAPTER 3:
Alter Ego

Mia kept looking at me to see if I was okay.

"Mia, I'll be fine. I *am* fine. I'm home now, and I knew this wasn't going to be easy. My family needs me, and they're expecting me to lay roots here. I guess it's time to join the local dating scene. Or maybe I'll just end up being a spinster."

Laughing, we both head back to the party to mingle.

Several more hours of chatting went by—and several glasses of wine—and exhaustion started taking over. It was already nine p.m. on a Friday night, and it had been a two-day drive from Montana. Bed was calling my name, so I made one more pass through to say good night.

I walked out on the back porch to find my family and the Lancasters talking. I was about to ask if Weston had already left, only to see him walking through the screen porch door. His parents asked him where Laura Belle was.

"Oh, I took her back to her hotel. She complained she was jet-lagged after her flight from Georgia."

We all kind of smirked at each other, trying not to laugh over being jet-lagged with a two-hour flight.

Weston then strolled over ever so calmly and put his arm around my waist like it was nothing. Though I tried to pull away, he only held on tighter. I tried not to pay it any attention as we talked about some business and Monday's meetings.

Noticing he'd been pulling me closer in to him, I couldn't help but think, *When did he get this domineering factor about him?*

As I was lost in thought, I felt my phone vibrate. It was a previous client from England, so I quickly excused myself to take the call.

"Hello, Mr. Hughes. How can I help you?"

"Miss Dupont, I heard you officially resigned from Colonial Corp to move back home. Is everything okay? As I remember, you briefly mentioned it, but I recall not taking it seriously. What can I do to make you stay and keep over my accounts?"

"Oh, that's very kind of you to say, but yes, everything's okay. I'd planned to email you and my other clients on Monday, but I had to roll off pretty quickly to get home because of some projects the ranch needs my help with. I promise, though, you're in great hands with Johnathan and Stacy. I went over everything in extreme detail with them."

"Well, Miss Dupont, I'm quite disappointed. I'll give those two a chance, but I can't promise that I won't reach out with concerns in the future. Oh, hell, I might even let you personally take on my accounts on your own."

"I'm happy to help in any way I can."

"I guess that also means you won't be coming over the pond in August. I was hoping to introduce you to my nephew. You two would be a very distinguished match."

"Well, thank you again for the kind words. I won't be there in August, but I hope to vacation there within the year. As far as your nephew goes, I wish him the best. I'm not looking to settle down or even date anytime soon, but thanks for considering me. That means a lot, as you've always treated me like family."

"Of course, Miss Dupont. My family adores you, and you've made me quite a bit of money. I'll let you go now. Good night."

After I hung up, I stared at my phone. I really loved my job and clients at Colonial Corp back in Montana and being able to travel to my clients. During the last year, I began working part-time for the ranch.

My Aunt Patsy was running most of it while I was off traveling and getting my degrees and real-world experience, but she'd recently decided to fully retire by the end of summer. So, I was beckoned home to fulfill my family duty. Even after being back for several hours, I still couldn't shake the feeling of uneasiness I had prior to arriving.

Weston

She's here. After all these years away, my Sam is finally back home.

I was supposed to be away on a business trip to New York that week before heading out to Oklahoma, but I couldn't miss welcoming her home, whether she wanted to see me or not. As I hid out in the corner of her parents' house, away from the crowd, I caught a glimpse of her as she walked in. Just catching that slight view of her made my mind and body go wild.

Get it together, Wes, I told myself.

I saw my father and mom eyeing me from the other side of the crowd, both trying to read my facial expression. I gave them a smile, as I'd decided earlier to hang back behind the crowd in hopes of catching her alone.

But I was quickly pulled out of those thoughts . . .

Shit! Why the hell is she *here?*

All of the attention had been pulled off my Sam and onto her—Laura Belle, the girl I couldn't seem to get rid of, no matter how hard I tried.

After walking over to Laura Belle, I quickly grabbed her elbow and whispered in her ear, "Why are you here, LB?"

"Why would I miss the welcoming home of your sister? Am I not family, Weston?"

I sighed. "Laura Belle, we've already discussed this. Our families are business partners, and there can be nothing more between us, no matter how hard you push."

"Oh, whatever, Wes. You know we're destined to be together."

I noticed Sam glaring at me, and I had no choice but to greet her. Adjusting my hat and facial expression, I strutted over to her. My eyes didn't waver from her face, though I admit, I quickly looked over her body. She was breathtaking, her silk caramel colored hair flowing down her back with those few strands that always hung by her cheek. She was wearing short—my God, I mean *short*—jean shorts with a tight, off-the-shoulder cinched top that showed just enough of her stomach to make my lower member burn. Everything showed all her perfect curves.

No one but me should be able to see her body like this. She's making me jealous of everyone here already.

Grinning as I reached her, I kissed her cheek and then tucked those loose strands of hair behind her ear. I leaned in. "You're lookin' great and all grown up now . . . and even more beautiful. I've really missed you."

She flushed as she gazed at me with those deep brown eyes with a hint of emerald green in them. I recalled that green taking over when she was happy and in love . . . when she was with me.

My thoughts were interrupted again by the blonde next to me.

Shit. LB introduced herself and threw the sister card at Sam.

Sam was keeping a straight face, so I was unable to read her thoughts. Before I could defuse the situation before me, Mia had already grabbed Sam's hand to walk off with her.

She must be pissed. This isn't how I planned on welcoming her home today.

Grabbing Laura Belle by the hand, I dragged her out of the Dupont's house. "You have some nerve showing up here today," I said. "Sam just got home and didn't need to be ambushed by some person she doesn't even know."

"*Tsk tsk,* Weston. Why are you so against me meeting her? The way you talk about the Duponts like family, and about Sam, 'the sister you never had.' Why would she *not* want to meet the woman you're dating and soon to marry?"

"There are no nuptials in our future, LB, so let that go. Speaking of which, *you* should go."

"I do feel tired from my flight. Am I staying in my usual room?"

"Um, no. The house is packed with everyone coming in for Sam's party. Let me get you checked in at a hotel in town."

"You are such a gentleman, Weston." She clung to my arm. "Will you be staying with me?"

"No, I need to come back here to help clean up later and be with my family."

"Then I'll just stay with you."

"No need. I can tell you're exhausted," I said as I led her to my truck.

After getting her settled in the hotel and prying her hands off me, I head back to the ranch. Finally, I hoped to see Sam and get some alone time with her.

I heard her voice on the back deck with our parents, and she noticed me as I walked in, but as soon as she made eye contact, she looked away as if ignoring me.

Okay, Sam. I can play this game.

Walking straight over to her, I wrapped my arm around her waist and pulled her close to me. Every time she tried to move, I'd pull her in even closer. A slight breeze blew, causing a trace of her scent to overwhelm my senses. Honeysuckle. I loved how she never strayed from it. My mind began replaying several intimate moments of us together, and it only made me want to pull her in to me more.

I felt a phone vibrating, breaking my thoughts. Sam answered her phone and excused herself, leaving me no choice but to release my grip. She walked off, and as I was about to follow her, my father summoned me over.

"My apologies if Laura Belle's showing up caught you off guard," he said. "I thought she told you."

"Told me what?"

"That we invited her, son. You seem to forget her parents are dear friends of ours, as well as business partners. We all approve of you marrying her."

"You've got to be kidding me. You had the nerve to invite her to Sam's welcoming home party? I'm not going to marry Laura Belle. I broke up with her several months ago, but now I know why she keeps coming around. You!"

"Son, are you really still holding out for Samantha? It's been over five years since you've been with her. You two no longer know each other, so I seriously doubt you can say you still love her. And right now, you need not to piss off Laura Belle and her family until you know for certain what you're going to do. Do you understand me, Weston?"

"Sure, Father, whatever you say."

CHAPTER 4:
Beach Party

The sound of the rooster crowing was not how I intended to be woken up. I'd forgotten about that annoying animal who didn't know when to be quiet and enjoyed chasing me every chance he got.

I was lying in my plush bed, swaddled up in my comforter with my head buried in goose down pillows, and scrolling through social media, when . . .

Bang!

My door flew open, and Jackson ran and jumped on my bed. "Hey, sis."

I threw a pillow at his head. "You're an adult. Have you still not learned how to knock?"

He caught the pillow. "Nope! Anyway, get up, and let's go. Everyone's waiting on us."

"I'm sorry, who? What? Where? I'm still half asleep, and I don't want to move today."

"The whole crew's heading to the beach at Palmetto to hang out. Camping, grilling, bonfire later tonight . . . Wait, have you forgotten our summer tradition?"

"No, of course not. I just didn't realize as adults that it was still happening. Not sure if I'm up for it, though. I need to get settled before Monday. You know Dad . . . He isn't going to let things slide just because I'm 'adjusting' to being back home."

"Ah, come on, Sam. It's your first weekend back after forever. Don't disappoint." He gave me his big green puppy eyes.

"Ugh. Fine. Give me ten."

Jackson rushed out of my room yelling with excitement. Even though he's older, I suspect I was the mature one.

Now, what to wear and bring . . .

Heading into the bathroom, I washed my face and brushed my teeth. It would be a makeup-free day. Not that I wore much most days, but it was a day for water and sun. I dug through my luggage to find my favorite bathing suit—a black bandeau top with matching black bottoms covered in silver lace design. Cute and classy. I threw on my cover-up and put my long hair half back with a clip. As I grabbed a change of clothes for later, I heard my mama say she had my beach bag packed with all the essentials.

I made my way downstairs to hug her. "Thanks, Mama."

"You're welcome, sweetie. Now, y'all don't get too rowdy today, and call if you need anything. Be safe."

"Will do, Mama. Love you."

I walked outside to see Mia already there with some other friends, Dawn and Jenny. The boys had just finished loading up the trucks, so it was time to roll out. I rode with Jackson and Lucey, along with Dawn and her boyfriend. Mia rode with her long-time crush, Dylan, and with Jenny and her new beau. We had about an hour drive, so we sang loudly to some old jams, cracked jokes, and had fun like there was not a care in the world. What I didn't know was that I'd have many things to care about before the day ended.

We finally reached our destination and unloaded the trucks as the boys put up the tents. A large portion of our crew had arrived earlier to stake out the usual area. My travels around the world, fancy dinners, and crazy parties would never compare to the amount of fun this group could have. They were always ready for a good time and didn't seem to miss a beat, even as we reached our mid to late twenties. This group consisted of college graduates, entrepreneurs, those running their family businesses, those who wanted to be CEOs, and some who wanted to live under the luxury of their parents' continued financial support. No matter what, though, we all had mad respect and support for each other, which was probably due to living in a small town.

Once we all are situated, I start catching up with old friends I hadn't seen in some time while also meeting the boyfriends or girlfriends who were new to the group. It was great to finally speak to people instead of keeping up through one of the many social media accounts we had.

After some mingling and a few drinks, Mia, Dylan, and I decided to go paddle-boarding. This was my favorite thing to do in Australia during the early mornings—get out there right when the sun was coming up and the wildlife was out and about, and enjoy the peacefulness before the beaches got crowded.

As I got up and stood on my board, I heard someone call my name.

"Sam! Sam! Over here!"

I scanned the beach only to find her, Miss Laura Belle, waving at me in her skimpy red bathing suit . . . with Weston swimming towards me.

"What the hell?" I shouted to Mia, who just shook her head.

At that point, I lost my concentration and balance, so I started wobbling on my board.

Splash!

I was in and under. Before I could get my bearings to swim up, I felt arms wrap around me and pull me to the surface near my board. I grabbed my board and turned around to see Weston holding me.

"Are you okay?" he asked worriedly as he scanned my body.

"Um, yeah. I just lost my balance. No big deal." I tried hard not to look right into his intoxicating blue eyes. As I turned back around to get on my board, I realized his hands were still clenched to both sides of my waist. He pulled me closer to him, and I could feel his hot breath on my skin. The smell of his aftershave was overwhelming my senses, and my body was heating up. He seemed to sense this and pressed closer to where I could feel him right up against me under the water.

"Why are you blushing, Sam?"

"I'm not. In case you haven't noticed, the sun is out, and my body is readjusting to this Texas heat."

I looked away because I learned years before that he could read me like a book when he looked in my eyes. He always knew me best, which was why it was so hard not knowing or understanding why he did what he did. I finally found my voice again and asked him to let me go so I could pull myself back on my board.

"Oh! Sorry. Old habit of not being able to let you go, I guess."

I was dumbfounded.

Old habit? It had been like five years since he laid his hands on me, let alone seen me. Not to mention the countless girlfriends he had during that time, one of which was swimming over just then.

Before she made it over, I let Mia and Dylan know I was heading in and leaving, ignoring Weston.

Laura Belle wound her arm into Weston's. "Baby, why did you leave me over there alone? You know I'm not comfortable around your friends by myself."

It was too hard to hide my laughter at that point, and I found myself mocking her sophomoric act, but hoping no one heard. I turned to look behind me. Laura Belle was sending me daggers while Dylan was trying to catch Mia from falling off her board because she was laughing so hard. Weston caught me off guard with a Cheshire grin I had never seen before. Oops, I guess they did hear.

Sitting on the beach and catching up with the ladies, a few guys came to sit with us. Two of them I knew belonged to Dawn and Jenny, but the third guy, I had no clue. He sat right next to me and offered his hand. I won't lie—he was pretty darn handsome at six foot two and with a lean but impressive shape, brown eyes, and wavy blond hair that fell a little past his ears. I could tell he was really embracing the summer hair and tan.

"Hi, I'm Richard," he said with a charming smile.

"Hi, Richard, I'm Samantha. But you can call me Sam. So, how do you know this group?"

"I work at the same law firm as Landon but actually knew Dawn before because we're cousins." He chuckled. "So, you can say I'm responsible for those two getting together."

Dawn placed a kiss on Landon's cheek. "Yes, Richard, I truly owe you one."

"Aw, how sweet and cool," I said. "Shows that it truly is a small world."

"Yeah, for real. I mean, speaking of small worlds, Dawn's been telling me you're the OG of this group but have been away traveling for several years."

"That's right. I actually got home yesterday."

Apparently, he'd traveled as well, so we sat there comparing notes and chatting about crazy stories and some of the sites we'd seen along the way. The whole time, though, I felt someone else's gaze.

Weston was out in the water, chilling with some of the other guys. I continued my conversation with Richard, not paying attention to how much time had passed or how many drinks I'd consumed.

Then Richard placed his hand on my arm—just a light touch.

All I could do was smile and look down.

"Hey, Sam, I've enjoyed getting to know you today."

"Yeah, me too."

"Could I possibly take you out one night this week?"

"Oh, um . . ."

Before I could even answer, I heard, "Samantha Jane, come here, now."

"You have got to be kidding me," I exclaimed, turning around to the voice. I stood up and looked at him. "What is your problem?"

"Seriously, you're just going to let some random guy put his hands all over you? Where is your decency?"

"My decency? You're the one causing a scene. This is not some random guy. This is Richard. And in case *you* forgot, you have no say in who I hang out with." I turned to Richard. "I'm so sorry. Let's go over there where it's less crowded." Taking his arm, we began to walk off, but Weston quickly stepped in front of us and threw a punch, taking Richard out.

"You are such a tyrant, Weston Lee! What is wrong with you?"

"You with him is what's wrong with me. You are mine, Samantha Jane. No one else. He obviously must be new in town because everyone else has been warned to stay away from you."

I was astonished by what he said, and we both yelled at each other, causing all attention on us.

"You asshole. What gives you the right to do that? I am not yours, Weston. You let me go a long time ago, and I don't recall you ever coming back for me, either. So, leave me the hell alone."

As I walked off, I heard gossiping around us and the wrestling of guys—including my brother, Jackson—holding him back and telling him to chill out as he yelled out for me. The girls were tending to Richard. Laura Belle was just stood there like she was waiting to hog-tie Weston herself and let him have it. Grabbing a drink from the cooler, I headed into my tent to blow off steam until Mia came and got me.

Later on, the boys started up the grills to cook dinner, and the bonfire was already going before dusk. The ladies were setting up the tables and putting out the dishes and dinnerware. As I looked around, avoiding Weston, I realized that the group had really grown since I'd been gone. We used to only use four picnic tables pushed together, but we now had two rows of five tables.

I sat down between Mia and Lucey. Dylan was on the side of Mia, and Jackson was on the other side of Lucey, and the other friends surrounded us. Dawn and Jenny sat across from us with their boyfriends and Richard.

I gave him a small smile and mouthed, "I am so sorry."

He told me it was okay and totally worth it.

Oh, boy. This could be more trouble than I signed up for.

CHAPTER 5:
Give Thanks

Dylan caught my attention by making a toast and reminding us of the rules of the "Thanks" game. Each person would say what they're currently most thankful for. We would all then cheer and take a drink. Simple as that. Before we got started, Jackson led us into the dinner blessing and ending with "Cheers to Sam finally coming home!" Everyone clinked their glasses and yelled, "Cheers!"

The game begins with Mia. "I am so thankful my bestie is finally home and home to stay. No more worldwide adventures, Sam, unless you take me with you."

"Cheers!" from everyone, and we clinked our cups.

It was my turn. "I'm thankful to be able to come home to this, to y'all. I'm blessed to have friends around the world, but no one compares to this crew right here that I consider family."

We kept it moving around the tables, and I realized this had become one long, intense drinking game. But at the same time, I loved seeing how happy and blessed everyone seemed to be. Finally, the game was coming to an end. Last up was Weston and Laura Belle.

Weston got up, nodding with his cup held high. "I'm thankful for new business opportunities on the rise at the ranch and Lans, as well. Also, I'm thankful for the moments we can find to lead us back to face our past so we can continue on in the future." He looked intensely at me.

Again, what was that supposed to mean? This man had a way with his words lately, and I wasn't quite sure what to think of him now that he'd become so outspoken and had this domineering aura about him. My thoughts were cut off by the cheers.

Lastly, Laura Belle stood up to speak.

This should be good.

"Hi, everybody. Thanks for having me. I would like to give thanks to my Weston, who I just love so dearly and cannot wait to set a date for our wedding with." She leaned over to kiss him.

Whoa. I didn't see that coming, and judging by the crickets in the background, no one else did, either.

My brother, Jackson, broke the silence. "Bro, why didn't you tell me?" he said through a laugh. "I'm just giving you a hard time. Seriously, congrats to you both. If she makes you happy, then we're happy for you. Cheers!"

All I could do was turn around and shove food in my mouth, then chase it with wine.

Mia felt my legs shaking under the table and took my hand. "You okay? Want to leave?"

"No, I'll be fine."

All I wanted was a no-Weston weekend, but this was way left field, even for him.

He held me so close to him just last night.

CHAPTER 6:

Paris

As we were finishing up, I couldn't help but feel a pair of eyes burning into my soul. I had Mia check for me, but she said everyone was lost in conversation, and she didn't notice anything weird.

Dinner was over, so after cleaning up, I went to change into some shorts and my favorite oversize sweatshirt. Everyone was hanging out around the bonfire, so I decided to clear my mind and take a walk down by the water to the jetties for a bit. I carefully walked out as far I could on the rocks without getting splashed by the waves.

"Can I join you?"

I slowly turned around because I knew that voice.

"Sure, they're public rocks. I can't stop you."

Weston chuckled and gave me his dashing smirk.

All I could think about was guarding my heart and wondering why he kept coming around me. He left me! His choice! And now he's engaged.

He sat right next to me as we both looked out into the dark horizon.

I broke the awkward silence. "Won't your fiancée be upset with you sitting here with me?"

"Nah, she passed out in the tent. Too much sun, and she's a lightweight. By the way, to clear the air, we're not engaged. I'm not sure why she felt she needed to say that."

"Weston, you don't have to cover it up. Whatever makes you happy is what everyone wants, right? That's how it's always been." Words came out before I could even stop myself. He now possessed an angry frown and grabbed my chin, making me look at him.

I tried to pull it back, but I was no match for him.

"Samantha, can you really say that to me? I'm being honest. We're not engaged, and I do not love her, nor am I with her. I've been trying to shake her for a while now, but she keeps showing up. She also seems to be very jealous of you, which has been quite amusing to watch."

"I'm so glad we can put this show on for you. But I'm not jealous of her. Besides, you're the one who seemed to be quite jealous earlier."

He turned my head back to look at him, and we locked eyes.

Dammit.

"I know when you're lying, Sam. You should know better than that."

"Whatever, Weston. Think what you want. I'm not sure we still have that connection. Just go do whatever you need to do or want to do, but leave me out of it. I'm going to bed, and I'll plan on seeing you in the office when you get back next week."

I got up and walked as quickly as I could off the rocks without falling. I make it on flat ground only to be pulled by him and pressed up against a tree.

"Sam, we need to talk."

"About what, Weston? We've both been drinking, and it's late. I just want to go to sleep."

As he glided his hand softy down my cheek, "but I need to tell you everything that happened. I know I hurt you, Sam, and I've never forgiven myself for what I did to you. When I heard you were leaving, I wanted nothing more than to come home and talk you out of it, but I couldn't."

"This is the conversation I'm not ready for, Weston. Not here, and not now. You need to let go of me. You shattered me before, and I won't let that happen again. I don't think I want to know your stupid excuses. I'm not sure I can bear it. Please, just let me be."

Wiggling out between him and the tree, I started walking away again, trying to keep him from seeing me cry.

"I went to Paris to find you after I graduated."

I stopped dead in my tracks and slowly turned to look at him as he ran his hand through his thick, jet-black hair. "Don't lie to me, Weston Lee."

I rushed towards him, and feeling overwhelmed with hurt and anger, my hand slapped his cheek. I looked at him with no remorse, and stunned, his eyes turned a dark blue. I'd been wanting to do that for a long time.

Before I could turn away, he picked me up, wrapping my legs around his waist, and pushed me up against the tree again. I couldn't even speak as his mouth smothered mine. I started to cry, hitting his back with my fists and wanting him to let me go.

My heart can't take this.

His lips finally separated from mine as he realized the distress I was in. He put me down. "I'm sorry, Sam. For everything. I've missed and wanted you for so long, and it's hard for me to control myself around you—to not be near you when I see you. Please give me the chance to explain, and then make up your mind about me . . . about us."

"There's not going to be an *us* ever again," I said, gritting my teeth.

Still trying to catch my breath, I stared at him. My heart was aching all over again, and I was unsure what else to say or do. I didn't trust myself to stay there at that moment, so I turned to walk away, back to my tent, and cried myself to sleep.

Weston

What a freaking day. Sam is pissed off at me, and I still can't believe she slapped me. Well, maybe I can, but does her anger prove she still has feelings for me? I think so. What about me, though? I have to sit back and watch her flirt with other guys in front of me. That guy deserved to be punched. They should all know by now that Samantha is off-limits—that no one can touch or speak to her.

I turned from my spot at the jetties when I heard someone approaching. My heart dropped when I saw Jackson instead of Sam.

"Hey, bro," he said, tossing me a beer.

"Hey, man."

"Bro, you, all right? It's been a long time since I've seen you take someone out, and that was after . . .well, you know when you came back from your dad's mission trip."

"Yeah, I'm fine. Besides, he deserved it. He was touching Sam."

"I get it, Wes. She's my sis. But you have to give her space or find a better way to approach her. It obviously shows she's not over what happened back then. You know you never shared all the details about what happened to you. Not that I want you to divulge if you're not ready, but bro, you really had all of us worried. You disappeared for weeks and came back looking like death. Then you disappeared for another month, only to show back up, fit to be a Marine . . . along with some serious anger issues. I guess I just want to make sure *that* Weston isn't about to make an appearance again."

"Well, I'm still not sure I'm ready to talk about it. Just know that my father is not who he seems to be and has been part of some pretty shady shit. It just so happened that I got caught in the crosshairs of it all, and I was used as a bargaining chip against him. Needless to say, it took my father longer than I expected to agree to the terms to get his own son back."

"Shit, man. I figured it had to do with the behind-the-scenes dealings of Lans, but damn. Sorry."

"No pity needed here, but thanks. I moved on past it, and now I have my mind on other things...... Dammit! I hate that I have to leave tomorrow. Let alone, LB being here has only made matters worse. I'm putting that woman on the first flight back to Georgia tomorrow morning and telling her parents to keep her there. That there is no arranged marriage between us."

"Oh, so that's what LB thinks is going on? And she wanted to throw it in Sam's face. Not cool, man. Glad to know you've not truly lost it, though. We were all shocked after that announcement earlier."

"You and I both, bro. This whole weekend has been a mess when I'm just trying to talk to Sam."

"Just give her some time. Let her settle in this week, and give her time to readjust with life at home. She's been through a lot, but I believe in you both. She'll eventually give in to the Lancaster charm."

"Thanks for the pep talk. Guess it's time to head to bed if I plan on heading out early."

We walked back over to the campsite, and I stopped in front of Sam's tent. I watched Jackson go into his tent with Lucey, then I leaned down to slightly unzip Sam's tent. She looked so innocent while sleeping, and maybe she was sleeping well after releasing some anger on my face. Quietly unzipping her tent all the way, I snuck in and just watched her breathe for a little while.

When I saw the sun wanting to come up, I knew it was time to leave her tent. I kissed her cheek and whispered in her ear, "There is no end for us, Samantha. You are only mine."

CHAPTER 7:
Family Secrets

The next morning, I woke up early to start packing. I needed to head home and settle in so I could be ready for work the following day. Looking across the way, I noticed both Weston's tent and truck were gone. Then I heard some rustling, only to catch Mia sneaking out of Dylan's tent.

I smiled. "You owe me details later."

Mia laughed. "Yeah, I know. But only in exchange for details on what happened to you last night."

"Ugh. It'll have to be later once I process everything myself."

Eventually, we load everything up and head home. It was a quiet ride, as most everyone slept, but I couldn't, so I kept Jackson company as he drove. He said Weston wanted him to tell me he'd be back on Wednesday.

"Oh, got it," I said. "Is there something I need to prepare for a meeting? I'm not sure why I need to know this. I thought I'd already accounted for all of my upcoming meetings this week."

"Come on, Sam. You know it's not business related. He just wants to talk to you. He sent Southern Belle home this morning with the hopes of her not returning again."

"Well, I hope he's happy with that decision. But I don't know why you're looking at me—like it was my doing."

"That's not what I am getting at. I just wanted to keep you in the loop. You weren't the only one who suffered when he didn't come back home. Wes also went through some crazy shit while you were away. I still don't know all the details, but I remember thinking, someone found a way to break this man. It might be why you're having to deal with his tough side demeanor these days. Even so, though he is my best friend, like my brother, in the end, you are my sister. I will have your back. But our parents have always taught us to listen to all sides before making a final decision."

I gave him a side glance, curious to know behind what Jackson just stated. "All right. I'll think about it."

It was about noon when we got home, and Mama had egg salad sandwiches with homemade chips and sweet tea ready for us. Jackson and I caught her up on the day before—of course, leaving Weston out of it. Though she did ask how it was seeing him again. I could only manage to say that it was fine. I hurriedly finished my lunch and went up to my room to shower.

When I came out, I heard some people talking outside. Quickly getting dressed, I walked over to my window and pulled the curtains back. The rooms on the corners of the house had large panoramic windows, and mine looked over the pastures and stables, with rolling hills in the background. I could see Weston talking to my daddy.

Weird. I thought he already left.

I turned my ear back to the window to eavesdrop.

"I'm sorry, Weston, give her time. I hope in the interim you can forgive your father. It's been many years, and he feels awful about it. I agree, his methods were quite unorthodox, but he just wanted the best for you and to see you succeed."

"Thanks, Mr. Dupont. Well, I'm about to head out to Tulsa to close that deal with the Annex Farmers Market. It's a great deal for both sides. Hopefully, this will push us into more market opportunities since more and more people are wanting to shop local and fresh. As we expand in Oklahoma, have we thought about the land we need to purchase and who's going to control that territory?"

"Yes, this is an exciting deal, for sure. I wish we had more of you and Jackson to help run it over there. I might have to look into pulling in a cousin or two to see who's willing to make the move. I know that's hard when we're all so close."

"Well, let me feel around and see if there's anyone trustworthy and willing to take over who's out there already. I know we typically don't bring in outsiders, but the more we grow, the more we'll need to lean on this."

"I agree, son. Some changes might be inevitable. All right, you have a good trip, and we'll see you Wednesday."

"Will do. Bye, sir."

It sounded like business was going as well as I thought, so that was a plus. But what was that about giving "her" more time? Was that about me? And I didn't realize there were issues with Weston and his father. He had always been a stern man and expected a lot out of Weston and his little sister, but I always thought he was gentle, as well. Mrs. Lancaster was as sweet as they come. Even when she spoke poorly of someone, it still sounded like a compliment.

I was now curious to find out what had been going on since I'd been gone. As a dual family business, there wasn't much room for animosity amongst us. There had been arguments throughout the years, but everyone always made peace and moved on. My understanding was that Weston didn't come home much while he was off in college.

All of our duties had been planned out for us before we could make a choice, and Weston was to become the family and the ranch's lawyer and take over Lans Enterprise. I know we used to talk about how much pressure Weston was under and that going to an in-state school wasn't good enough for his dad. His sights were set on Weston attending Yale and becoming a lawyer with a minor in business. Though Weston received a full ride to Texas between academics, football, and debate team, having a prestigious lawyer in the family from Yale was what his dad wanted. So, Weston complied. Though I don't think any of us would think that him going away would be the wave that caused the rippling effect. I'd ask Mama or Jackson about what happened while I was gone.

It was Sunday evening, and we'd just finished the traditional Sunday dinner, ending with chocolate and pecan pies. The five of us were still chatting it up around the table when we realized it was getting late. Daddy reminded Jackson and me that the following day would be busy getting me caught up on everything.

I turned to Daddy, who had his arms wrapped around Mama. He loved her, and even after almost thirty years, together he still would've moved Heaven and Earth for her. I can see he'd lost weight and looked more haggard than when I saw him two years prior, but I push it off that there must be a lot going on—and that if something was really going on, Jackson would know and tell me.

I hugged and kissed everyone good night, then headed to bed. Every time I closed my eyes, though, I saw Weston and scenes from the previous night replaying in my head. He said he came to Paris to find me. When and how? I never saw him. And why didn't he contact me?

CHAPTER 8:

Workday

*M*onday in the office on the property started promptly at eight a.m. The grandfathers had turned one of the old barns into an office. As soon as we open the barn doors, we're greeted by hardwood floors, marble countertops, several meeting rooms, and offices, as well as a loft turned into an open breakroom, all equipped with water and electricity. There were top-of-the-line computers and a large TV that always played the news.

The first meeting of the day was to touch base and determine what was going on and who was needed where. I met with Aunt Patsy so she could get me caught up on all the financials, spreadsheets, and charts. Though I was part-time for the last year, I still found it astonishing how we had two ways of doing the same thing and how she stayed organized.

By the end of the day, I had begun to move all her information to the format I used for years and which was highly useful at Colonial when dealing with multiple accounts for the same client. Aunt Patsy didn't seem to care—she was just seeing the light at the end of the tunnel.

"Oh, my darling niece, I might even retire before the end of June at this rate."

"We'll see, Auntie. I might need you to remain available on speed dial."

We laughed as we made our way out of the office barn.

It was about 5:30 p.m., and I saw the ranchmen finishing up for the day as they headed to their house to get washed up and ready for dinner. I did notice my dad riding his horse, Chance, with the guys. I wondered where he was most of the day.

Mama always had the table already set for dinner—pot roast with all the fixin's, rolls, and salad—so I washed up and took my seat next to Jackson. Dad came in, washed up, then sat next to Mama. As we were passing the food around, I asked him what he was doing out on Chance today.

"I was just out helping the guys. One of the bulls got out earlier chasing the heifers we got in. So, we had to wrangle them up before a mess was caused. Remember, never forget your craft and what you were born to do. Getting in the saddle to work hard is where your roots lie—not just sitting in an office all day."

"Yes, Daddy. Be careful out there. I know you're rough and tough, but you're not getting any younger. I know how crazy it can get out there herding cattle, and I know Chance has your back also, but just saying . . ."

He smiled. "Yes, dear. I sure have missed your worrying self around here. Funny how you travel the world on your own like it's nothing but worry the most about your dear old daddy."

"Well, of course. I love you."

I headed up to my room after dinner to send out the emails I'd promised my old manager I would do on Monday. Luckily, we had a template for that sort of thing, though I added a personal touch to it for several of my closest clients.

Weston

I was sitting in my hotel room in Tulsa, wondering what she was doing now. I hated leaving my Sam after the weekend's events. Jackson told me he would put in some good words for me and let her know LB was gone for good. At that point, I would take all the help I could get. It was Monday night, and I was already longing for her. I found ways to suppress that feeling over the years with her gone, but now that she was home, this was going to be a problem. Maybe I could move several meetings to the following day and get home sooner than Wednesday. One less day away from her would be time better spent.

I needed to close the deal out, and we were set in Oklahoma as we expanded across the western states. That would be my last main job to complete for the ranch since becoming VP of Lans Enterprises, and it would take endless hours of my time.

Jackson would be taking over the full reign of the ranch soon, and I'd stay on as their lawyer and business advocate, with Sam handling the back-end of everything. There would be all these changes, plus expanding our cattle and sales across city and state lines, and we were in discussion with the families to pass off a few of my shares to Jackson, since he would be running the roost. Of course, Sam had her own shares, but would also have my shares once she married me, so she'd always be taken care of from a ranch and Lans Enterprises perspective. What's mine would be hers. I could've been jumping the gun on all of it, but the paperwork was already signed and ready to be submitted—once she married me. We would be tied together in every way possible.

Speaking of, maybe I should text her good night, at least, and let her know I'll be home early. It's the perfect excuse to see her. Now to come up with a plan to get her alone so she'll listen to me. I might have to bring Mr. Dupont and Jackson in on a game plan. First, I do need to take Jackson's words to heart from the other night and tone it down. No one truly knows what happened to me for those several weeks I was captured in Egypt by Anhur Maher's men. I rarely have a good night's sleep anymore because of the flashbacks my mind likes to throw my way when it goes dark.

My whole body turned cold, and I shuddered at the mere thought of it all.

CHAPTER 9:
Guess Who

My phone began buzzing like crazy, so I pulled it out to see four text messages. One was from Mia, checking in on me and asking if I wanted to have dinner the following night so we could catch up on our weekend encounters. I texted her back, stating I'd meet her at Mabel's at five p.m. The other three were from Weston. I was unsure if I wanted to read them, so I headed downstairs to grab a glass of wine first. Jackson and Lucey were in the kitchen eating dessert and gawking at me.

"One glass is not enough tonight? Huh, sis?"

Lucey punched him in the shoulder for me.

"Possibly not." I looked back at my phone, puzzled, then tipped my glass back to drink. "Hey, what do you know about Weston and his dad having a falling out while I was away? I can't imagine that actually happening."

They looked at each other with wide eyes, as though I wasn't supposed to notice.

Jackson coughed. "Where did you hear that?"

"I overheard Daddy talking to him Sunday evening about forgiving him, but then they started to talk about business. Just curious. It seems everything was okay with everyone when I got home, and no one has told me about any family drama happening."

"Well, there was an argument, but I'm still not sure what it was about. I'm sure if you ask Weston, he'll tell you."

"Okay. You both know I have a feeling there's more that's gone on around here than anyone lets on. I will find out, and you know I will find out." I pointed to Jackson with a threatening look. "Have a good night!"

After refilling my glass, I went back to my room with my wine and phone, knowing they were hiding something from me. I wasn't going to pry for, now, but maybe I'd ask Weston when he got back.

Looking back at my phone, I opened the text messages.

HELLO, BEAUTIFUL!

HOPE YOUR FIRST DAY BACK IN THE FAMILY BUSINESS WAS GOOD.

I HEARD WE'RE DOING OUR JOINT FAMILY DINNER WEDNESDAY NIGHT. CAN'T WAIT TO SEE YOU.

Was this man trying to drive me crazy? I threw my phone down on the bed and took a sip of my wine. Well, the sip turned into chugging the whole glass.

Well, shit. Now I'm out.

I decided to respond, but I tell myself to make it short and sweet.

Day was good. Safe travels home.

He responded . . .

Sweet Dreams.

I turned my phone off and threw my head into the pillow and screamed. The nerve of him. I made up my mind to talk to him and lay out the rules that we were colleagues and family friends only. I needed boundaries, or I feared I'd end up shattered like years before.

CHAPTER 10:
Day 2

Tuesday came and basically mimicked Monday. At lunch, I checked my personal email and saw several responses from clients. I opened them and began responding. There really were some great ones. Daddy came by to see what I was doing on break and began reading the emails behind me.

"Sounds like they lost a good one, kid. Can't say I blame them for being upset you left. You worked hard to accommodate them, and I know you were close to several."

"Thanks, Daddy. Yeah, crazy how they responded, but I left them all in capable hands."

I opened Mr. Hughes's email. It was a video of Mr. Hughes, his wife Clara, and his daughter Sophie telling me hello and how much they would miss me in August but that they hoped to see me soon. I decided to send them a video later that evening.

I loved their daughter Sophie, who was then eighteen. She was so smart, talented, and funny. We always had a lot of fun together when her dad decided to have crazy business trips in the oddest places. I clicked out of the video and found a photo attachment, and I opened it up to see a photo of a charismatic, handsome guy—tall, olive skin, sandy hair with deep brown eyes. He had a clean, rugged look to him and was in a black-and-white tuxedo. Unsure of who he was, I went back to the email.

MEET MY NEPHEW, NATE. TAKEN AT MY NIECE'S WEDDING LAST WEEKEND. HANDSOME, RIGHT?

My daddy just stared at me in disbelief, and I started laughing. Mr. Hughes really was trying.

"Have you met his nephew before?" he asked.

"No, he was studying abroad in Scotland, and then I know after graduation he went to Singapore for the family business the following year. He must've recently gotten back. They are good people, Daddy, but honestly, I have no interest in men right now. I have work to do here after doing my own thing for several years."

"Okay, honey. I want you to be happy, but I also don't want you disappearing for some guy overseas. We just got you back."

"I won't, Daddy. I promise."

Lunch was over, so I decided to respond to Mr. Hughes's email later. I had some work to finish so I could meet Mia for dinner.

After going through all the folders Aunt Patsy handed me for the day, I told everyone bye and let Dad know I was going out for dinner.

At 5:00 pm, I see Mia strolling up to Mabel's.

"I actually beat you here for once."

She blushed. "I was held up."

I grinned and pushed her into the diner. "Mia Scarlett, what have you been up to?"

She giggled. "We are finally together! You know I've been in love with Dylan for years. We've always flirted and hung out, but nothing serious ever came about. I was starting to think he only liked me as much as he liked his own sisters. So, when you left us out there paddle-boarding and he had to rescue me from falling, he leaned in and kissed me! Eeek! I was in shock, Sam. Because I didn't react right away, he began to apologize and was about to head back in. I knew I had to do something, so I flipped him off his board. When he resurfaced, he asked me what that was for. I just grabbed him and kissed him. I don't know what came over me."

"Good for you, girl! I'm proud of you!"

"Thanks! After a mini make-out session, I told him I'd been waiting a long time for that. He said he wasn't sure about my feelings, but he wanted to make sure the time was right before he tried anything. Dylan said he wanted to wait to be done with college and secure in his career before he was serious with someone. And he was hoping when the time came, I'd still be around."

We both squealed like little girls.

"So, what's next?"

"We're taking our time, finding a routine that works for us with our careers and social life. He's taking me out on our first official date next Friday night, so you have to come over and help me get ready."

"Of course. I'm so happy for you guys and wish you all the best."

The waitress finally came over to take our order. She said she didn't want to interrupt the girl talk, which we appreciated.

"Oh gosh, I'm so hungry. How about a double fudge shake with chicken fingers and cheese fries."

Mia said, "Ditto."

As we waited on our food, Mia said, "So, your turn. What happened the other night with Weston?"

I told her all the details about that night and through to the text messages from the previous night.

"Oh, good. Our food's here!" I shoveled food in my mouth because I knew a gazillion questions were coming.

"What is his deal? What are you going to do, Sam? He broke up with Southern Belle? I wonder what's going on in that head of his. He actually showed up in Paris? Are you going to forgive him? Have you asked Jackson about any of this?"

"Mia, I don't know where to start with all those questions! All I can say right now is that I'm still trying to process it all. Was he not bringing girls home constantly when I was gone, let alone always seeing him published or on the news with a girl next to him? And when did this possessiveness start? I didn't see him that way with her. He was always the gentleman when we first got together. I just do NOT understand it. He left me, right? Disappeared, never to be heard from again. And now he wants to act like we should be okay?"

"What I really want to know is, how was the kiss?"

"Perfect . . . passionate. I don't trust myself around him right now with the way he's acting. I'll talk to him tomorrow night and set some boundaries. He doesn't get to break this heart again, with whatever that damn man is up to."

"Well, I know something happened to him a few years ago. Everyone was told that Wes was on a business trip, but I was over there with my dad not long after he got back. He looked like hell, Sam. Then he disappeared again, came back all super muscly, like even more than he was, and just seemed . . . different. Jackson told me he was just going through some stuff and not to worry about it, but also not to say anything to you about it. I figured if you asked about him, I would tell you, but you never did, so I never brought it up."

"Jackson said something along the same lines and that he really didn't know the details, but it really messed with Wes for a while and to not take to heart this harsh demeanor I get from him sometimes. At times, he seems like the gentle teddy bear I know him to be, but then the next thing I know, he's flying off the handle like an angry gorilla."

"I don't know, Sam, but y'all will figure it out. You two always do. But hey, what I do know is, we need a girls' night out, tomorrow night. Let's head over to the bar at the edge of town. They have ladies' night on Wednesdays."

Trying to push Wes out of my mind for a while, I said, "Sounds like an awesome plan to me."

After dinner, I found Mama and Dad on the couch watching TV. Jackson was apparently staying at Lucey's, so I grabbed some water and headed to my room with Maddox.

Ping! Ping!

I wondered who was texting me at almost 9:00 at night.

Oh, Weston . . .

HOW WAS YOUR DAY?

I waited a few minutes before responding.

GOOD.

I took out my laptop to set up my video for Mr. Hughes and his family.

Ping! Ping!

GOOD TO HEAR! I CLOSED THE DEAL WITH THE ANNEX FARMERS MARKET, SO I WILL GET WITH YOU ON THURSDAY ON ALLOCATING FUNDS, AND WE NEED TO LOOK AT PURCHASING PROPERTY FOR THE CATTLE OVER HERE SO THEY TRULY CAN SELL FRESH BEEF.

Now you're just texting me about work.

THAT'S GREAT NEWS. SOUNDS GOOD.

I turned my ringer off and proceeded with the video.

"Hello, Hughes family! Thank you for the sweet video, and I miss you all very much. Yes, it's a bummer about August, but I plan to be that way hopefully in the spring, and we can meet up then. Very Sneaky, Mr. Hughes, though the photo was lovely. The handsome genes must run in the family. Hugs to everyone, and keep the videos and messages coming! Talk to you soon . . . Bye."

Save and sent.

I grabbed my phone to put it on the charger, and there was another text from Weston.

SWEET DREAMS, BEAUTIFUL.

Yep, I was definitely going to have a talk with him.

CHAPTER 11:
Wednesday Blues

It's Wednesday, so Jackson and Dad were at the cattle auction up the road for the day. Aunt Patsy decided to take the day off, so I didn't have much to do, as I needed her to organize this mess before I could even input it in the system. After answering some emails and realizing it was only 9:00 a.m., I felt my phone buzzing at my desk.

"Hey, Daddy."

"Hey, honey. Huge favor I need to ask of you."

"Sure, Dad."

"I need you to pick up Weston from the airport."

"I'm actually really busy today. Can't someone else do it?"

"Well, Aunt Patsy would always pick him up, but she's out today, so . . . Sam, honey, are you still there?"

"Yep, right here. Not wanting to leave."

"Please, honey, his plane gets in at noon, so that gives you plenty of time to head to Corpus with all the morning traffic."

"Fine, Daddy, but you owe me. I love you."

Can I just sit here and pout for the next thirty minutes?

Between traffic and me driving purposely slow, I got to the airport with about twenty minutes to spare. I found a place to park near an exit and stood by the car. At that point, I wasn't paying attention to anyone coming out of the doors, as I was playing a game on my phone to pass time. For some reason, popping bubbles is so satisfying. Who knew?

I suddenly felt a presence near me, and before I could react, I was engrossed in a hug and kiss. I inhaled his cologne, and my knees went weak.

"Hello, beautiful."

"Hi, Weston." I glared at him. "You know, you shouldn't do that. I could've really hurt you if I didn't realize it was you."

"You wouldn't hurt me, and even if you somehow did, I'd forgive you."

On the drive home, he kept staring and smiling at me.

"Weston, can you stop? It's distracting."

"What? Me looking at you? I can't help it. You've been gone for so long, I only had our pictures. Of course, your mom would share her pictures of when she was with you, but then you blocked me on social media. So, I'm just soaking in how much more beautiful and tempting you've become."

"Seriously, Weston. Do we need to do this now?"

"Stop to eat lunch? Sure. There's a Whataburger up here on the right."

We went inside, and I excused myself to the ladies' room. I needed to have a pep talk with myself before this conversation began.

After five minutes, I decided that it was now or never.

He waved me over to the booth, and to my surprise, he'd already ordered our food and even remembered my favorite items. He caught the look on my face and smiled.

"You remember?"

"How can I forget? It's been the same thing since we were kids. A number four with a Dr. Pepper Shake and extra ketchup."

"That is true."

We both chuckled. It was nice not to have so much tension around us.

I decided to keep some peace between us and not say anything yet. We talked about business and how his trip was out to Tulsa. I could handle casual conversation. He brought up the need for someone to run the ranch out in Tulsa, then he said he might request to do it himself and hire ranch hands to take care of it when he traveled for his lawyer duties.

"Why would you volunteer to do that? And just leave? Hire someone local to do that who needs a job. That way you and Jackson can take turns checking in."

"I don't know. I feel like a change of scenery will be good. Unless there's something or someone here worth sticking around for . . ." His eyes pulled me in, and I needed to look away, so I dipped my fry into the ketchup to avoid his gaze.

I felt like I was being tricked into showing him that I care. "Weston, what do you want from me? I'm so confused about everything that's happened, yet you act like we need to move on and be fine. If you need to tell me something, then just say it."

"I do, Sam. I have a lot to tell you, but not here. Meet me later tonight by the pond after dinner?"

"I can't tonight. I already have plans with Mia after dinner."

"*After* dinner?" he shouted, looking at me sideways.

I was taken aback. "Yes, we're having a girls' night, but I can meet you tomorrow after dinner."

His eyes turned dark like the deep ocean. "Sure . . ."

"Fine, let's go."

We hit the road, and Weston was being unusually quiet and deep in thought. I dropped him off at his house and headed to mine.

CHAPTER 12:

Family Dinner

After heading into the house and thinking I'd caught up with most of the day's work, I check my phone and see multiple missed calls from my old company, Colonial, and Mr. Hughes.

This can't be good.

Once I listened to the voicemails, I called Stacy back immediately.

"Sam! Where have you been? We have a big problem and need your help!"

"What happened? I have missed calls and emails from Mr. Hughes."

"We need you to convince him to stay with us. He's threatened to leave Colonial and take his business elsewhere." Stacy started crying. "He said we're incompetent fools."

"Calm down, Stacy. Walk me through what happened, and let's figure out what can be salvaged. I'd like to have a game plan before I return his call."

She began to tell me Johnathan got a lead on a new company, SIR, which was going live that day. That the company had a lot of large investors and how their product was state-of-the-art, with the promise of the return being over triple the dollar. She said Johnathon wanted to jump on it for Mr. Hughes to earn a big win for them. Unfortunately, Mr. Hughes was in flight that morning, so they made the decision without him so they wouldn't miss out. With only a few hours into multiple investors jumping on this, the stock price went through the roof. This was right after a video was sent out to all the news stations that showed the CEO having an affair, after hours, in the factory on one of the assembly lines. Everyone was backing out, and the stock price was plummeting.

I logged into the stock market and started doing research on the product, then I had Stacy send Mr. Hughes's file and timeline of events.

"I can see why he's pissed! Not only did he lose money, but y'all caused him to be the leader of the crusade. We're not going to sell today. Everyone is in a panic, so let's give it forty-eight hours, after the dust has settled to where the price lands. Call me on Friday, and we'll go from there. Do not touch anything else on his account until then. And I'll try to figure out how to gain the losses back. Let me call him for damage control. Talk soon."

Deep breaths, Sam. You've dealt with an angry Mr. Hughes before, and this time it has nothing to do with you.

I dialed Mr. Hughes.

"Miss Dupont!"

"Hello, Mr. Hughes. Sorry I'm just now getting back to you, but I wanted to gather all the facts before I called you. I told Stacy we're giving this forty-eight hours before the dust settles before doing anything rash, since everyone is panicking right now. I have your profile in front of me, so I'm looking to see how we can earn back gains for the losses by the end of the week—if SIR doesn't fall out, at the very least."

"Thank you for taking the initiative, Miss Dupont. I've already moved all of my money out of Colonial and into my own mutual funds headquarters that you're going to run."

"I'm sorry. What do you mean that *I'm* going to run, sir? I'm a little shocked you've already moved everything over."

"Exactly what I said, my dear. I have a very big surprise that should be greeting you in a couple of weeks, along with a contract to sign. I don't think you'll be able to turn down my offer."

"Mr. Hughes, I am practically speechless. If the headquarters are in England, there's no way I can agree. I just got home, and my family needs my help. The offer does sound generous, and for that, I appreciate you, but—"

"Dear, the headquarters will be where you are."

"Oh."

"Does that change things for you, Miss Dupont?"

"It certainly gives me more to think about. Are you sure you want me to run this new business adventure for you and control your funds?"

"I only trust you, my dear. I will provide everything you need . . . you name it. From the space to the staff, everything is at your disposal. Now, I must go for my morning tea. Hope to hear good news later."

"Thank you, Mr. Hughes."

"What just happened?" I said aloud to myself.

Daddy walked in and heard my solo conversation. "You okay, honey?"

"Yeah, it was Mr. Hughes. He opened his own Mutual Fund business and wants me to lead it. He said I can do it from here."

"That is pretty wild, Sam. He must think a lot of you."

"I guess. He really treated me like his own family when I lived out there. He said I'll have a surprise delivered to me in a couple of weeks with a contract to review and sign."

"Well, don't sign anything until Wes reads it over. Also, I want to make sure you're not going to be overwhelmed by taking that on . . . on top of the ranch. Family does come first."

"Yes, Daddy. I understand. And really, it's just managing his funds. I can hire staff if it gets any bigger than that." I looked at the clock. "Oh, I'm going to be late. Let me go get ready."

I ran up to my room to take a shower and get ready for the night, pushing the last hour behind me. The dinner was a weekly thing, so dressing casual was fine. I slipped on my skinny jeans with my lightweight, off-the-shoulder blue tee. It would look fine for the hometown bar that night, also. Light makeup, with some added curl to my hair for volume. Finally, I felt ready and headed downstairs. Before I reached the dining room, I could hear everyone's laughter. There didn't sound like any tension to me, I walked in, and everyone stopped and stared at me.

"Oh, gosh. Did I forget to take out a roller or something?"

"No, Sam, you just look stunning." Weston came over, placed a kiss on my cheek, and walked into the kitchen.

Yep, I was blushing through my blush that night.

Can this guy not leave me be?

I needed an escape. "Mama, do you need help with anything?"

"No, sweetie. Lucey and Jackson are grabbing the rest."

All of a sudden, I heard a squeal come through the kitchen door.

"Sam, you're home! I hate that I missed the other night, but I was on a school field trip."

It was Weston's sister, Maddie, and she gave me a big hug.

"Hey, Maddie. How's it been going?"

We sat down at the table covered in food and caught up. My daddy and Mr. Lancaster sat on each end of the table, and their wives sat next to them. Filling in the middle was Maddie, myself, and Lucey on one side, with Jackson and Weston sitting across from us.

Dinner went off without a hitch, though I did notice that Weston and his dad weren't really speaking to each other directly, but more in a roundabout way through Daddy and Jackson.

Lost in thought, I felt a piece of bread hit my face.

What in the world?

"Earth to Sam!" Jackson said. "Are you here? Mr. Lancaster asked you a question."

"Oh, I'm so sorry, sir. Just reminding myself to reply to some emails tonight. What was your question?"

"I was just saying how nice it is to have you back at the ranch and working. But I wanted to know if you have plans to travel soon or go back to the corporate world."

"Um, I'm not sure what you mean. I might travel back to England next spring to visit with some old friends, but that would only be for a week or so. And I can definitely work while I'm over there, if that's the concern. As far as going corporate again, as long as my family and the ranch need me, I will be here."

"No, no, that's no concern. I know you're excellent at your job and won't let things fall to the side. I didn't know if you would be leaving again or if you've been serious with someone that might cause you to leave down the road. Your dad told me about that picture your old client sent of his nephew and wanting to set you up."

I felt offended and caught off guard.

Weston said, "Father, not now. She's home, and it's our first dinner with her back. Can we not?"

"Mr. Lancaster, again, I'm not sure what you're getting at, but I can say I am home for the near and far future unless I'm not needed anymore. I may have left suddenly, but I had my reasons, along with my parents' backing. I have to say I have learned a lot about the ranch business from all over and have grown as a person—mentally and spiritually—and that will only help me in the long run. I worked for one of the top global companies before leaving to come here, and I've seen more in the past five years than most can see in a lifetime. With all that said, I'm content with being home. As for dating someone, rest assured, there is no one special in my life right now or in the near future that can take me away."

"I'm sorry if I offended you, Samantha. That's not what I meant to do. I just know everyone is so happy to have you back, including myself."

"It's okay."

I looked at Weston, who had a clenched jaw, so I kicked him under the table to get his attention. We locked eyes, and I could see he was calming down.

"All right," Mama said. "Who's ready for some cake?"

I got up to help clear the table with Lucey as Mama prepared dessert. We all sit back down again to eat cake and drink some more wine. Shortly after, Jackson leaves to take Lucey home, and Maddie heads back to her house.

I got a text from Mia. It was time to go.

"Hey, Mama. Mia's here. I'm heading out."

I told everyone goodbye and felt Weston's glare. Quickly turning around, I hustled out the door and into Mia's car.

CHAPTER 13:
Whiskey Girl

Dawn and Jenny already had a table for us, so we sat down and quickly ordered a round of drinks. We were in a small-town bar, so it seemed I'd be taking some rounds with Jameson that night. Being that it was ladies' night, they had the country-to-club mix playing, and several rounds in, we found ourselves on the dance floor, laughing and having a great time.

Before we knew it, several guys joined the circle. At first, they were being gentlemen and staying a nice distance away, but they kept coming in closer to make conversation. I was quickly called out as the single girl, so one guy made his way over for casual conversation. I let him know I was heading to the bar for another drink, so he decided to follow me. He was about six foot three with silk back blonde hair and a clean shave. It looked like he and his crew came after work—they were all wearing suit pants and long-sleeve collared shirts, but the sleeves were rolled up and ties were off. After some basic Q&A, I learned his name was Blake Sircy, and he discovered I was a Dupont related to the Heart of Kings Cattle Ranch.

"Aren't you considered a princess around this town?" he asked.

"Oh, gosh. You've heard of me? I would think Lancaster's daughter would be considered the princess of this town. I actually got home a few days ago from being away."

"A rebel, I see. Couldn't take living under scrutiny and left?"

"Um, that couldn't be further from the truth. I had a wonderful childhood, but I felt the need to get away, so after I graduated, I went abroad for several years, seeing the world and completing my studies. I got a job in the States that I loved for a couple of years and then was summoned home by my family and business. So, yeah, I'm far from being a rebel."

"That's pretty cool."

"So, what brings you here?"

"Business. I'm looking to expand my company's brand into the surrounding cities of San Antonio."

"Okay, so you're a Texas native?"

"Born and raised in Austin but fell in love with San Antonio in college, so that's where I live now. I'm expanding my business model for healthy drinks and smoothies. Ever heard of SIR?"

What are the damn odds?

I tried to keep a poker face. "I actually lost a lot of money for my client recently. Please tell me you're not the CEO that was having an affair in the factory," I said, half-laughing, half-serious.

"That was my father. He's now been kicked out of the company, and I'm taking over the upper Northeast for now."

"Sorry to hear that. That couldn't have been easy to handle in the spotlight. But I'm glad to hear you're making a comeback. Is that why you're here?"

"It's fine. My parents hate each other anyway. And yeah, I'm trying to calm down investors and create new contracts. Who would've thought the last twenty-four hours would be such a tidal wave? Besides, hiding out in a small town for a few days doesn't seem so bad now. But enough with the hard stuff. I think you're gorgeous and would love to dance with you." He took my hand and led me out.

I was feeling buzzed anyways and not like I belonged to anyone, so I thought . . . why not? The ladies were still out on the floor, having fun and teasing me. I'm not sure how planned it was, but immediately after getting out the floor, a slow love song started. Not even having a moment to reject, I was pulled into Blake's arms. We began to sway, and he was telling me jokes until my face hurt.

"Is this supposed to be a romantic moment?" I ask in between giggles.

In a husky voice, he said, "You can come back with me tonight, and I can shower you in romance."

"Well, we'll just have to see about that."

He leaned down and placed a soft kiss on my lips. "Guess we will."

At the same time, I felt a shadow had formed over us. Looking off to my right, I saw Mia making a face as she stood next to Dylan.

Why the hell is Dylan here? Wait a minute, I see the other guys, too.

I lifted my head to look up past Blake, and I was met with angry, dark ocean eyes.

"Samantha Jane." I hear a growl coming from Weston. "Outside, now!"

I decided to slowly follow, looking back at my friends in disbelief and trying to figure out what the hell was going on.

"What the hell, Samantha?"

Trying to keep myself together, I try to act like I don't care for this man in front of me. "Why are you here, Weston?"

"Girls night, huh? Are you trying to break my heart? Who is that guy?"

"You just threw a lot of questions at me, Wes." In my drunken state, I was trying to comprehend what he said to me.

"How much have you had to drink tonight? You're drunk. Are you going to let every guy take advantage of you tonight?"

"First, quit using my full name like you own me. Second, I can be with whomever I want because I'm single. You left me! It's girls' night, and we're having fun. Well, until you decided to show up. Besides, who cares how much I drink or what I do?" I poked him in the chest. "Do you think you can march in here like you own the damn place and treat people a certain way? You are my co-worker, Wes, and my neighbor.

Nothing more. Do you hear me, Weston Lee? Nothing more! I am fully over you, so quit coming for me, dammit!"

It seems drinking gives me more courage to tell him off, *way more than expected*. We were standing toe to toe, and he was looking down on me. I kept backing up until I hit the brick wall, and he put his hands against the wall on either side of me.

"Darlin', I can own this bar right now or even have it shut down. Would you like me to?" He smirked. "I can ruin that guy's business and reputation with a snap of my fingers if you keep this up. As for you and me, this is far from over, as there is no one else for me other than you."

He pressed himself closer to me and lifted my chin. His kiss started off as subtle but quickly deepened and hardened against my lips. Like he was starving for my affection. I felt myself slipping into his magic, but the lack of oxygen pulled me back to reality, and I pushed him off.

"Weston, this cannot happen!"

Completely ignoring me, he slung me over his shoulder, "I'm taking you home, now. Don't even protest!" Carrying me through the bar with one arm, I heard Blake asking if I was okay, and then I heard yelling and something hard hit the ground. Weston didn't stop, so I looked up to see what was happening. Blake was getting up from the ground with blood gushing from his nose. Several men in black suits were holding Blakes friends along with keeping Blake from retaliating. I found myself in a state of shock between what just happened and being carried out in Weston's arms. Looking back at Mia, she gave me a goodbye wave and a smile, hollering that she would call me the following day to check on me. All I could do was look at her disbelief—like a traitor. It's like this whole group was in it together. As I was put into the passenger seat of his fancy McClaren, then buckled in, I called him a tyrant. He only looked at me with his eyes as dark as the bottom of the deepest ocean, then locked me in as he walked around the car. Weston soon entered the driver's side, and we sped off.

Refusing to talk to him, I dozed off while staring out the window.

I found myself in an old familiar room the next morning. With my head pounding and buzzing from the previous night, I soon realized I was in Weston's room. Right when I was getting up to sneak out, the door opened.

"Here, drink this," Weston said. "It'll help with your hangover."

I gave him a side glance and took the drink from him. "Thanks." After a few sips, I put it on the nightstand and stood up to grab my shoes. "I'll just see you later. I need to get to work."

"I already called in sick for you. There's nothing that you need to do today."

"You did what?"

"Sam, you need your rest. It was a late night, and there's nothing that requires your attention today. You're welcome to stay here, or I can drive you home."

"I think I'll walk home alone, thanks." Gathering my stuff up, I quickly headed to the door.

He reached for my hand. "Sam . . ." His low voice caught my attention, so I turned back around to face him. All I could do was stare back at him despair. He didn't say anything else, but I noticed pain and longing in his eyes. Before I got sucked in, I turned around and left. Thankfully, I could walk home in peace and go to bed.

A few hours later, Mia showed up for lunch. She filled me in on the events from the previous night on what I seemed to have blocked out—that Weston had called the boys to do a guys' night, only to find out Dylan and the others were planning on going up there to hang out with us. I soon felt awful for being mad at her and everyone and for how I handled the situation. Part of me still thought he deserved it all, but it didn't take away from the fact that I looked like a drunken-ass fool. My emotions and feelings were all over the place.

"Mia, I'm supposed to meet him tonight so he can share his side of things. If he even wants to still talk to me, this isn't going to be awkward at all, right?" I looked at her for some reassurance.

"Girl, that man will never give up on you. If you want him, take him. He's only yours to have or deny. You were both wrong for how things went last night, but I also don't blame either one of you. You've suppressed your broken heart for so long, and he's been pining for you to come back. Sam, it's you that has full control of this relationship."

"That's what I am afraid of."

Mia headed back to work, and I went to crawl back into bed for a while but was woken up by a text from Wes.

MEET ME BY THE POND AT 7:00 P.M.

CHAPTER 14:
Confession

Post-dessert, my parents were engaged in their own conversation, so I excused myself from the table. I walked onto the porch, and in the distance, I saw Weston walking towards the pond.

I guess it's time.

Luckily, the pathways were well lit, so we weren't completely immersed in darkness. There were hanging lanterns by the pond that I saw had been turned on.

I sat down on the bench next to Weston. "So, I'm here to listen, then I'll talk."

Weston looked at me with both sadness and desire in his eyes. "First, I want to apologize for what my father said and how he acted last night at dinner."

"I'm fine. I mean, I was caught off guard for not knowing where it was coming from, but whatever."

"Well, I'm going to tell you where it came from. He currently blames your leaving for our fallout. When he made his demands, no one expected that you'd leave and be gone for years. This also caused some issues among your dad and him."

"Weston, I'm so lost. What the hell has been going on?"

I could tell he was nervous, and he stood up.

"My father threatened me with you. Remember for a while after I went to Yale, I came home every other weekend to see you? It was hard to concentrate when I was at school and not knowing if you were safe . . . Not having you close to me. It was like going one hundred to zero in a split second when leaving you. We've seen each other every day since I can remember, and we officially got together that summer before I left. Needless to say, I kept asking him if I could come home and attend Texas because I wasn't happy there, my grades were slipping, and right after the holidays, I was put on academic probation. My father was pissed. So that last weekend I was home, before heading back for the next semester, we had it out. He stated that I was no longer to come home until my grades improved and I proved that I was serious about being up there to become a lawyer. He said he would be monitoring my calls and messages so that I should be careful."

"Weston, why didn't you just call and tell me? We could've figured it out together."

"It gets worse, Sam. When I flew back to school that day, there was a big party happening that night. My roommates dragged me out to go. I had a few drinks, honestly. I don't remember doing anything crazy, but the bad thing is, I don't remember much from later that night. What I do remember is waking up the next morning with some girl in my bed. Neither of us had clothes on."

My face turned red, and my body started shaking with rage. I got up, and he started walking towards me. "Don't touch me!"

He backed off. "Sam, I was horrified! I didn't remember any of that night or that girl at the time, and I just ran out of there. It took me all day to find the nerve to even text you. I knew I couldn't call you because you would know something was wrong, and this was not a conversation I wanted to have over the phone. Classes started the next day, so there was no way I could've come home. The next morning, I got a phone call from my father asking me how my weekend was. I told him I screwed up and that you would never forgive me for what I did. I thought it was strange that he was so calm and said, 'Well, good for you for trying new things. But it's Sam.' He said, 'Son, if it's meant to be, she'll be around when you come home. I suggest you take advantage of this little situation.'" All I could do was let out a gasp of shock.

"Sam, it almost felt like a threat from him. I was so lost and perplexed that I didn't have the energy to fight him anymore. A few weeks later, I was sent pictures of that night—of me and her in bed together—like it was a threat. I talked to my buddies, and they thought I should buckle down to finish through these next few years and move on. I couldn't even forgive myself for what I'd done to even try and ask for your forgiveness. So, I became a coward and started to text and call you less and ignore you. I was an idiot for how I handled the situation. I was an idiot to choose not to fight for you. Jackson would check in on me occasionally and wanted to know what happened with us because he said you were deeply depressed—that you just threw yourself into your studies, losing weight, and never wanting to do anything with anyone. My heart was breaking, but I couldn't tell him why. He would've flown up there to kill me with his bare hands. I kept it short and said I was just slammed with schoolwork and trying to graduate early so I could take the bar early and come home sooner. But I asked him to keep me updated on you and the family. I tried to come home for your graduation, but Dad still denied me and said it wouldn't be a good time, plus, you were getting ready to head abroad the following week. I asked how long you would be gone, and he said for a while." He took a pause to study me, to see if I was okay before he continued. All I could do was stare back while the tears filled my eyes. He finally takes a seat next to me, and I find my body finding comfort with him so close. Taking a heavy deep breath, Wes continued.

"Fast forward to the end of the following summer, I ran into that girl from that night. She came up to me and asked how life had been. I apologized to her for leaving abruptly and having no reconciliation of what happened. Her name was Ava, and she told me not to worry and that we didn't do anything. She was paid to drug me and then make it look like we'd had sex for pictures."

Now losing my own temper, "Excuse me? Who would do such a thing to anyone . . . especially to you? You don't have enemies, and I'd especially think not at school, states away from home! Weston, this is too damn much."

"Sam, it was my dad! It took some investigating, but it was him. That's why I didn't come home until Christmas that year and only because my mom begged me to. I hate that she was stuck in the middle of this. I was also hoping you'd be home, but I heard your mom flew out to Scotland to see you for the holidays. I didn't think it was time to call my dad out, so I endured the week and headed back to Yale before the New Year. I sent you a text, but you never replied—though I didn't expect you to. I stayed gone until the following summer, while Jackson kept me updated on where you were. I had one more year left to graduate and was set to take the bar exam that upcoming April. I was working on a plan to find you, no matter where you were. At that point, I still hadn't told my dad that I knew, and he was acting like a proud father should be of his son. Now that I was about to graduate, he thought it was time to start looking for a woman in my life that would help build our side of the family for generations and be great for the social aspect of corporate life. Lans Enterprises is now reaching its all time height; trampling every company and everyone in its way. Deciding to play by his game, I would bring random girls home—girls who were full of themselves—gold diggers, city girls. I acted like I was serious about some of them just to get a reaction. By the time I took the bar and graduated in May, I heard you were in Paris. I came home for the graduation party with family and friends. I saw your mom sharing some albums of her adventures with you over the couple of years, so I walked over to her, and she happily let me look at them. You were breathtaking, Sam. It seemed over time you'd gained some weight back and your body had filled out beautifully. You still make my heart skip a beat when I look at you."

I looked away. "I'm still hating you right now, so don't make me blush."

"Your mom let me know you were spending the summer in France and had been in Paris for the past month, getting ready to head to Toulouse mid-June. I figured this was my chance. I asked her all the details about where you were staying because I wanted to visit you, but told her not to say anything to you. I wanted it to be a surprise so I could beg for your mercy without you having the chance to dodge me. Now that I did what Father requested of me, I had my freedom back.

He said I could take the summer off since I was a year ahead of the plan anyway. I took the red-eye out the following night to Paris. Once I arrived, I went out on the street of your apartment, walking around and getting myself together. After some time, I stopped at a café to grab a coffee. When I turned around, I thought it was fate . . . There you were. Just as I was about to call your name, a man came up behind you, wrapping his arms around you and kissed you. You were smiling and looked so happy. It seemed that you had moved on. I stayed in Paris for twenty-four hours, following you to see what this was with him. You seemed genuinely happy, and I didn't want to cause you any pain, so I flew back home. I let your mom know what happened, and she said he was probably some guy you'd met there—that it probably wasn't anything serious. She said I should give you time until you came home. I was heartbroken when I got home, so I let Father have it. He didn't even deny it and said he did it for my own good . . . to look where I was now. I'd graduated as a lawyer, top of the class at Yale, a year early. Mom was shocked. All she could do was cry and pray for all of us. I needed time away, so I got a job with Jacob's dad in Austin for a year before being summoned home and told that my help was needed for running the ranch business and becoming vice president of Lans Enterprises. All during this time, I swore that once you came home, I would do everything in my power to have you back in my arms—to not let you go again. So now, another year later, here we are. I love you, Sam. I always have and always will. Those other girls were nothing other than filling a void. You were what I dreamt of and thought of while we were apart, especially during the most darkest experience of my life." As he can see my wheels spinning, with my mouth agape wanting to speak, he pressed my chin up to close my mouth.

"That is nothing I want to discuss right now, to take away from this current conversation, nor do I want your pity. Please forgive me, and let's start our future together." Weston put his hands on my face and leaned in to kiss me.

I tried to dodge him. My emotions were everywhere. But his lips met mine, and I could feel the passion coming from him. He was biting and sucking on my bottom lip feverishly and then moved to kissing my neck. His hands gripped my waist, pulling me into him. I was getting weaker in his arms as my body heated up. My heart was racing, and I couldn't think straight.

Get it together, Sam.

I moved my hands up to his chest and tried to push him off, panting for breath. "Weston!"

He pulled back and looked at me. His eyes glistened with desire and love, but I knew he could only see the pain still in my eyes.

"Weston, I appreciate you telling me all of this, and I hate that it's taken this long for us to get here, but I need time. You shattered me by just disappearing like that, and no one—not even your mom or Jackson—could give any explanation. And I am so disappointed in your dad. Did he really think I would keep you from fulfilling your duties, or is it that I'm not good enough for his son? We all come from humble backgrounds. I know your dad has other businesses from the ranch to better secure your family. Hell, I think y'all might be one of, if not *the*, richest family in this state. Lans enterprises owns everything. But why does that give him the right to judge me? What was that shit at dinner about me leaving? Is he trying to see if I'll leave again so he can find someone more suitable for you?"

"I just don't know, Sam. I really don't. But I also don't care what he thinks. You are it for me—the only one I want to be with. If you need time, I'll give it to you. But just don't push me away anymore or leave again."

With that, he embraced me, so I decided to put my arms around him, as well. It felt good. It felt right. But I felt my heart aching about the past and what the future might hold. I longed to ask what happened to him a while back but decided I could wait for another time. I believed we were both emotionally spent.

It was late, so he walked me to my back door and kissed me on the cheek before we told each other good night.

I fell asleep dreaming about him . . . about us.

Weston

I was lying wide awake in bed finally feeling more at ease than I had in a long time, but still unsettled. Luckily, she didn't ask about my time away, as Jackson let me know he hinted to her that I'd gone through some things in hopes she would ease up. I couldn't even be mad at the guy because he was just trying to help. The past always finds a way to show itself, so I knew eventually she would ask. Then I would tell her, and only her. Until then, I was going to keep trying to win her back.

I loved hearing her laugh at dinner the previous night, and I loved seeing her eyes sparkle with joy. Oh, and how she looked tonight in those jeans.

I needed to cool off in the shower. My mind kept replaying those innocent looks she gave, those soft lips when she talked, those jeans when she walked and bent over . . . us kissing. After the cold water calmed my body down, I began to think of how the night went.

Sam had now heard the truth and my side of things. She didn't flat out tell me no afterwards, so this added to my reasons that she still had feelings for me.

Now, to make her fall in love with me all over again and to forgive me for the past.

This should not be too hard, right? It was Samantha . . . *my* Sam. She may have been all grown up now, but she was still her under all that elegance and charm. Since she'd asked for time and space, I was unsure I could give that to her. Having her back and so close, it took every effort not to be near her every moment. I needed to plan something that weekend. Maybe she would let me take her out on a date.

No, I'm not even asking. I'll just tell her when and where. Wait, that won't work. I'm just going to show up at her front door. See how she turns away from me then.

I looked at the clock. It's already 2:00 in the morning. The next day would be busy, but at least it was almost the weekend.

My mind started racing.

Has Sam been paying attention to my name in the news? This is something I need to check in to. Not that I think she would believe what anyone says about me, but if so, she might end up fearing me before I can win her heart over again.

The positions my father and I hold could be dangerous when sitting on top of the temple, as there are always those, who instead of benefiting, want to see the temple fall. Those who went against the Lancasters tended to be the ones who fell—or even paid with their lives. Behind the scenes of running an empire can be truly brutal at times, but my family worked too hard not to keep pushing forward. Our name was also linked to the ranch, so I had a lot to protect.

CHAPTER 15:
Forget-Me-Nots

*I*t was Sunday night, and I had stayed hidden in my house all weekend, hiding behind a few good books. Luckily it was rainy and muggy the entire time, so the need to venture outdoors was null. Yet, that didn't stop Weston from making a few appearances or sending reminders of his existence. After our Thursday night discussion, I really needed to take some time to just process everything from his dad, to him going to Paris, and everything in between. We both had changed, too. I was no longer that shy girl who took a seat in the back to be unseen all of the time. I was independent, and he seemed to be more ruthless than I remembered.

Weston showed up a quarter to 6:00 p.m., with roses in hand, dressed in one of his many fancy tailored suits, and stated that he was taking me out. Stubborn me, who just got off work and was excited to have no plans, told him no. I just wanted to relax and hang out with the Bronte sisters that night.

He chuckled, knowing what my life's go-to was. "Some things never change, do they?"

I smirked. "A good book puts me in the best of moods."

Along with him being persistent, he said he'd leave after helping me put the roses in a vase so I didn't prick myself. But Mama was cooking in the kitchen and couldn't help but admire the roses. She struck up a conversation with him, which then led to him staying for dinner. I found it funny that the date he wanted with me turned into a double date with my parents.

After dinner, hoping to send him on his way, we realized it had started raining and that his truck was at the end of the drive. So we sat on the front porch swing, waiting for it to at least come to a drizzle so he wouldn't completely ruin his suit. We talked about our day and family. It felt like we were an old married couple chatting about life while swinging with our faithful dog at our feet.

Weston tucked my hair behind my ears and asked me what my fears were about us. He wanted to know so he could reassure me. I told him everything as he patiently listened and held my hand. Once I finished, he said he understood, kissed my cheek and the top of my head, and then left in the pouring rain. I was dumbfounded and sat there for another hour with Maddox until Mama came and got me. To avoid any overthinking, and taking advantage of the space, I threw myself into a re-read of *Wuthering Heights*. It always puts me to sleep.

Upon awakening Monday morning, I was met with an overwhelming floral smell. As I sat up in bed, rubbing my eyes open, I was astonished to see my room covered in different colors of roses, mixed in with pink and blue forget-me-nots. Not one arrangement was alike, and they were all so beautiful. Walking around my room admiring the flowers, I soon found a note taped to the door.

My Sam,

Please accept the roses and forget-me-nots as me showering you with hugs and kisses as I give you space. I saw your face when I got in my truck yesterday and realized I must have left you wondering what had happened. It was me absorbing your thoughts and fears as well as hating myself for hurting you so badly in the past. I cannot erase all your fears and doubts overnight, but I can promise to you that I will spend my life proving to you that you need not fear anything or ever doubt my love and faith in you. I spotted what you were reading, so here is one of my favorite fitting quotes.

"In every cloud, in every tree-filling the air at night, and caught by glimpses in every object, by day I am surrounded with her image!" —Heathcliff

Love always and waiting,

Weston

On Tuesday, there were copies of *Wuthering Heights, Pride and Prejudice,* and *The Great Gatsby* on my front porch. Flipping through them, I realized they were the ones we used when I was helping him with his senior AP literature course in high school. All of our notes and favorite quotes were circled. As I started flipping through the books, I found colored sticky notes in between the pages—pages that identified our own faults and losses, along with identifying his love for me throughout. He was a man who not only was spectacular with his own words but knew exactly how to use others' to pull at my heartstrings. I read through all three of them and documented his colored sticky notes with my own.

Knowing Jackson was heading to his house shortly to deliver some maps of land, I wrapped them up and asked him to deliver them to Wes. I did add my own note, of course.

Weston,

Thank you for the beautiful flowers. They smell divine. I can assure you I don't need forget-me-nots to remember you, but I appreciate the symbol and gesture. Also, I had forgotten about those copies of the books and cannot believe you still have them after all this time. Thank you for the stroll down memory lane. I am sending them back so you may enjoy reading back through them as I have.

All best wishes,

Sam

It was Wednesday, and I hadn't seen Weston since Sunday. That night was the large family dinner, and Mama said she hadn't heard that he was not coming so to assume he was.

Before I knew it, it was 6:30 on the dot when I heard the front door open. My heart started to race so fast I feared a panic attack was ahead, even though my mind was trying to be calm, as it was the one that had been making the decisions and asking for space. So, what was the big deal if he was there? Of course, my heart dropped every time someone from his family walked in and it wasn't him.

Mama noticed my anxiety taking over and asked where Weston was. His parents looked at each other and said he had to head to Dubai the previous night for an urgent matter and wouldn't be returning until Friday, at the earliest. The look of disappointment on my face seemed to be blunt, as they all tried to console me with the "He will text or call when he can" nonsense. I just nodded my head.

I didn't stick around for wine and dessert but headed to my room to shower and crawl into bed with Maddox to watch TV. Around 9:00 p.m., my phone dinged. It was a message from Weston.

> A LITTLE BIRDIE TOLD ME YOU MISSED ME AT DINNER TONIGHT. I'M SORRY I COULDN'T BE THERE AND THAT I DIDN'T TELL YOU I WAS GONE. I WAS TRYING TO GIVE YOU SPACE AS REQUESTED. I KNOW IT'S LATE THERE, BUT MY DAY'S JUST GETTING STARTED HERE. HOPEFULLY THE DEAL IS CLOSED TODAY SO I CAN FLY HOME. BY THE WAY, THANK YOU FOR ALL THE READING MATERIAL. I HOPE TO SEE YOU SOON. GOOD NIGHT.

Trying to rack my brain about which family member sold me out, I decided to respond back.

> WELL, GOOD MORNING TO YOU, THEN. I WOULDN'T SAY I MISSED YOU, BUT I WAS A LITTLE TAKEN ABACK THAT YOU WEREN'T PRESENT AT DINNER. ENJOY YOUR READS, AND HAVE A HOPEFULLY PRODUCTIVE DAY. I'M SURE I'LL SEE YOU SOON. BYE.

~✧~

Weston's POV

I laughed to myself.

I see what you did there, Sam. I can read through the lines, with you trying to act like you really don't miss me.

I could only smile, hearing from Maddie and Mother on how sad my Sam was at dinner and how she didn't even stay to socialize afterwards. It pulled at my heartstrings. I meant to let her know I was leaving, but I was torn between giving her space or pissing her off, and the last thing I wanted to do was make her even madder at me. Hopefully this deal would be closed today so I could get on a plane to start heading home. This nine-hour time difference didn't make things easy when communicating with anyone back home.

I was ready to be back home, to hold her in my arms, and move on with our lives. Surely, she had plenty of time to think things through, and based on her notes in the novels, I had a good idea of where her heart lay. It was just that stubborn mind of hers I had to convince.

Knock knock.

"Come in, Carl."

"Yes, sir. Your car is ready when you are."

"Well, let us get this show on the road and close the deal." I was boasting with confidence as I exited the penthouse, knowing what I had waiting at home.

CHAPTER 16:

Not a Date

The next couple of days were busy with work. The guys were out for meetings, and I was still processing Aunt Patsy's mess. But finally, the weekend was here. I promised Mia I would help her get ready for her date that night, so I went to her house and dolled her up.

She was so cute with her button nose and defined features, long, wavy brown hair and green eyes. At five foot four, she was a bit shorter than me at five six. I gave her a loose French braid with light makeup. She already had a nice summer tan. We chose a short black dress that complemented her figure without revealing too much and that would show enough to tease her new beau.

Mia slid on her wedges and was ready to go. I was still dressed in my work clothes, so I was now determined to rush home into my pajamas for the night. Walking her out of the house, we heard Dylan drive up in his Camaro. Then right behind him, I saw Weston's black Chevy truck. Mia looked as confused as I felt.

I quickly walked over to Weston. "Why are you here? Is everything okay at home?"

"Everything's fine. I didn't mean to cause panic. Just here to pick you up for a date."

"Um, we don't have plans for tonight. When did you even get home from Dubai? I was about to head home and catch up on some movies . . . in my pajamas."

"Literally four hours ago. I went by the house, and your dad said you were over here helping Mia for her big date, so I thought I'd accompany you home or to dinner. We can pick your car up tomorrow. I have to be out this way dropping some fence posts off for Mia's dad."

"Nice gesture, Wes, but I'm not sure that's a great idea." I walked to my car and told Dylan to be careful with Mia or I'd hurt him, then I watched them drive away.

As I opened my door, it was slammed back shut, and I felt an alluring presence behind me.

Weston turned me around to face him. "Woman, you have officially hurt my ego. How are you going to apologize?"

"Woman? Apologize? For what? Because I turned you down in front of our friends? I told you I need time, Wes."

"You did, and I'm trying, but you make it so hard." He gently pushed a few strands of my hair back behind my ear and inched closer until I was pinned between his body and my car.

I scrunched up my nose and looked down.

"What are you confused and overthinking about now?" he said.

I looked up at him. "You! I'm trying to figure *you* out. One minute you pour your soul out to me, and the next, you're surrounded by this dominant-aggressive aura. It's been years since we've been around each other, so I know we've changed, but you . . . There's something different about you now."

Wes pushed himself completely against me, his head bent down and his hot breath on my neck. "Is it a bad difference? Or does it turn you on more?"

"Wes, what the hell?" I tried to push him away, and I caught him off guard, so he stumbled back a few steps, only to keep his eyes locked on mine as I tried to look away. Before I could speak, his mouth was covering mine, then his insatiable lips found their way to the corner of my mouth, over to my neck, and down to my clavicle.

"You are mine, Sam, and no one else's. I'll give you time to come to this realization, but I wouldn't take too long, my dear."

"Are you threatening me? I do have a say of who and when I'm in a relationship. Don't get too high up on that horse of yours, cowboy."

He kissed me on the cheek. "Oh, don't you worry, darling. I won't fall. So, back to how you're going to apologize to me . . ." Giving me a wink.

"Ugh, fine. You can hang with me to eat pizza and watch a movie. Keep your hands to yourself, though."

He just smirked and walked to his truck.

I climbed up into the cab of Weston's truck and needed to break the now-awkward silence. "Well, I'm so happy for Mia, and I hope it ends well for them both. Did you know he's been waiting for his life to settle before he asked her out?"

Weston nodded. "Yep, he knows he doesn't come from the same type of influential family as Mia does, so he wanted to make sure he could support them and prove to her dad what kind of guy he is and that he loves his daughter."

"Good ol' Dylan. He's always been one of my favorites. He's always had a good head on his shoulders, regardless of his upbringing. Well, I pray for them. Mia's dad is pretty reasonable and didn't say too much about her going out tonight with him, so we shall see."

Weston reached for my hand across the seat. "Enough about them. What's the entire plan for tonight?"

"Other than my original plan of binge-watching movies with pizza and ice cream?" I laughed and tried to pull my hand back. "Did you think I was joking?"

"Well, let's do it. I'm game and won't even complain about the movies you pick."

I gave him a silly smirk.

We stopped by my favorite hole-in-the-wall pizza place, Nik's Pizzeria. We grabbed pizzas, some appetizers, and drinks to go. Mama already had the freezer full of my favorite ice cream. We arrived back at the house, and my parents smiled as we walked in together.

"It's nothing. We're going down to the movie room to catch up on some movies and eat dinner."

"Okay, sweetie. Y'all have fun," Mama said.

Before I closed the door, I heard Mama tell Daddy, "I hope it works out this time for the two of them. They really are a perfect match."

I closed the door and smiled.

Weston was already getting settled in the theater recliners. I remembered I was so happy when Daddy created this space for us years ago. It was like having our own little theater without leaving the house. We had our own candy concessions and popcorn maker that my mama kept stocked. We started scrolling through the movies. There were so many I'd missed seeing the past year because of working so much overtime. The first movie was "The Secret," a Josh Lucas love story, which sounded good to me.

Weston smiled and didn't say a word. Of course, by the end of the movie, my face was all puffy from crying, and I was ready for ice cream. Weston volunteered to run and grab it. Returning with my favorite flavor of double chocolate swirl and cherries and waffle cone pieces. Weston had a bowl of rocky road, meaning it seems my Mama kept his favorite in stock, as well. He even brought a blanket down since it was getting cold and I had a tank on.

I decided to choose an action movie next, so we went with "Wonder Woman." Halfway through the movie, I was snuggled up in my blanket and fighting sleep.

"You can lean your head on my shoulder if you want," Weston said. "I won't mess with you."

"Thanks." I thought about it for a minute then moved slightly closer to him, and then laid my head on his shoulder. He smelled so good with his usual mixed musk of wood and bourbon that all my senses crave. Also, I admired his muscles defined down his arm as the lights reflected off of him. Eventually I found that I was way too comfortable and began to drift off.

Some time must have gone by because I woke up in my own bed. I tried to sit up and found something heavy was on me. It was Weston. He had his arm around me, asleep next to me. I remember thinking, *o' my, he must've carried me to bed.*

I tried to twist my body, and his arm tightened around me, pulling me closer to him. Even in his sleep, he wouldn't let go. I didn't want to wake him up, so I got as comfortable as I could and fell back asleep.

CHAPTER 17:

Sneaky Man

The damn rooster crowed, and I was back awake. Though that was the most peaceful sleep I'd had in a long time. I was finally able to roll over, so I sat up on my elbow facing him. He was still asleep. Such a gorgeous man. In my eyes, I'd never met another who could compare.

I gently began tracing the outline of his face with my fingers, then I carefully pushed his black hair back off his forehead. I moved around to his defined cheekbone and down his chiseled jawline. He hadn't shaved in a few days, so he had this sexy, rugged beard coming in. My fingers reached his lips, and I glided across them. They were the most perfect tint of red and smoothness to match his dark features. I began smoothing out the lines in his furrowed brow and brought my fingers down the other side of his face. I was taking it all in since it had been so long since I'd been near him.

As I did this, I saw his eyes flutter open. I'd been caught, but he grabbed my hand into his and smiled. "Enjoying the view?"

I whispered with a smile, "Um ,well, you had a feather in your hair . . . from my pillow." I tried to sit up, but he moved fast, pinning me to my bed. One of his hands was holding both of my wrists together above my head, as he straddled me. His eyes had an intense darker tone to them than usual, and all I could do was look at him with wide, questioning eyes.

Almost like he could read my mind, he said, "I know what I want, and I'm no longer going to let anyone take away what is mine. I have had to be ruthless these past few years in dealings with my father and the business, so it has taught me some things. This does include you, Miss. Dupont."

"Weston, you know I still have a lot to think about before committing." I wasn't able to speak further because he muted me with his own mouth. The kiss was hard and intense to where I couldn't catch my breath. He bit my lip again, and this time I could taste the blood. He lowered his body onto mine so I could feel his excited lower presence. His mouth moved from my lips to my neck as his hand slid under my shirt, and he cupped my breast in his hand. I was still trying to catch my breath and control my body's urge to be with him.

"Oh, Sam, you taste and smell so good. You don't understand how much I've missed being with you. I dream about that summer all the time."

I let out a soft moan, and my back arched when he squeezed my breast and kissed my neck again. This only seemed to excite him more, and he moved both hands to my waist, inching my shirt up slowly while softly kissing every inch of my abdomen.

Now that my hands were free, I brought them down and pushed on his chest. "Weston, as tempting as this moment is, we can't do this right now. There will be no going back for me emotionally. I can't handle the unknown right now."

He stopped and gave me this look like he was trying to control my mind and body with his. "I'm serious, Weston. We need to stop." He saw the panic on my face, and almost like he was in a trance before, a frown appeared. "I'm so sorry, Sam. I didn't mean to . . . The urge to be with you is so strong. I promise I won't push you any further and to be better about controlling myself until you're ready."

"What if I'm never ready?" I tried to read his face, wondering if I offended him or made him sad.

The side of his lips curled up. "I promise you, Sam, you will be mine again. I know you know this. But I'll give you time to stop resisting what you feel in your heart." He rolled over next to me and sighed. "I love you, Sam. No time will ever change that."

There was a knock on my door.

"Sweetie, are you awake? Breakfast is ready."

"Oh, no. It's Mama." I felt like I was eighteen again and panicking.

"Relax, Sam. We're grown adults. Besides, we didn't even do anything to be ashamed of."

I blushed as the door opened and she poked her head in. "Oh! I was wondering where you were, Weston. Breakfast is ready if you want to join us."

"Sure, Mrs. Dupont. That would be great."

"Okay, well, I'll see y'all two in a bit, I guess."

I threw my face into my pillow, again dying of embarrassment.

Weston laughed as he stood up to get ready to head down. "Come on, darlin'."

Getting up, I headed to the bathroom to get ready. He met me there, and for some reason, he still remembered there were always brand-new toothbrushes in my drawer. We stood there brushing our teeth together like a married couple, him grinning ear to ear. I pushed him out so I could dress, then I threw on some athletic shorts and my old UT shirt Jackson sent me from college. I put my hair in a ponytail. Even up, it still reached my mid back. It might be time for something new, I thought as I splashed cold water on my face and wiped it off.

I walked out to him waiting on me.

"You could've gone down without me."

"Nah, I'd rather escort you to the kitchen so I can make sure you're safe."

"Um, okay," I said, laughing. "Just down the stairs and to the right. I think I can manage the path I've made since I could walk."

"All right. Suit yourself." He grinned and walked past me and down the stairs. Not even four steps down, my foot slipped, but I caught myself on the railing before completely sliding down the stairs on my ass.

Weston picked me up and cradled me in his arms. "See?"

"Please, put me down. There's no need to carry me." I glared at him.

"You said that earlier, and you just slipped. I'd rather be cautious than have something happen to you."

Weston carried me into the kitchen and set me down in my seat. I was about to jump up to make my plate.

"No, I'll make it. Stay there."

My parents and Jackson were staring back and forth between us and smiling.

"Hey, bro, can you make me a plate, too?"

I threw a biscuit at his head. "Jackson, shut up."

"If you were as delicate and beautiful as your sister, I might consider it," Weston said with a chuckle.

My parents were now laughing at our banter, and I was turning redder by the second. Weston finally came over with our plates and sat down next to me. I chose not to say a word and shoved food in my mouth.

Daddy asked, "Do y'all have plans today?"

I shook my head no, but Weston quickly responded back. "I need to take Sam over to Mia's to pick up her car, after I load up some material Mia's dad needs for the new fence he's putting in. After that, I thought about heading into San Antonio to take Sam out for the weekend . . . if I have your permission, sir."

I kept my head down and shook it side to side. Daddy wasn't sure what to think of it, but he thought I seemed to be happy.

He smiled at Weston. "Sure, son. If Sam wants to go, y'all have fun."

"Thank you, sir. Hey, Jackson. Do you and Lucey want to join us? And Sam, you can ask Mia and Dylan."

"Um, sure . . . Let me text her now."

I texted Mia and basically demanded that she and Dylan come. I couldn't go away that weekend with him on my own. No way. Luckily, Jackson told him they were in.

"Maybe we can have girls in one room and guys in the other," I said under my breath.

The boys just glared at me. Worth a shot, I thought to myself.

"Breakfast was great, Mrs. Dupont. Thank you. I'm going to head home to shower and pack up. See you in about thirty minutes, Sam?"

"Yep, that works."

Ping.

It was a text from Mia.

> OUCH! WE'RE IN SINCE YOU TWISTED MY ARM SO DAMN HARD. WE'LL MEET YOU AT YOUR HOUSE. I'LL FOLLOW DYLAN IN YOUR CAR. MY DAD IS ABOUT TO CALL WESTON, SO THE DELIVERY CAN WAIT UNTIL NEXT WEEKEND. SOMETHING CAME UP WITH WORK, AND HE'S HEADING TO LA TODAY.

I texted her back.

> SOUNDS GOOD. SEE YA SOON.

Just as I did, Weston's phone rang as he was walking out the door. "Hi, Mr. Miller . . ."

He left, and now I felt the stares.

"Sooo . . ."

"What, Mama? Nothing happened. We're taking it slow so I can make up my mind. My heart is still very guarded right now. Leave it be."

"Well, I know it was nice hearing all those laughs last night and seeing you two together again. I'm not pushing, but we just want you happy, no matter if it's with him or not. But don't push love away because you're scared."

"Got it, Mama. I guess I'm going to go pack since Daddy just couldn't say no to him." I playfully punched him in the arm.

"What did I do?"

We women glared at him, then laughed.

I ran upstairs to pack and decided not to change since we would be driving for the next two hours and would want to be comfortable. I packed my cute jumper and sandals to walk around in later. I packed a pair of jeans with my pink laced top and also my long pant jumper that hung low in front in case we ended up somewhere fancy for dinner. Bathing suit and clothes for tomorrow? Check. I packed my makeup and toiletries and headed down to wait on everyone.

I curled up in the porch swing with Maddox, the sweetest, biggest white lab I'd ever met. My parents got him for me the spring I graduated high school, and it was love at first sight. It was hard leaving him all those years while I traveled, but my parents took great care of him, and we FaceTimed a lot. When I returned, he was so happy and would rarely let me out of his sight.

I scratched his head. "I promise I won't leave you again, boy."

"Can I have that same promise?"

Maddox and I both whipped around to find Weston walking up.

"Geez, you scared me."

He gave me a hug. "Sorry. Oh, wow, you smell so good." He dipped his nose into my neck, and I could feel him breathing me in.

"Okay, lover boy. You need to tone it down some. Oh, good, here comes everyone now." I escaped from his embrace and ran to hug Mia, as we had a lot of details to exchange about our nights.

"Ya'll, Mama said we can borrow her Tahoe so we don't have to take as many cars. Does that work for everyone?"

Everyone agreed, so we loaded up the Tahoe, shuffled some cars around, and headed out.

I let Weston drive, and Dylan sat up front in the passenger seat. Jackson and Lucey were in the middle, with Mia and me in the very back. Like we were teenagers again, we wrote on notepads and kept to ourselves. Though I got glances from Weston in the rearview mirror when he heard our squeals and laughs.

CHAPTER 18:

The River

We were almost there, and at that point, Mia and I were pretty much filled in on each other's nights and excited and shocked about what lay ahead. We decided to enjoy the weekend with no worries—at least she was trying to convince me to do so. This wouldn't be a problem for Mia.

I wrote on the notepad: *We need to find a place to dispose of the evidence as soon as we arrive.*

She laughed and nodded, trying to keep a straight face.

I was looking out the window, catching a beautiful view of the River Walk. It had been so long since I'd been, and it was as lovely as I remembered. I figured we would stay at one of the chain hotels on the river, but I turned to see Weston pulling into a different hotel.

"We're here!"

The boys grabbed our things, and Weston handed the keys and a tip to the valet.

When we walked in, we were greeted by a large sign: Hotel Contessa. It was immaculate. I was so busy taking it all in, I didn't see Weston passing out keys to everyone. It was only noon, so I wasn't sure what the plan was.

Lucey said, "How about we chill and swim since it's so hot out, and then we can venture out later once it cools down a bit. The River Walk is best at dusk."

We all agreed to meet down at the pool, and we headed to our rooms on the top floor. First, we reached Jackson and Lucey's room, and a few doors down was Mia and Dylan's. Weston and I walked to the end of the hallway, and when he opened the door, and I was blown away. He'd booked the Contessa Suite for us. It had its own dining area and lounge area.

I ran inside; running into each room. "Look at that porcelain claw tub! You can fit at least four people in it!"

Weston smiled, watching me take it all in. Don't get me wrong, I had stayed at some swanky places over the years— and not some—but I was always so excited being somewhere new.

"You haven't even seen the best part!" Weston waved me over and pulled me out onto the balcony overlooking the River Walk.

"This is stunning, Weston. Thank you!" I shyly turned to face him.

He lifted my chin and kissed me softly on my lips.

"I knew you would want a view of the river, so why not the best view for my best girl?"

I snuggled my head into his chest as he hugged me. We stayed like that for a moment, but our phones started going off.

"I bet they're looking for us," I said.

We went to put our bathing suits on. I decided on my black and pink, low-cut, one-piece bathing suit. I walked out of the bathroom, and Weston picked me up and threw me on the bed.

"I'm not sure I can let you go out looking this good for everyone to see."

I covered my face with my hair so he didn't see me blush.

"It's just a bathing suit, Wes. I bought it in Prague. You like it?"

"Like you can't tell . . ." He pressed up against me in between my legs. I realized I provoked the beast within and could feel his lower member harden.

Weston's phone rang. Thank goodness. Saved by the bell.

Weston looked perplexed, and in a deep, disturbed voice, he said, "We're coming down now. Yes, order us two, thanks." He hung up. "They apparently started the party early. Let's go." He pulled me up off the bed and handed me my cover-up. I grabbed my pool bag, and we walked towards the elevator. Once inside, I was pushed up against the back wall with my arms pinned down next to me. Feverishly, we kissed, and he must've sensed me loosening up, so he brought my arms up around his neck. I ran my fingers through his silky, jet-black hair as I was caving to his needs, to my body's heated needs. The elevator started to open, as I tried to escape Westons embrace. I have never been one for public display. Luckily, no one was waiting to come in. I rushed out to the pool area before he could touch me anymore. *God, help me not give into him!*

We had a great time chilling by the pool and swimming, and around 3:30, we all opted to head up and rest before going out that night. Weston said he was treating us to a delicious dinner, so everyone needed to look on-point. We planned to meet at the hotel bar at 5:30.

Once in our room, I decided to lie down for a bit before taking a shower, and he had some emails that apparently needed his attention by the end of the day.

Weston woke me up at 4:45 so I could shower and doll up. Wes said "on point," so that meant I would wear my black jumpsuit that cut low in the front, with a low back and a silver chain across it, with my silver heels. I straightened my hair to give it a sleeker look and brushed a light amount of powder on my face, going with the smoky-eye look with my plum lipstick. I grabbed my wristlet and walked into the lounge area, where Weston was working.

"I'm ready."

"Give me five more minutes to finish this . . ." He looked up from his computer. "Holy shit, Sam. There are no words to describe how incredible you look right now."

I playfully bowed to him. "Thank you, kind sir."

He chuckled, got up, kissed me on the cheek, and left to get ready himself. Of course, it took him less than ten minutes, and he was walking out of the bedroom.

Dear, God! I thought to myself. A six-foot-five cowboy in fitted dark jeans with a black belt latched through his prized rodeo buckle, he looked like he just stepped out of an old-school Stetson catalogue. He wore a pressed, white, button-up collared shirt with a fitted black sports coat that was obviously tailor-made for him. He topped off the look with his black cowboy hat and black cowboy boots.

I felt flushed and unsure if I could stand up.

Please don't grin at me like that. It only makes matters worse.

He took my hand and pulled me up to be in front of him.

"You look mighty handsome tonight, sir."

"Why, thank you, ma'am." He tipped his hat towards me, and we laughed and walked out arm in arm to the lobby.

As we walked to the bar, our friends started to catcall and whistle.

"Damn, I don't think you'll find a finer couple in this great state," Mia said.

We rushed past them. Me, blushing wildly, shaking me head at Mia.

"Y'all are too much," I said. "Let's go."

We began our descent up the river, stopping along the way to take pics and enjoy the view. Though we were a great-looking group all around, I sensed the stares of women and even some men towards Weston. He kept his head forward and didn't acknowledge any of it. I decided to tease him about it. Just as quickly as the words came out of my mouth, he turned to me and pulled me close.

"Let's give them a show, then."

Before I could even guess what was about to happen, he took his hat off, then proceeded to dip me while kissing me—all in what felt like one motion. He slowly lifted me back up with his lips still attached to mine. Once he knew I was stable, he released me from his mouth, then he put his arm back in mine, and we strolled off like nothing just happened. Though he flashed that cheshire grin my way. The one I still wasn't sure what to say or do with.

We headed to the corner of River Walk and took a right. It seemed we'd found our way to the restaurant, Bohanan's.

"Wow, this looks high class and smells amazing," Lucey said.

Weston went to check on our reservations, and we talked Jackson into taking a picture of just us girls.

Mia was dazzling in her fitted, open-back silver dress that had a split all the way up to her mid-thigh. Lucey was rocking her short, sequined, dark blue dress that hugged all her curves with a v in the back. She was five foot nine and had killer legs and the body of a model, but she was the most down-to-earth, easy-going person, and loved the ranch and rodeo life. Jackson definitely picked a great one.

Weston returned, and we were taken to a private room. The boys were gentlemen and pulled our chairs out for us. The girls sat on one side of the table and the guys on the other. We could hear the classical jazz band playing outside, really making it a romantic evening. The waiter came by to take our drink orders, and I was about to order when Weston piped in.

"She'll have a bourbon, neat, and I'll take one, as well, thank you."

I stared at him. "How did you know that's what I would order, let alone that I would even drink that?"

"I won't lie to you, Sam. I've done my research on you so I could know the new, mature Samantha that was coming home. To be prepared . . ."

"So, you had someone investigate me?"

He winked at me. "I have my ways."

I wasn't sure whether I should've been creeped out or admired this tactic. "Hmm. What else do you know about me?"

He winked at me. "I guess you'll just have to wait and see."

After dinner, we were all stuffed, tipsy, and tired. Weston graciously covered dinner, so we thanked him, and I gave him a hug, stepping up on my tiptoes to kiss his cheek.

We headed back to the hotel, laughing and enjoying the remainder of the night. The River Walk was now completely lit up along the way, and we watched gondolas float by as the city itself was getting ready to sleep.

CHAPTER 19:

No Turning Back

With hugs and kisses, we all parted ways and headed to our rooms until morning. I turned to Weston. "Not that I or anyone else is not appreciative of what you've done this weekend, just know that I'm as happy having a picnic by the lake or sleeping in the bed of the truck under the stars. But I will say it is nice to get fancied up and go out every now and then."

"Every now and then. Got it." He put his hands on both sides of my face and leaned down to kiss me. It started as gentle but quickly turned heated. My whole body was tingling and my heart was lit on fire. Unsure how much longer I can deny my want and need for him. Scooping me up in his arms, he gently laid me on the bed this time. He took my shoes off for me as he also stepped out of his boots and put his sports coat on the chair.

Dear God, now he's unbuttoning his shirt.

Between the alcohol and the man in front of me, I was having hot flashes and couldn't stop staring as he got to the last button and pulled his shirt off. He was toned all over like a Greek god. Tan and toned all over. I hadn't seen his body in five years, and he'd filled out even more nicely. Even to the perfect *V* that his pants hinged on. Though he was a businessman by day, he was always helping on the ranch or anyone that needed a helping hand and was well aware of his routine of running 5 miles every morning. It was Weston's big heart and gentle soul that I always admired most about him, and looking like a cowboy angel sent from the Heavens was just a bonus.

Now lying in bed next to me, I looked over and got lost again in his scintillating ocean blue eyes. Some of his hair had fallen over his right eye, so I went to swipe it gently back over.

He then cupped my face with one hand and gazed into my eyes. "I love you, Samantha Jane, and you truly are the most stunning person I have ever known."

I shifted my eyes down and back up to look at him while biting my lip. I was unsure what to say, and he still made me feel so shy sometimes. I looked away again. He then kissed me, demanding my attention.

I felt myself caving to his inner beast. "Let's go slow, okay?" I placed my hand on his chest.

"No pressure, Sam. You're in control, so at any time, tell me to stop."

I nodded and smiled, thinking to myself that might be easier said than done. Thinking, *I love this man, but if he breaks me this time, I will always be broken.*

He gently slid off the top half of my jumpsuit, leaving me quite exposed. His hands cupped my breasts as his kisses began lingering down my neck to my chest. His lips were over my right breast, biting my nipple. I arched up and let out a slight moan. He then turned his attention to my left breast, handling it the same way. Minute by minute, I could feel myself losing control and becoming more wet. He had me stand up to shimmy my way out of the rest of my jumpsuit, left only in my black, lacey panties. Wes stood up to remove his belt and jeans, and we were both left standing there in our underwear.

He pulled me closer to him, bringing his hand down between my legs and up against my panties. "You are so wet," he whispered in my ear.

I let out another moan as this man I've missed for so long started to explore my entire body, inside and out. His fingers interlaced with my panties and pulled them down as I stepped out of them. Weston bent down, gently rubbing my legs up and down while placing soft kisses all over them as he made his way up to my inner thighs.

He must've felt me get shaky, and he asked if I was okay. I nodded, and in a low husky tone, he told me to sit on the bed. As I sat, he was still pressing his palm between my inner thighs. His mouth inched closer, causing me to fall back on the bed, and then his wet tongue entered my slit, causing my core to quiver. With one of his hands, he reached up and caressed my breasts, and the other hand was pressed on top of my lower stomach to hold me in place. Groaning himself "you taste amazing Sam. Better than I remember." I couldn't help but arch my back and let out several moans as he brought me to my peak, sucking and licking me dry. The vibration of his groan into my core had me wanting him more. There was no going back now, I thought to myself. My thoughts were quickly interrupted with a heated kiss, his tongue sliding into mine. I kissed him back just as feverishly, tasting myself on his tongue. I pulled him closer to me while running my fingers through his hair, almost pulling it. It took one look from me as our eyes locked, and he knew I'd given in to the desire. He disregarded his *Derek Rose* briefs in a single motion and was back on top of me, moving closer to me with his pulsing member. With his eyes locked in on mine, he slowly pushed himself inside me, allowing my walls to expand to his girth.

He groaned. "Fuck! Sam! You're so tight. It feels incredible." The rhythm was slow at first as we adjusted to each other, but we soon found our stride, now moving in a vigorous, harmonious motion. I pushed my hips into him to be closer and deeper. We both moaned and panted as if we couldn't get enough of each other. As if we could not get close enough. Not wanting any space between us.

"Weston, I'm about to—"

"Me too, baby, me too. Just hold on."

I wrapped my legs around him while grasping and clawing at his back, trying not to lose complete control, until we both come to our release together. We tried to catch our breath, and covered in sweat, Weston kissed me softly on my forehead. "That was amazing, Sam. It was more phenomenal than any of my dreams about you. I love you so much." I looked back into those bright ocean blue eyes. "I love you, Weston." He looked as if he might shed a tear. Leaning in to give me another kiss, we start over again. The need to make up for lost time and explore each other more was evident.

CHAPTER 20:
The New Normal

A couple of weeks had gone by since Wes and I became intimate and announced to our family and friends that we were officially back together. Everything was happening so fast, as I was still trying to figure out this new normal I'd been thrown into. I was helplessly in love with this man, so if my heart broke a second time, it was on me. My heart and body constantly yearned for him to be near, and in reality, in my twenty plus years of being around him, when had I ever been able to tell him no?

Jackson had been traveling quite a bit while expanding the ranch's business, so I was constantly drowning in paperwork and crunching numbers. Weston's dad sent him to New York to deal with some of the family business and was supposed to be home by Thursday night. It was only Tuesday.

The weekly big family dinner was moved to Thursday to accommodate Weston being back home, plus Jackson and Lucey had been busy looking for houses and wedding planning. Mama and Daddy were trying to convince them to build on the property up the hill since the ranch would be left to both of us. I hoped they would so we could continue growing the place and stay close together.

Mama and I sat down in our PJs to watch some TV together post dinner, while dad was in the study working. We heard the doorbell ring, and Maddox took off to the door, barking.

"Who could that be?" I said. "It's after eight."

My daddy strolled out of the study. "I'll answer it." He opened the door and said, "Son, do you have any recollection of what time it is? What can I help you with?"

"I am so sorry, sir, but I'm looking for Miss Samantha Dupont. Does she live here?"

I heard a very strong English accent, so I headed to the door quickly, and stood next to my daddy.

"I'm Samantha Dupont. What can I do for you?"

The man was stunning, almost unreal, and he looked vaguely familiar, but I couldn't seem to place him.

"Please forgive me, Miss Dupont. I'm running later than expected. You truly live out in the middle of nowhere."

I couldn't help but giggle, but I asked again, "What can I do for you, sir?"

"That's right . . . Let me start over. I'm Nate Hughes, Mr. Hughes's nephew."

He extended his hand, and as I went to shake it, he lifted my hand and kissed the top of it.

"I knew you looked familiar. Please, come in. Tell me he didn't send you all this way for paperwork that could've been expedited or emailed."

"You know my uncle, Miss Dupont . . ."

"Call me Sam."

"Sam, he likes to be over the top. He also thought this would be a great opportunity for us to get to know each other since you will be leading the headquarters, and he's appointed me president of the company."

"Oh, very well, President Hughes. I hope we can come to terms and work together. I'm unaware of what your uncle has told you, and he doesn't know about my current dating status, but if he's still trying to play matchmaker, I'll have to decline. I'm already taken. Long story, but he has my heart, fully. Though I am sure with looks like yours and your brilliant mind, you're not at all lonely or lacking women by your side."

"I will take it as Miss . . . Sam finds my looks appealing. Yes, you are correct. I'm not lacking in that area. But it is time to find a suitable wife and start a family, as told by my own family."

"I understand that, Mr. Hughes."

"Please call me Nate. When you call me Mr. Hughes, it feels like you're speaking to my father or uncle. I'm not that old or distinguished yet."

Mama brought some tea out as we continued talking in the living room. My phone started going off. It was Weston. I texted him back saying we had company and that I would call him back shortly. After a little more time passed, Nate stood and stated that he would be going, as it was later than expected, and he was hoping to find his way back into town without getting lost.

Mama spoke up. "Nate, we have a guesthouse out by the pool, and you're more than welcome to stay the night. It's very dark out there, and a lot of deer and critters like to be out on these roads."

"Thank you, ma'am, but I couldn't possibly intrude."

"No bother at all. We always have guests, so everything you need should be there already. If not, just ask. Breakfast will be at seven thirty if you care to join us."

"Thank you, Mrs. Dupont. This must be what they call Southern hospitality. I greatly appreciate it. Before I go out, Sam, here's the contract. Please read over it carefully, and we can discuss it tomorrow."

"Thank you, Nate. Good night."

My daddy walked him out to the guesthouse to help him settle in. I took the contract, grabbed my phone, and headed to my room to call Wes.

"Hey, babe. Sorry so late. Were you asleep?"

"No, I was finishing up some paperwork and waiting for your call. Who was there?"

"Oh, such a crazy day. Mr. Hughes's nephew Nate is here. He brought me a contract to look over to run a mutual funds business for him."

I went into detail about the day to Wes, and when I finished, I heard, "So you're telling me he sent his nephew from England to meet you and deliver paper? The boy he wants to set you up with? How old is this kid?"

I giggled. "Do I perceive a dash of jealousy in your tone, Mr. Lancaster?"

"Do I need to catch a red-eye and be there in a few hours?"

"What? No. You're crazy. Nate is now the president of the new company. I want you to review this contract with me when you get back. He wanted to introduce himself and family orders. The best thing is, I can stay here. I may have to travel to England every so often, but then you can come with me. The Hughes will love you!"

"Sure, we can look at it tomorrow. Just promise not to sign anything before I return."

"Yes, dear," I state with an eye roll and smile that he can see.

"I heard that eye roll, miss. I will make sure to punish you for that later, because I need to finish this before the morning's meeting, so I'll let you go. I love you, Sam."

"I love you, Wes. Sweet dreams." Still looking at my phone, giggling. There is not a punishment he gives, that I don't enjoy.

It was Thursday morning, and Weston was coming home, so I had that to look forward to. I texted him before heading downstairs, as I was sure he was getting ready for the meeting.

Good morning. Can't wait to see you tonight! XOXOXO

It was another day at the ranch, and I had the contract in my hand to review later with Nate and Weston. I heard the horses going crazy outside, so I looked out my window to see what the fuss was about. The baby goats were out causing havoc in the stables and for the ranch hands. It was pretty amusing to watch as the guys were falling over trying to catch the little guys.

Something caught the corner of my eye, so I looked to the left, and it was Nate stepping out of the guest house while pulling a t-shirt over his head.

Oh, this isn't good.

I ducked before I thought he saw me. Thinking, *damn, that is a body that should be appreciated.* I quickly heard a shrill, so only to look back out, I saw that evil rooster chasing Nate around in circles. Good, he found someone else to pick-on. Laughing, I ducked back down, crawled on my hands and knees over to my bathroom and closed the door, before getting up and ready for the day.

Lucey and Jackson were already at the table having breakfast, and I was surprised to see Nate there with a plateful of food.

"This is so good," he said. "I might never have tea and toast again for breakfast."

We all chuckled and started talking about the day's meetings and tasks. I was supposed to ride with Jackson to the bank and get my name added to the accounts since Aunt Pasty got her wish and was retiring at the end of June in two weeks. All of a sudden, I heard the back screen door open and shut, so we all turned around.

"Oh my God, Weston! You're home early!" I ran and jumped into his arms, wrapping my legs around his waist. He hugs me back like it's been forever apart.

I had to get home to my favorite girl. It's been too long."

Daddy chuckled. "Son, it's only been four days."

"Well, sir, after five years apart, any minute without her is too long."

"Ain't that the truth, son. Well, welcome back early. Did your dad come home with you?"

"No, sir. He'll be in later this afternoon, so we should see him at dinner."

Weston put me down and looked up to say hello to everyone else. I saw his gaze stop at Nate, so I took his hand and walked him to Nate.

"Weston, this is Nate Hughes. Nate, this is Weston, my boyfriend."

They shook hands, but I believed everyone sensed the tension between the two of them.

Breaking the silence, "Well, it's time to head to the office. Wes, what are your plans this morning? I was going to go to the bank with Jackson to add my name on the accounts, unless you want to take me. And then when we get back, the three of us can look over the contract together. This way, I can give Mr. Hughes an answer by the end of the day."

"I'm all yours, babe. Let's go."

"Are you good, Nate?"

"Yes, I'm about to head into town myself to grab some supplies and check in to my hotel. My number's on the contract, so just text me, Sam, when you want to meet up to discuss."

As soon as we walked out the front door, Weston stopped me.

"Why is he here this morning?" he asked with a scowl on his face.

"It was late, so Mama offered him the guest room last night. No big deal. Are you trying to accuse me of something?"

"No, I'm not. But you're mine, Samantha Jane."

"Wes, you do *not* own me! I make my own decisions, and if me taking this job and working with him is going to be a problem, then we are going to have a huge problem." I glared at him as he frowned back at me.

Even when he was mad, he still looked sexy, especially now that I noticed the five o'clock shadow on his face. I placed my hand gently on his cheek, as he wasn't used to me talking back and being so independent. But that is what roaming the world solo does to you. It makes you grow up and deal with the world for what it is and take a stance when needed.

He cupped my face with his hands and kissed me. It was the type of kiss that I'd been longing for from someone for so long—gentle and hard at the same time. He pulled back slowly, leaving my lips lingering for more.

"I'm sorry, Sam. I'm being irrational and over demanding of you. I just can't lose you again . . . not after everything."

"I appreciate your willingness to fight for me. Just know that it's you I've chosen. Let's just enjoy this and see where we go from here, okay?" I stood on my tiptoes to kiss his cheek, and he picked me up and carried me bridal style to his truck.

CHAPTER 21:
Something New, Something Old

Wes and I ran our errands at the bank, then I was all squared away on the accounts. He also stated he had a surprise for me. For a moment, I thought we were going home, but he turned early onto Ashford Road. I was wondering where we were going, as it used to be a dirt road that came to a dead end, with only a handful of houses on it. Now it was paved. As we were driving, I remembered Mia, the boys and me riding our bikes down there all the time to play in the lake behind several of the houses and thinking that these Victorian houses looked abundant and majestic. We reached the end of the road, where there was only one house that sat not far from the water. I remembered it used to have white with black shutters, but now it resembled more of a grayish-blue with dark blue shutters. It had two stories with a large, gleaming white porch that wrapped its way to the left and around with Victorian trim on the top and bottom. To the right, there was a Juliet tower covered in scalloped shingles that faced the lake and a sunroom coming off the backside. It truly was breathtaking, but now I was out of my thoughts as I turned to Weston.

"Why are we here? Was this another Lancaster project? It's definitely been updated."

He nodded. "Do you like it?"

"It's breathtaking, Wes."

"Come on, let me show you around the place." He stepped out of the truck and took my hand to lead me around the house. I noticed all the intricate details on the house and porch, and even the flower beds were pristine and vibrant with life. Someone must have been living there because this place had been very well kept. As we walked towards the back, there were beautiful stables with open pastures that opened up for several acres. I also noticed the stables weren't occupied.

"Oh, I guess the owners don't have horses. That seems like a waste to have all that with no horses or animals to use."

"I believe they're having horses moved over soon from their old place. So serene, isn't it?"

"It truly is! But should we be here? What if they come back while we're here?"

"No worries, babe. I know the owner. Want to check out the inside?"

"Um, sure, if it really is fine," I said with an awkward face, as he pulled a key out to unlock the door.

He pulled me inside, and I could tell that someone had really put in an effort with the decorations. It truly felt like I was walking back in time, but with a modern flair. The colors and trim on the walls were immaculate in a cream farmhouse with black trim. The furniture looked untouched but also looked like it might be very comfortable. I was in awe walking through the downstairs while we made our way up the spiral staircase to a large opening at the top. When we entered the upstairs, there was a large sitting area, two bedrooms with a Jack and Jill bathroom on the left, and a very large master on the right. Every room was unfurnished but large with tiered ceilings. The master ceiling had a stunning and intricate Victorian lace design.

I made my way into the master bath, which was covered in marble and stone, had an open waterfall shower, an old-style deep claw tub, and a double vanity with black-trimmed hanging mirrors. There was another door, so I stepped in. It was a closet as large as one of the bedrooms across the hall.

I found my way back into the bedroom, where Weston was standing by the French doors that I must have completely missed earlier. We walked out, and I realized this bedroom had its own balcony.

"Whoever you had working on this house did an amazing job, Wes. It truly is a dream."

"Thanks, Sam. A lot of time and effort went into restoring this place to make it perfect."

He quickly turned to me, took my hands, and I felt his palms sweating. "Are you all right?" I asked, worriedly.

The last time I remembered him being like that was when he kissed me that summer and confessed his feelings, but even then, it was after several drinks that I was sure gave him liquid encouragement.

With a nervous smile, he said, "Samantha Jane . . ." He got down on one knee. "Marry me! Move in here with me, and let's start our life together. We've been apart for far too long, and I don't want to go another day without you officially by my side. I love you."

"Weston, I . . . I . . . We just got back together after being apart. You really want to jump right into marrying me and living together?"

"Even more reason, Sam. Can you really tell me this isn't what you want? All of this with me?"

I could tell he was getting anxious since my initial response wasn't yes. There was nothing I had wanted more in my life than to be with him in every way possible. Was this too soon? Were we ready for this? We both had the family business to run, as well as outside careers, but this had been the plan all along, even five years earlier. As a million thoughts ran circles in my head, I opened my mouth to speak . . .

"I love you, Weston. My answer is . . . Yes. Yes, I will marry you!"

He picked me up and spun me around, slowly put me down, then dipped me into a passionate kiss. After he pulled me back up, he reached into his pocket and pulled out the most simple and gorgeous ring that I had ever laid eyes on. He placed it on my finger, and I lifted my hand to admire it closer. It looked so familiar, though. Before I could even ask, he said, "It's your mom's engagement ring. She gave it to me when I asked for their permission. She knows you've always admired it and thought it would be a great heirloom to pass on."

Tears streamed down my face. I played with that ring so much growing up. It was a 1.5-carat oval surrounded by mini diamonds on a band that looked like two vines intertwining. I used to imagine getting married and having one just like it.

"Thank you, Wes. I will cherish this forever and pass it down to our little girl when the time comes." I hugged him as if I would never let him go.

After being overwhelmed for an hour or so, we realized it was almost one o'clock in the afternoon, and we were starving. Knowing that we still needed to review the contract, I found Nate's number and texted him to meet us at Mabel's for lunch so we could review it there. He texted back and said he'd meet us.

~✧~

Weston's POV

My Sam was about to be officially mine. She said yes. I almost couldn't believe it, it seemed so surreal. I watched her grin from ear to ear while she sat next to me in the truck. To some, it might have looked like a quick engagement, but for me, this was years in the making. I hadn't expected to propose that day, but it felt right in that moment. Plus, the ring had been wearing a hole in my wallet. Now I had to convince her to have a short engagement so we could be married by the end of the year. *Gosh, she's beautiful*, I thought to myself while stealing glances of her while driving. She had on a cute yellow dress with her dark, caramel hair blowing loosely in the wind.

My thought was to wait before I had shown her the house and proposed. I wanted her to feel confident in us and her decision. I felt like that day was the day. Sure, you could've said the English kid pushed me over the edge, but I also wasn't sure how much longer I could've kept it a secret. The house needed to be a surprise.

I bought the house right after I became vice president of Lans Enterprises. The owners were reluctant at first, but money talked. I would've paid five times over the price I paid if I needed to. There were too many memories in that area, and I would never forget how my Sam would look at that house when we would come down to swim and ride trails. I would watch her take in every detail, closing her eyes as if she were snapping a photo of it in her mind. There was no doubt in my mind that she would love it. Now we could decorate together and make this our home for our family to grow. Sam being pregnant and us having kids . . . wow. There was nothing more I wanted than to build a life with her.

CHAPTER 22:
Not Giving Up

We reached Mabel's, and Nate already had a table. I noticed people were staring at him (probably because he wasn't from around these parts), plus I was sure his looks caused some attention, as well.

Wes and I walked in hand in hand, like we were floating on a cloud. Nate stood up to greet us, shaking Weston's hand and kissing both sides of my cheek. Out of the corner of my eye, I saw Wes's clenched jaw, so I gave him a look to settle down.

We sat down, and I pulled out the contract. As soon as the waitress took orders, we got down to business. I hadn't even looked at it, fearing I might've been too excited and signed my life away. Mr. Hughes had already given me the gist of the contract, and I had faith he would never try to screw me over.

As we turned the pages, we came to the fourth page, and my mouth gaped open. This page had all the numbers on it: salary, percent of the company, as well as other benefits.

"Nate, this is crazy! This salary is triple what I was making at Colonial, and I'm not even doing half of the work. Your uncle is my only client right now, correct?" I was taken back, as that now increased my salary to half a million dollars.

"Sam, my uncle has extreme faith in you. And you'll be taking over and managing all the family's stocks."

"Oh, wow. But still, I'd rather earn this salary over time. This is too much to start off with. Can we push that down?"

Weston whispered in my ear, "Sam, what are you doing? Know your worth."

"I do, Wes. But I also don't want the pressure of knowing what expectations go into place with making that kind of money. I need to earn this figure and let the whole family trust me as much as Mr. Hughes does. This world can be very finicky, and one little mistake, they lose hundreds of thousands—or more—as quickly as they can make it. Plus, there's finding the best investors for their companies and properties."

I figured Nate could hear us. "Sam, I will respect your wishes if you choose, but know that my uncle believes this is your worth . . . and then some."

"Thank you for that, Nate, but yes, I would like to amend the contract. Based on what I was making at Colonial, let's push down to $265,000 for the next six months. I think that's reasonable for everyone. We can review after the first two quarters and then annually after that. Sound fair?"

"As you wish, Sam." Nate amended the contract with his fancy, gold-plated pen. "Anything else?"

"Wes, how do you feel about this? Did you see anything in the contract that needs further review?"

"No, the contract is sound. Mr. Hughes seems to be a generous and smart man. Everything looks good."

"Great! All right, Sam, I'll have the amendment added and bring you an updated copy to be reviewed and signed."

"Perfect. Thank you, Nate."

The waitress delivered our food, and the next hour was spent discussing staffing plans and what supplies and access would be needed. The goal was to have everything set up by the end of the following week. Dad had already said I could take one of the offices in the barn because I would have multiple monitors and equipment. I could also fit at least two other people in there comfortably.

Wes asked, "Well, Mr. Hughes, how much longer are you in town?"

With a smirk, Nate said, "Oh, please. Call me Nate, Mr. Lancaster."

Why do men have such egos?

And Wes grinned with a clenched jaw. "Well then, Nate. When are *you* going home?"

I side-kicked his leg under the table.

"I actually fly home tonight to make all the arrangements, and then I'll be back in two weeks for some time, just to oversee the startup and make sure Sam has everything she needs. I'll also deal with any difficulties she runs into."

Before Weston could say a word, I spoke up. "I am sure my mama will let you stay in the guesthouse during that time, if you wish. That way, you don't have to trek between town and the ranch." I held Weston's hand under the table, hoping to squeeze it hard enough to indicate that he should not say anything.

"That would be very kind of your family, Sam, and I will certainly take you up on that offer."

"Sounds good, President. We'll see you out. We both have tasks to complete at the ranch before the end of the day."

We walked out of the restaurant, Weston in front of me, and Nate pulled me back by the hand.

"Sam . . ." He held my hand now adorning the ring, and he had an icy look in his eyes. "Congratulations on the pending nuptials."

"Thank you, Nate, I appreciate it. Wes and I grew up with each other and dated years ago, so I assure you this isn't sudden."

"I see . . ." He moved in a little closer and whispered in my ear. "I'm still not sure I want to give up on you just yet." He pulled back, gave me a grin, and kissed my cheek, then he walked away. "I'll see you in two weeks."

I was dumbstruck and totally caught off guard by what this man said to me. What the hell? I decided not to tell Wes about it, as I really wanted this corporation up and running and didn't need any man's ego interfering. Besides, we were about to move in together and get married. I just needed to let Mr. Hughes and Nate know that there wasn't a possibility.

Suddenly, I felt a wave of fear. Mr. Hughes was a very powerful man, as were the Lancasters, both in their own respective worlds. I hoped these two would never clash—especially over someone like me.

I walked back to the truck where Weston was standing. He opened the door, and I jumped in. Once he got in, he looked at me with a solemn expression, like he knew what Nate said. Or maybe he saw the fear in my eyes.

It was a quiet drive back to the ranch, so I figured I had better speak up.

"I only stated he could stay at the guesthouse because I figure we will be moved in together. I want to do that as soon as possible."

"Really?" He gave me a shocked smile. "I figured you'd want to wait a bit."

"If you don't want to yet, we can wait, but I am ready to start my life with you."

"Sam, I've been ready to wake up to you every morning and love you every night. since all those years ago. So, are we going to make the official announcement tonight at the family dinner?"

"I think we should. We have a lot to celebrate!"

I could tell he was in a much better mood, and he held my hand as we turned onto the long driveway to the ranch. Since it was 4:30 p.m., we decided to part ways for a bit to prepare for dinner.

CHAPTER 23:
Not All News Is Good News

I headed to the kitchen to help Mama finish up dinner and set the table. My ring was in my pocket, and I was ready to make the announcement with it after everyone arrived. Since it was such a special occasion, I decided to wear my cream cotton strapless dress that had pockets on each side. The bottom, waist, and hem were trimmed in black. Comfy and cute, I couldn't go wrong with that.

Jackson and Lucey had arrived, and through the window, I saw Maddie running up the walk. Daddy was already at the table looking weary, so I hugged and kissed him on the cheek.

"Hey, Daddy."

"Hey, honey. How was your day?"

"It was good. What did you do today?"

"Oh, you know. I visited some of the other properties to check on the cattle, helped fix some fence posts down at the Lowry farm, and then I came back to handle some paperwork."

"Sounds like a busy day. Take it easy the rest of the week. You look tired, Daddy."

"I will, Sam. Thank you for always worrying about me."

The Lancasters walked in with Weston behind them. He had a big grin on his face as he made his way over and put his arms around me, then leaned down and gave me a kiss on the forehead. Mama brought the last dish out to place on the table, and we'd all found our spots.

Daddy said the blessing and gave a toast to the family, health, and the ranch. Once he finished, Weston squeezed my hand, and I realized he wanted to do this right then. I carefully slipped the ring on my finger as Weston stood up and clinked his glass with a butter knife.

"Speaking of family . . ." He motioned for me to stand up next to him. "We have an announcement."

Everyone was smiling, except for Mr. Lancaster, who stayed straight-faced.

Wes said, "I asked Samantha to marry me, and well . . . she said yes!"

I threw my hand up to show off my ring.

"Also, I showed her the house, and we're moving in together soon."

Mama winked at me, and everyone got up to hug us.

"It's about damn time!" Daddy said.

I gave him a big hug and whispered, "Thank you. You will always be the number-one man in my heart."

Down the table, Mrs. Lancaster hugged her son and slapped Mr. Lancaster on the arm, telling him to be part of it. Confused by what was going on, I stood next to Weston while his parents congratulated him. As I took his arm in mine, Mrs. Lancaster gave me a big squeeze and asked when the date would be.

Wes said, "I prefer sooner than later."

"I always wanted a fall wedding outside, with sunflowers out by the pond, but I don't want to take away from Jackson and Lucey, either."

"Oh, no, Sam. You won't be. I promise we're good if you marry before us. We have some announcements, as well."

"Thank you, Lucey. We appreciate that. Please, spill the beans!"

"You want to tell them, Jackson?"

Jackson took her hand. "How about you say the big one after I announce the first one?"

"Well, we're taking Dad and Mama's advice and decided to build up on the hill. We already have the plans drawn up, and the contractor is ready to start next week."

We all yelled with excitement but quickly quieted down, waiting to hear what the next set of news was.

Lucey smiled as she pulled Jackson's hand to her belly. "We're having a baby!"

"That's incredible, you guys!" I started crying with happiness. "I'm going to be an auntie!" Then it clicked. "Lucey, how far along are you, and what about the wedding?"

"We're about to complete the first trimester next week, so three months. By the time of the wedding, I'll be pushing eight months. Definitely not how we planned this, but God has His reasons. So, Jackson and I have already gone to the courthouse and gotten married. But we're also aware that a lot of time and money has been spent on planning the wedding, so after talking with my parents, they still want us to go through with it so we can celebrate with everyone." Lucey laughed. "May I not be as huge as a whale, come that day."

"I seriously doubt that, Lucey. You're still as thin as a toothpick, even at three months."

It was an evening of joyful surprises. As we ate, I looked around at my family and Wes, and my heart was beyond full. I needed to cherish this moment in my heart forever. Though we were all chatting across the table, I saw Mama paying extra attention to Daddy, who had really been quiet since after the excitement. He seemed to look ragged and pale. I wanted to think it was due to too much excitement for one evening, but my heart ached knowing it wasn't that.

I kicked Jackson under the table for his attention and whispered, "Is something wrong with Dad you're not telling me?"

"Cross my heart, Sam. I know nothing," he whispered back. "I've seen him get tired easily, but he really has been doing too much."

We looked at each other, then Jackson turned to Dad. "Hey, Dad. I was thinking we should wake up and go fishing in the morning before we start the day. What do you think?

"Sure, son. That sounds nice. You sure you wanna be out-fished by your old man again?" Daddy chuckled.

Jackson turned back to me. "He seems fine."

Feeling eyes on me, I noticed Mr. Lancaster staring at me with worry in his eyes. I just chose to smile and look back down at my plate.

Mama brought out dessert: homemade apple strudel pie with vanilla ice cream. The smell wafted through the whole house, and I could already taste it. Once I helped Mama pass out all the dessert, we dug in, chatting about all the upcoming events in our lives.

It was 9:00 p.m., and the Lancasters were getting ready to leave, so I walked them and Wes out to say good night. We were standing on the front porch, looking up at the sky and listening to crickets, until we were interrupted by Mama screaming and then Jackson yelling for me.

"What on earth is going on?" I tore into the house and then the kitchen. "Mama!"

She was kneeling on the floor and shaking with my dad's head in her lap while Jackson was calling 911.

"Mama, what happened? Is Daddy okay?"

Wes and the Lancasters were behind me.

"I sure hope so, honey," she said, crying and whispering every prayer I'd heard since I was a baby.

Jackson said, "Sam, we literally got up from the table to take the dishes into the kitchen, and he went pale and down so fast, no one had time to react. I'm not sure if he had a stroke or why it looked like he was having a seizure."

Jackson was shaking, and Lucey took him outside to calm him down as I took the phone from him. Luckily the ambulance arrived quickly, and they came rushing inside.

I felt like I finally took a breath after they said he still had a pulse.

"Mrs. Dupont, are there any recent injuries or medical history that we need to be aware of?"

My mom looked at me as if scared to speak.

"Mama, do you want me to handle this?"

"No, dear. Weston, can you just be there for her now and keep her calm?"

"Of course, Mrs. Dupont . . . Anything." He tightened his arm around me as if to never let go.

I stared back and forth between the two, trying to figure out what the hell was going on.

My mama began speaking to the tech. "Um, yes, he had a mild heart attack about eight months ago. Nothing major." She looked at me. "But we had to get his blood pressure and cholesterol down. So, now he takes medicine for both. We also found out he has onset Parkinson's with early stages of Alzheimer's."

"What?" I yelled.

Jackson ran back into the kitchen. "Did something happen?"

"Yes, something happened! Where were you when Daddy had a heart attack and was diagnosed with Parkinson's and Alzheimer's? Or did you just not *think* to tell me?"

I turned to look at Weston. "You need to let go of me, now!"

"I can't do it, Sam."

I started kicking and punching any place I could reach on him.

"Quit resisting, Samantha. I'm not letting you go."

I stopped, but as soon as he thought I was being obedient, I bit down on his arm, drawing blood.

"Shit, Sam!" With him having to let me go, I made a run for it, off the porch and to the stables.

Before Weston or Jackson could reach me, I was hauling ass, bareback on Admiral, one of our horses. He had always been one of my favorite and most trusted.

The men were now yelling at me to come back, but my choice was to run—run as far as I could to escape the feeling that was burning a hole in my heart.

I came to the water's edge of the large creek and took a deep breath. Jumping off Admiral, I let him drink some water while I pulled my phone out for the flashlight to check the surroundings.

"Great. Of course my phone is dead. What are we going to do now, boy? Huh?"

Admiral let out a neigh and nuzzled against my shoulder.

It took some time to digest what my mama said and seeing my daddy like that. The thought of losing this man was unfathomable to me. I needed to calm my anger from being kept in the dark about it all. After sometime getting myself together, I decided it was time to head back.

"All right, boy. Let's try to find our way back." I pulled myself back up on his back. I was thankful the night was clear so the moon and stars could offer some light in the darkness.

After about an hour of wandering around, I saw porch lights in the distance from Wes's house. It was late, and I was exhausted after making it back to the stables to settle Admiral in. Someone grabbed my arm and pulled me over as I was walking out of the stable.

I tried to scream, but my mouth was muffled as I was turned around. My eyes grew wide until I locked eyes with Weston. I started punching him in the chest.

"Sam! You need to calm the fuck down! I'm going to remove my hand. Please don't scream."

"What the hell is wrong with you? Why would you come at me like this?"

Grabbing my wrists, he pinned me up against the wall in the stable. "Are you crazy? You just take off on a horse in the dark like you have no sense at all! Where's your phone? Did you forget how to use it?"

"Please let go of me. It hurts!"

He released my wrists, then pulled me into his chest and held on tightly. "I was so worried about you. You can't just run off like that, especially in the time of a crisis."

"I know, and I am sorry," I said as I buried my face into his chest. "It was too much. That's my daddy, and no one thought to tell me he was sick for so long? Who all knew about this? Have you gotten an update from anyone?"

"It seems my parents knew about it, but the four of them have kept it to themselves all this time. Your mom did call and said he was stable, and that they were waiting for the attending doctor. She'll call later when she finds out anything new."

"Okay. Is Jackson still here? I need to apologize."

"No, he and Lucey were stopping by the hospital to drop some stuff off for your mom, and then they were heading to her place."

"Oh. Well, can you stay the night? I really don't want to be by my-self right now."

"Of course, babe. Let's go inside."

We walked inside and started cleaning up the mess that was left. Maddox seemed to have helped himself to some dessert as well when everyone ran out.

"Maddox, was it yummy?" I bent down to run his belly.

Once completed with chores, the three of us headed upstairs to my room. Deciding to take a shower, I left Wes and Maddox hanging out on the bed watching TV. I let the hot water pour over me and relaxed. At once, Weston wrapped his arms around me and whispered in my ear, "Can I join you, beautiful?"

I nodded.

I could feel his strong hands maneuvering up and down my back in a deep but gentle motion. With his breath on the nape of my neck, my body started tingling all over. My mind was telling me that I was tired after the last several hours, but I could already tell my body's desires were betraying me.

Wes turned me around to face him, and before I could say a word, his hand was on my chin, tilting my face up towards his. He kissed me gently on the lips. I kissed him back more feverishly, nibbling at his lip as he let out a groan. We were now standing under the waterfall shower, caressing each other's bodies and kissing. Wes was kissing and sucking my neck and sucking harder with every moan I released. His hand slid down over my breasts and down my stomach until it settled between my legs.

"You're already so wet for me, Samantha."

"Take me . . . now." I said in between kissing him and moaning. I wanted to put this night behind me and forget all that had happened in the past several hours.

"Not yet. I enjoy exploring your body too much." He inserted his fingers inside of me. Needing to distract myself, I took hold of his shaft and gently massaged back and forth while kissing his chest and neck.

"Oh, baby. Now you're making it hard to wait."

I enjoyed the fact that he hardened and enlarged more in my hand with each movement.

"You can give in anytime," I said as we were both trying not to cave first.

His fingers began moving quicker inside of me while his other hand grabbed my ass and his tongue grazed across my nipples. "Come on, Sam. Just let go for me."

My back arched, then I pressed my body up against his again, finding my release as my body shuttered in his arms. As our wet bodies clung to each other, he kissed me hard on my lips, then lifted me up, wrapping my legs around his waist.

I was lost in his eyes as he stared back at me with intense desire. He carried me to my bed, sat down upright, then slowly lifted me up just enough that my core slid down on his member. It almost seemed to hit me at the center, and I let out a loud moan as we found our rhythm with each other. We were moving hot and heavy until I felt his warm release inside me as he let out a pleasurable moan by my ear.

I dismounted him. "Where do you think you're going?" He asked with a smirk.

"Another shower."

"I'm not done with you yet!"

In one motion, he flipped me over so I was now lying on my back in the bed with him hovering over me. My body betrayed me again as it yearned for him. With one of his hands on my left breast and his mouth on my right, he entered me slowly. I tilted my hips up to allow him deeper inside me as I clawed his back up and down, clinging to him like my life depended on it. My room was like a sauna from the shower and sweat.

"I will never have enough of you, Samantha."

In the midst of my moan, his tongue slipped through my lips as it rolled in circles over mine. My body was so tense as I neared release and tried to catch my breath. I bit down on his lower lip.

"Oh shit, Sam . . ."

But he continued. I could taste the sweet iron flavor of blood in my mouth as Wes pushed me to my breaking point again. I pooled over him as he kept intensely pounding against me until he spilled inside of me again.

I panted. "Sorry I bit you so hard. I needed to breathe."

"No complaints here." He licked the side of my mouth where some of his blood remained.

He used his muscular arms to stay hovering above me. "Ready for more?"

"I'm not sure I can even move at this moment." I chuckled and bit down on the side of my own lower lip.

"You asked for it, Sam." He flipped me over.

"Wait. What? No, really, Wes. Time out."

"I don't think so, babe. You don't realize how irresistible you are already, and then you bite that lip like a tease. I think now's the time to teach you a lesson—especially since it's been over a week since I've had you."

I looked back behind me, and his eyes were now a darker shade with a hint of wildness in them. Pushing my hips and butt up in the air, he entered my core slits from behind. My body quickly tensed up from already being sore from overuse.

"Damn it, Sam. I love how your body reacts to mine every time. It's always wet and ready for me. You're so tight, every damn time, too."

I held onto a pillow that I'd moved under me as the pain and pleasure heightened. I wasn't sure if my body or moans gave me away, but Weston knew I was reaching my peak.

"Hang on, Sam. Don't you come unless I tell you to." He smacked my ass and then slapped it again even harder, making me even wetter. Tears leaked from the corner of my eyes. I could feel the pain, but it also felt so good.

He was still penetrating me hard from behind while his finger circled the tip of my inner folds at the same time.

"Holy . . . I can't hold it anymore."

"Not yet, Sam. Not yet!"

I was seconds from not being able to control what my body did next.

Again, he smacked me on the ass, and I lost all control, unraveling around him. He moaned while slowing down and pulsating within me. Then he slowly pulled me back towards him and turned me over slowly so I could face him. "Are you good? Sorry if that got too intense. I'm not sure what came over me, but it is so hard to control myself when I'm near you—especially in such an intimate way."

Gathering my strength to even speak between my hoarse and panting voice, I said, "I'm fine, but no promises that you won't be carrying me everywhere tomorrow."

We both laughed. Being so sore and tired, I hobbled over to my closest to grab panties and a T-shirt to throw on. Moving over to my bed, I checked the time. It was already 3:00 a.m.

Wow. We've been at this for hours. Crawling into bed, Weston pulled me in close to him and snaked his arms around my waist. We fell asleep like there was nothing else going on around us.

CHAPTER 24:

Men Hiding

*I*t had been about a week since Daddy's incident, and he was finally coming home. Mr. Lancaster had been dealing with his businesses abroad but luckily left Weston to help Jackson and me with the ranch. Aunt Patsy had already headed out to California with my uncle to celebrate her retirement. Mama had been running around the house getting everything clean and ready for Daddy to return. Even though the doctor discharged him, he stated that Daddy needed to be on bed rest for at least another two weeks to completely heal from his cardiac bypass and for his body levels to return to normal.

Needless to say, it had been a crazy, stressful week. On top of that, the equipment for Mr. Hughes's business had started coming in, so I'd been working on setting that up. I was just exhausted.

"Hey, babe. Why don't you go lie down? Everything is caught up, and your dad will be home in a few hours."

"Thanks, Wes, but I still have all these résumés to go through. I need an assistant and at least one other person to run data and reports."

"Why don't I help you with that? I have accountable assistants, and I can easily lend one to you. That way you have time for everything else."

"Are you sure?"

"Of course!" He called out to Carl.

Where did this guy just come from?

He noticed the shock on my face.

"Did this guy appear out of thin air?"

Wes laughed. "No, this is Carl, my most trusted assistant. He's always around but may not always be visible. I'll tell you now, there are always bodyguards around the property. I tell you this because once we move into our home, there will be some, as well."

I was speechless, thinking, *Is he not just a corporate man?*

Wes took me by the hand. "This isn't how I wanted this conversation to happen, but we're having it now. The bodyguards are for everyone's safety. Though we are a towering, respected company, it also means we have quite a few enemies. There's always someone who wants to take the top dog down. Do you understand?"

"I do . . . It's just that, hmmm. I never thought I'd be living in a world where I'm surrounded by bodyguards. It's something I've only heard of and sometimes witnessed with my high-money clients and their entourages."

"Good." He kissed me on the forehead. "Now, you already have Carl's number in your phone, and he has yours. This is in case you need me but can't reach me."

"All right."

"Carl, please send over Lans' top three assistants for Sam to choose from tomorrow morning."

"On it, Sir. Anything else?"

"Please send me over details from my father's meeting this week."

"Yes, sir." and Carl walks off.

Still trying to wrap everything that happened in the last several minutes around my mind, I said, "I think I'm going to lie down for a bit."

"Do you want me to come with you?"

"I'm sure you have plenty to do. I'll go by myself. See you for dinner later?"

"Of course," he said as he kissed me gently on the lips. As I headed out of the office to walk back to the house, Jackson was driving off. He must've been going to pick up Dad.

I made my way into the kitchen. "You need any help, Mama?"

"No, sweetie, I'm good. Everything is ready for your dad, and I've already started working on dinner. How are you? I know we haven't had much time to talk since everything."

"Um, I'm fine. Trying to deal with it as it comes."

"I heard you ran away that night." Mama looked at me with concerned eyes. "You can't leave again, Samantha. No one's heart can take it. You've been gone way too long."

"I don't plan on going anywhere, and I did not run away last time. I went on an adventure that I thought you and Daddy supported? Besides, I was upset that night, and felt once again as though everyone was keeping things from me."

"We did, and we do support you, sweetie. But I'm not going to lie. It took an emotional toll on everyone with you not being here. I'm thankful you had those opportunities, but knowing how your heart ached when you left and were out there all alone . . . It was nerve-racking. On top of that, when your father started getting sick, we didn't want to add any more stress or pressure on you kids."

"I understand, Mama. But I'm here now, and Jackson is taking over. So, no more secrets. We handle everything as a family, okay?"

"Of course, sweetie." Mama gave me a big hug, then she pulled back.

"Speaking of family," I said, "are you aware of the bodyguards around the property and that follow the Lancasters?"

"Oh, you finally noticed them?"

"Um, not exactly. I met Carl, Weston's assistant, today. Weston told me that we're always surrounded."

"It's nothing new, Sam. They've been around long before you babies were even born. It's mostly to protect the Lancasters, but also the ranch since it's also a lucrative business for them. I will say, I have seen an increase since Weston started taking on more over the past year. Rumor has it he's a fierce and violent man no one wants to tangle with."

"Weston? Fierce and violent? That's hard to believe."

"I know. I just laugh it off when I hear rumors. Did you stop keeping up while you were away?"

"Yep. After a while, I made myself stop looking. It wasn't easy, but it hurt too much to know. To read articles of him with a new girl on his arm or being called hottest bachelor of Texas. No, thanks!"

My mama laughed. "Well, I guess that's all about to change. But do me a favor. Take everything with ease. Being thrust into the limelight isn't easy, so don't listen to the rumors or any nonsense that comes from it."

"I won't. I'm also going to try and hide my face as much as possible…. Well, I am going to lie down for a bit."

"Okay, sweetie. Daddy and Jackson should be home in a couple hours."

It didn't take me long to fall into a deep sleep, only to dream a nightmare of the possible future: Bodyguards, cameras, photos, headlines about us. Him travelling all the time. Running two businesses on my own.

I was so hot and flustered in my dream, I didn't realize I was actually sweating.

"Sam, wake up! Sam!"

My eyelids fluttered, and eventually, his face became clear. "Wes?"

"Sam, are you all right? You're burning up! Stay here. Let me grab a cold wet cloth."

He returned and gently wiped my face with the cloth, and all I could pay attention to were his glistening eyes.

"You need to see a doctor. Let me call Dr. Adams to come over."

"No, I'm good." I pushed his phone down. "I'm tired and didn't have the best dream. I used to do this all the time. It's no big deal."

"You mean, because of me?" He looked down.

"That's not how I wanted that to come out." I put my hand on the side of his face. "I just wanted to let you know I'm fine. I don't need a doctor, but thank you for caring."

He quickly pulled me into his embrace. "I'm so sorry, Sam, for all the hurt I've caused you. I will spend our lifetime making it up to you."

I climbed over to sit on his lap as his hands began moving under my shirt to take it off. I quickly did the same to him, then I sat back up for a moment to take all of him in.

"Do you need me to send you a picture later?" he said.

I laughed. "No, this is embedded in my memory." I pushed his upper body back down on the bed.

We were hot and heavy in a make-out session with only underwear on. My body craved his and wanted more. In one fell swoop, he ripped my panties off. I was on my back, and he looked as if he were about to devour me.

Maddox started barking loudly, and there was an eruption of voices coming from downstairs.

I froze and looked at Weston. "Oh, my goodness. It sounds like Daddy's home."

Jumping up quickly, I threw my clothes back on and was about to run out the door, but I realized he was still sitting on the bed, looking stunned.

"Sorry, babe, but we have to go down now."

He slowly got up and dressed, steadily making his way to me. Then he placed his hand behind my neck and pulled me to him. "Don't worry, babe. I'll have you later," he stated with that Cheshire grin, and then he strolled out.

I heard Weston say, "Mr. Dupont, I'm glad to see you home. Sam will be right down. I just woke her up."

I flew down the stairs and threw myself into Daddy's arms. "I'm so glad you're finally home."

"Me too, sweetie. Me too." He kissed the top of my head and walked to his chair in the living room.

The Lancasters were at our home, as well as a few other family friends.

"Mama, I didn't realize we were having a whole event this evening."

"No big deal. You know how everyone stops by. We have more than enough for everyone anyways."

I smiled at her and remembered that our home had never lacked company or food. Mama was always prepared whether there were four or one hundred people.

Lucey and I set up all the tables outside and pulled out the porch awnings for shade. I walked back in the house only to hear a familiar voice.

"Sam!"

"Mia!"

Simultaneously, we said, "Where have you been?"

We both started giggling and gave each other hugs.

"Where's Dylan?"

"I left him in the den with the other men. They were talking business. My dad is in there, too." She looked somewhat frightened.

"Really? Well, your dad knows who he is to you now, right?"

"Well, not exactly."

"Mia, no! Let's go spy on them."

Mia and I headed off to the den and hid around the corner. My mama, who most always knew what we were up to, brought me a tray of bourbon-filled glasses to deliver.

"Thanks, Mama."

"Anything to help my favorite girls."

I walked in slowly and said good evening to the men. I put the tray on the table, so I could pass the drinks out . . . and eavesdrop. They were talking about expansion, and Dylan seemed to be making a good impression. Even Nate was in there making talk with the Texans on business. I soon saw Wes, who gave me a wink, so I decided to quicken my pace. I announced that dinner would be ready in thirty minutes and that appetizers had already been set out if they wanted to take their conversation to the bar area in the kitchen. All the men left, but as I was about to walk out, Weston stopped me.

"Excuse me, sir. Appetizers are that way, and I need to go get ready."

"Oh, really? Need help with any of that?" He pushed me up against the wall.

"Wes, settle down. We're surrounded by people."

"Doesn't it make it that much more exciting? Come on . . . Just one kiss?"

"Don't give me that face. One kiss." Standing on my tippy toes, I planted a quick kiss on the side of his mouth.

"Now you're asking to be punished." He pinned my arms above my head with one hand. "Would you like to try that again?"

Play the innocent card.

I looked at him and bit the bottom side of my lip.

"Dammit, Sam. Are you trying to be punished right here, right now? You are not allowed to bite that lip of yours like that."

"Do you not hear Mama calling me? I need to finish setting up."

Right on cue, Mia walked in. "Hey, Sam. Oh, sorry . . . Um, I can come back later . . ."

Weston said, "Yes, please."

"Wait, Mia." I gave her a side-eye. "What's going on?"

"Your mom needs our help in the kitchen and wanted to make sure you had changed your clothes before dinner."

"Oh, no, I still haven't changed. Tell her to give me five minutes, and I'll be there."

I quickly took off up the stairs and shouted, "Be down in a few."

"Sam," I hear through Weston's gritted teeth.

As soon as I was in my room, I locked the door.

I thought to myself, *He is going to eat me alive*. I could barely move the last time he had his way with me.

I quickly grabbed a cute sundress that had a teal ombré effect and dipped low on my back and adorned all my curves. Then I pulled my hair half back and applied some perfume.

I peeked my head out the door, then quickly made my way to the kitchen. The men made their way out to the deck, and everyone started spreading out. I could count at least thirty people.

Mia and I told jokes and stories about our love lives, over a few rounds of bourbon and laughs.

As we brought the dishes out to set up on the buffet table, I felt that burning glare again. I turned around to see Weston glaring at me, but I just smiled at him and went on with what I was doing.

CHAPTER 25:
Family Announcement

*C*ling! Cling!

"Attention, everyone," Mama said. "My lovely husband would like to say a few words."

My daddy stood up and began speaking, but off to my left, Carl appeared to deliver some documents to Wes and was whispering in his ear. They must have felt my eyes on them, as they both looked at me at once, so I quickly turned back to look at my dad.

He thanked everyone for coming out and visiting him in the hospital. He thanked his family and the Lancasters for dealing with the ranch and business. At the end, he started getting emotional and asked the kids to come up and stand with him and Mama.

"This family is my backbone," he said, "as well as the backbone to this ranch. You all know Jackson and Lucey are expecting a little Dupont this year and that their house is already on its way to being built up on that hill. We will be celebrating their marriage in November. We love them so much and could not be prouder of the man Jackson has become and the woman he has chosen to spend his life with."

"Cheers" rang out from everyone.

"Now, y'all also know my baby girl finally made her way home a couple of months ago. She has made me so proud with her accomplishments and how she's stepped up taking over Patsy's position. What many of you may not know yet, since we didn't have a chance to announce it due to my hospital stay, but there will be a big party in two weeks to officially celebrate . . ."

All I could do was smile while looking around the room.

"My sweet Samantha is engaged!"

The look of shock on people's faces was quite amusing. They were holding their breath, looking to find out who the groom was going to be.

"She is officially engaged to the guy I consider a second son, Weston Lancaster."

Everyone cheered and looked back and forth between the two of us, but all I could do was smile back and turn my attention back to Daddy.

"Okay, okay . . . I have just one more announcement. My kids have grown up, and now is the time to pass on the reign. Therefore, Jackson and Samantha, I am officially stepping back for you two to take over."

"Oh, Daddy, really?" I squeaked out, having mixed emotions.

This was a joyous time for our family, so I went with it and hugged my family tightly.

"Now, let us eat!" Mama announced.

Everyone scattered to find their tables and make their plates. Thinking back, midway through Daddy announcing our engagement, Carl had disappeared, along with the stack of folders he had.

Weston's face looked ashen.

Mrs. Lancaster distracted me from my thoughts, asking me to sit with her, Mama, and a few other ladies from church. I pulled Mia with me, and we sat between them.

"Sam, I am so excited for your engagement party. Your mama and I are pulling out all the stops!"

"There's really no need. You know I'm simple."

"I know, sweetie, but you're becoming a Lancaster, officially joining the Duponts and Lancasters together forever. It deserves to be a big deal."

"As you wish," I said with a smile.

The other ladies at the table interrogated me, inspecting my engagement ring and asking about the wedding date, colors, theme, when we would have kids, and on and on and on.

I felt a strong hand on my back, and one of the ladies exclaimed," Have you ever seen a more handsome groom? Speaking of which, did the two of you get back together while you were away? I remember what poor shape you were in when you left, but you've only been back a short time."

Before I could give an answer, Wes stepped in and asked if he could borrow me for a little bit. Of course, everyone obliged him.

Getting up, I whispered "Thank you" to him. I knew the ladies meant well, but I wasn't in the mood to share that story.

He started to lead me off the deck and to one of the large oak trees that had a swing on it. Before we made it, I heard his mom say, "Smile, you two lovebirds!"

We turned around, and he wrapped his muscular arms around me.

"Perfect," she said, then walked off.

"I'm happy to have your mom excited for us, but I'm not too sure about your dad."

Weston's face looked perplexed.

"Hey, what's going on with you?" I asked.

He sat me in the swing and started to push.

"I have to go abroad to deal with some things over the next week."

"Okay. Did something happen?"

"My father was just there, and then today, one of the warehouses caught on fire. Luckily, no one died, but several were injured. Now I need to meet with the injured's families and investigate."

"Oh, so was that why Carl was here earlier tonight?"

"Yes and no. He had a deliverable, and then that also came up. I'm heading out first thing in the morning with Carl. He's already arranged the assistants to come interview with you in the morning, but also, I'm leaving Andre to personally watch out for you. Just say his name, and he will be there. Whatever you need, ask. I might be unreachable at times but will reach out when I can. I'm serious, Sam. I just got you back and will not lose you. Understand?"

"Yes, Weston. But why are you giving me the feeling that something bigger is going on?"

"It's mostly me being overly cautious about leaving, but when I know more, I promise I'll tell you. All right?"

"Okay, I trust you." I leaned back into him on the swing.

"I also know we're supposed to start moving in next week, so Andre and the guys will help with that, also."

"We still need to buy bedroom furniture before we officially move in. But we're good with everything else, I believe. We can wait until you're back. I don't want to be there without you."

"Well, here . . . Take this and go buy whatever you want for the house. I know you'll turn it into our perfect home, and then we can spend the first night there when I'm back."

I looked down to find that he was handing me the elite black card.

"Um, Wes, that I definitely cannot take. Your family is apparently worth more than I could have imagined with you flaunting that around."

"What's mine is yours, Sam. Take it, and use it."

"Um, ok." Deciding in no point to argue this one out.

I looked towards the large gathering still going on.

"Hey, I do need to grab some items from my apartment downtown before heading out," he said. "Do you want to accompany me tonight?"

"Of course. Let's go say goodbye to everyone first."

~✧~

Weston's POV

Those last twenty-four hours had been ruthless, and I wasn't looking forward to the next several days. Not only was I having to leave Sam's side, but my father seemed to be wreaking havoc with several of our business partners overseas by cutting corners and adding stipulations to contracts that were signed months before. Now, due to his reckless behavior, several employees had been injured and needed to be assessed, immediately. My men had been following him around for several months, with little to report. It's nothing I couldn't handle over a quick virtual meeting and investing more money when needed, but this time, corners were cut in labor and materials, causing a small fire in one of the new warehouses in Sicily.

I was happy that Mr. Dupont was home and better now. That's one less thing weighing on my girl's shoulders. She'd been beside herself those last several weeks, on top of spearheading a multi-million-dollar project for Mr. Hughes and keeping up with everything at the ranch. She sure is something special. My heart aches for having to postpone us moving in together. Just a few extra days, though, and I'd feel better knowing that she's staying at home with her family and that Andre was looking after her. Between my dad's shadiness and the random letters with pictures being sent to my office about Sam and us together, I was now on high alert, and so were my men. I hoped I didn't worry her too much about the bodyguards and sticking to Andre. She might have just noticed them, but they had been more present since she came home.

Then there's my Sam, the little minx who'd been teasing me all day, leaving my body suffering from sexual frustration. I would definitely be taking my revenge on her that night. Even just looking at her, my body burned for her. She was so innocent while she slept, but I knew better. I was catching on to her cat-and-mouse games. Soon enough, she'd understand that she would always be caught and ravished by me. And by me only.

CHAPTER 26:
All in the News

I ended up falling asleep on the way to his apartment, only to be awakened once we were inside as Weston carried me in. He sat me on the sofa while I got my bearings. It looked to be a true bachelor pad and basic.

Once he was done packing his bag, he sat next to me.

"You awake now?"

"I believe so," I said with a smile.

"As I recall, you still need to be punished for today."

"Punished? What did I even do?"

"Let us run down the list, shall we? You left me right when I was about to have you, and no interrupting either."

It took all I could not to speak or bite my lip, but my eyes were wide open. "Then there's the sad little kiss on the cheek after you promised me a kiss. But you escaped when I was about to receive the kiss I wanted. And to top it all off, you came downstairs wearing this dress and smelling the way you do. It makes me think you've just been teasing me all day."

I tried my hardest not to giggle. "Can I speak now?"

"Yes, you may."

"I can assure you nothing was done to purposely tease you today. Well, except for the dress, hair, and perfume." I state, winking at him.

"That's it. You are mine, Samantha Jane." He suddenly lifted me up and carried me to the bedroom.

I quickly pulled my dress down, only for him to discover I'd been bra and pantyless all night.

"You, my dear, are naughty. Were you also waiting on me all night?"

I bit my lower lip and looked up at him, and the last thing I remember was him ravishing and devouring my body for most of the night.

My phone woke me up. It was Mia. "Hello."

"Oh, my God, Sam! Have you seen the news?"

"No, I literally just woke up. What's going on?"

"You! You and Weston are what's going on!"

"I'm sorry, what? Hold on . . . let me look." Sure enough, as soon as I opened the news page, my and Weston's picture from last night was front and center. "What the hell, Mia?"

I was wide awake now and realized I was in Weston's apartment, but without Weston. "Mia, let me call you back in a few minutes."

He must have left early that morning and didn't want to wake me. I tried to sit up, only to realize my whole body was aching. I managed to make it to the shower, feeling refreshing water rush over me. As I finished my shower and got ready for the day, I heard a knock at the door.

"Weston?"

As I opened the door, a petite older woman said, "Hi, Miss. I'm Betty, Sir Lancaster's housekeeper. I came to bring you these clothes he had delivered this morning, along with this note. Also, breakfast is almost ready."

"Thank you, Betty. I appreciate that. What time did he leave this morning?"

"It was about four a.m., Miss."

I nodded my head and smiled as she walked away.

I couldn't believe he had clothes picked out for me, the right size and style of everything, down to the underwear. I put the letter on the counter as I threw on a pair of jeans and a green soft tee with cuffed sleeves. I took the letter and headed to the kitchen for breakfast, which was a large spread on the counter.

"Miss, please have a seat and let me know what you would like."

"Betty, I don't mind getting it myself. And this is also way too much food. Some eggs and bacon in the morning is good enough for me."

"Good to know, Miss. But I insist on serving you."

"Okay." I told her what I wanted, then I opened the letter.

Sam,

Please forgive me. I didn't want to wake you this morning. You looked too peaceful to disturb, but I did steal a kiss from you anyway. Last night was amazing, and I will hold on to those memories until I'm back home with you. Remember what I told you last night, and don't hesitate to ask Andre for anything. Also, stay as long as you like at the apartment. Betty and others will assist with your wants and needs. I will call you when I land. I love you

—Wes

This guy, I thought to myself. *He's all mine and almost too good to be true.*

My phone rang again.

"Good morning, Mr. Hughes. Isn't it late over the pond?"

"Well, good morning to you, Samantha. I just wanted to call and congratulate you on the upcoming nuptials. Seems like lots of great things are happening for you right now."

"Thank you! I will say I am very blessed and appreciate all of it. Did Nate tell you?"

"Oh, did he know prior? I found out like everyone else—on the news."

"That is just . . . wow. Good to know. I honestly didn't expect the news to be posted outside of my state, let alone on the other side of the world."

"The Lancasters are a big deal in the corporate world. Not only in the States, but they've definitely made a name for themselves overseas, as well. To be honest, I'm not too fond of the father, having not met your fiancé. Rumor has it he's a brutal businessman also. I find it hard to visualize someone like you, Samantha, with someone deemed like that."

"I assure you he's not like that with me or his family and friends. He definitely keeps business and pleasure separate, as I believe most of us try to do. He treats me very well. As for his dad, he's definitely changed over the years, so no argument from me. But enough about the Lancasters. Mr. Hughes, did you receive my monthly report of earnings, with a twenty percent increase, despite the whole SIR ordeal?"

"I did! Very good, Samantha. That is why you're managing my money and the company."

"Thank you, sir. Well, if there's nothing else, I need to head in to complete interviews for your company."

"Very well. I appreciate all you're doing there. Keep up the great work. I also believe Nate will be back there by the end of the week."

"Thank you, again. And I'll have my assistant retrieve all his travel details so we know when to expect him. Have a great day, sir."

"You, as well."

It was now 9:00 a.m., and I needed to head in.

"Andre!"

"Yes, Miss?"

"Agh! Where do you hide out? You scared me. Stay visible, please." I panted, trying to calm myself down.

"Yes, Miss. What can I help you with?"

"One, please call me Sam. I'm not that formal. Second, Weston said you'd drive me to work today. Also, have you seen the news?"

"Yes, mi— I mean, Sam. I'll take you over there if you're ready now. And yes, I have seen the news and have contacted Carl to let Sir aware of what's going on when he lands."

"Thank you, Andre. And I'm ready, so let's go."

After getting to work, I needed to call Mia back.

"Mia, are you free for lunch today?"

"I can make myself free. I think this situation trumps everything else I had going on today."

"Agree, and that's why I love you. Meet me at Mabel's at eleven, and then after lunch and figuring this out, we're going furniture shopping."

"Sounds like a plan. See you in a bit."

It was time for me to greet the assistants Carl had sent over. As I looked them over, I was slightly skeptical but was told these were the top three assistants in the company. Two of them, Kiera and Calhoun, seemed to be a few years younger than me, and the other, Mrs. Bennett, was in her mid-forties. Surprisingly, during their interviews, they all blew me away with their résumés and answers to not-so-easy questions. At the end of the day, I knew I needed someone who had my back and was willing to put in the work. I decided to go with Kiera, as she seemed to enjoy crunching numbers and wanted to learn more about the money world. Andre had her sign the documents that Weston left. The gist of them being a no-competition clause, as well as a hefty fine if they divulged any information about either company. I set her up in the system and started figuring out President Hughes's travel schedule, along with ranch tasks for the day.

There was a knock at the door.

"Come in."

"Hey, honey! How are you holdin' up? I saw the news this morning, and my phone has been blowing up with local reporters. Have you heard from Weston yet?"

"No, Mama, not yet. He left early this morning. I'm not sure if he's landed yet or if he knows what's going on. Who would've released that photo and news to the major press? And Mrs. Lancaster is the one who took the photo. Hmm. Mama, you don't think it could've been her, do you?"

"Oh, my. I hope not, but it is possible. Let's call her now. It's ringing . . . I'll put her on speaker."

"Good morning, Clara."

"Good morning, Arlene. Have you seen the news this morning?"

"Oh, of course! Who do you think submitted the picture and announcement?" Hanging my head, looking dumbfounded at my mama,

"Mrs. Lancaster, why did you do that? And no warning?"

"Hello, Samantha. How can you be upset? You're marrying the most eligible bachelor in the state, as well as becoming a Lancaster. You need to get used to your life in the spotlight, sweetheart. Our clients need to know this information, and every woman needs to know he's taken."

"Um, I totally understand where you're coming from, Mrs. Lancaster, but Wes is out of town right now. A fair warning would've been nice. Not only is this state and national news, but worldwide news! We wanted to make this announcement together when we felt it was right and necessary."

"Did you just say he's out of town?"

"Yes, he's out on business, and that's honestly all I know. I need to head out for a lunch date now, so we can talk later."

"Samantha, please tell Weston to call me when you hear from him. And I am sorry for any problems or tension I've caused. I promise it wasn't intentional, but I'm excited you'll finally be my daughter-in-law after all these years."

"I understand, and it'll be fine. We'll talk to you later. Goodbye."

"Oh dear," Mama said. "Well, at least it's settled. It'll be all right."

"I know, Mama. Thank you. Well, I need to go meet Mia." I gave her a hug and walked out to the car with Andre.

CHAPTER 27:
Who Is He?

After a long day of dodging reporters and furniture shopping with Mia, we were both exhausted. Hoping not to cause any problems at home, I decided to sleep at Weston's apartment. Mia accompanied me for the evening, and we ordered in. I dismissed Mrs. Betty and the rest of the staff except for Andre. We still hadn't heard from him, but Andre confirmed they did land safely and that Weston would call as soon as he could.

The doorbell rang, and before I could even get up, Andre rushed to the door. "Miss, please let me grab it. No one needs to know you're here."

"Okay, thank you."

Mia turned to me. "This has been a weird day, especially with having that guy around. Are you used to it?"

"I don't think I'll ever be used to it, to tell you the truth. It's like the man I'm madly in love with has an alter ego in the business world. I almost feel like I'm marrying into the mob with all this going on recently."

Mia rolled on the floor laughing as Andre brought over our food, and I grabbed a crab roll from my box and threw it at her.

"I'm totally serious, Mia!"

"I know, but you have to laugh. He's definitely not part of the mob. I think he can control all the mobs with that elite black card of his."

"Oh, my gosh. Other than hearing about certain celebrities, who all possess one of these damn things?" I took it out of my wallet and put it on the table.

"I still can't believe you barely used it today."

"I'm just not one of those girls. I work too hard for my own money and want us to be equal."

Mia laughed.

"Well, shit, as close to equal as I can to a billionaire." I chunked another roll at her, but this time she caught it and popped it in her mouth.

After some more girl talk and wine drinking, we concluded our evening. I set her up in the guest room and headed to mine to take a shower. It was already almost 1:00 o'clock in the morning. I texted Wes good night and that I loved him, hoping everything was fine.

A few minutes later, I received a text.

> HI, SAM. SORRY I HAVEN'T CALLED YOU YET. IT HAS BEEN A DAY. I LOVE AND MISS YOU. I KNOW IT'S REALLY LATE, AND I STILL HAVE MEETINGS FOR THE NEXT COUPLE OF HOURS. I'LL CALL YOU TOMORROW. GO GET SOME SLEEP, AND DREAM OF ME.

The next morning, we were greeted by a large breakfast buffet. Once finished, Andre dropped Mia off, and we headed into the office. Soon it was lunchtime, and I walked to the kitchen only to notice my parents sitting down with President Hughes. Seeing me walk in, he quickly got up to bow and then kissed my hand.

"Good afternoon, President. We weren't expecting you until tomorrow. Can you make sure your assistant updates my assistant with these changes? I would hate to send her into a panic thinking she was in the wrong."

"Of course, Miss Dupont. Also, my apologies for not heading out there to greet you first. Your mother saw me drive up and asked me in for lunch and tea. It wasn't something I could say no to."

"I understand. I was just coming over to grab myself some lunch."

Mama handed me a wrapped plate and a tea.

"Here, Sam. Let me walk you back over, and we can catch up on everything."

"Sounds good."

He turned to thank my parents for lunch and followed me out while taking the things from my hands and carrying it to the office for me. I could sense all the guards on us and the tense aura surrounding the place.

We sat down in the breakroom and went over all the recent changes and upcoming goals. President Hughes seemed satisfied with everything.

"Miss Dupont, are we still playing the game of being so formal with one another?"

"Well, there is a distinction between our rankings as well as keeping business separate. But if you feel you'd like me to address you another way, that's fine. Of course, you're more than welcome to address me by Samantha or Sam."

"As before, please just call me Nate. Again, I am not old like the men before me."

That put a smile on my face.

"Now, with formalities aside, I have a few other things I'd like to discuss with you."

"Okay, like what?"

I watched him pull a folder from his briefcase and stand next to me. I decided to stand up as I hated the feeling of people hovering over me.

"Sam, before I hand this file over to you, I really want you to take it and make an intelligent decision from it. I would not and will not lie to you, therefore I feel I need to share this information with you. Please know I'm here for you."

I took the file from Nate's hand and opened it, and I was shocked to see it was a file on Weston and his bodyguards.

"It's a file on your soon-to-be husband. I don't think he's told you things you should know before you actually marry him."

In the file, I found pictures of Weston from years ago in fights, holding a gun to someone's head, and his men beating people up in random places. "I can't look at this, Nate. I appreciate you trying to bring things to light, but I don't want to know what happens within his business. And if he feels he needs to tell me, he will tell me. I'm not going to question who he is based on some file full of violent pictures. I've known him my whole life, and so has this whole town. Please don't try to ruin him. What do you even gain by showing me this?"

"It's *you* I'm hoping to gain. I've heard about you and seen your pictures for years, Sam. I admit I am a playboy, but it's only been until I could get to you. I hate to think I was too late to even get my chance to make you happy. We are a force to be reckoned with alone, so just think what we can accomplish together. Not just as business partners, but as a couple . . . as lovers."

"Nate, have you lost your damn mind? Taken or not, this is not how you win over someone's heart. And I'm sorry you didn't get your chance, but my heart has always belonged to someone else. It has and will never be mine to give away."

"Sam, not even one kiss to let me prove otherwise?" He stepped closer until I was backed up against my desk.

"No, we can't. Besides, it won't change anything for me. I have been with other guys before. No one makes me feel the way Weston does. So, I think we need to end this conversation and go back to work."

Before I knew it, I was locked in Nate's embrace with his mouth on mine. As soon as I could free a hand, I slapped him. "What the hell, Nate? I said no! Do I need to quit my job already because my boss can't keep his damn hands to himself?"

"You let that man do whatever he wants to you, but you never say or do anything but slap me over a little kiss? Screw you, Miss Dupont!"

"Are you kidding me, Mr. President? That man is my fiancé, and we have history. You are a nephew to a client of mine that I've known for a handful of weeks. How dare you! I'm calling Mr. Hughes right now to turn in my notice. Please leave me before I call my bodyguard in here."

"You don't need to call anyone. I'll leave and settle this with my uncle. He'll be furious if he loses you. But this is also not over, Miss Dupont."

I fell to the floor in tears as he walked away, then I quickly made the decision to leave for the day and head back to the apartment. Mia came over after work so I could explain everything to her and so she could keep me company.

CHAPTER 28:
Not Meant to Be

*I*t was 8:00 o'clock in the evening, and my phone had been going crazy from texts from Nate apologizing, almost as if he was a completely different person earlier that day. Totally over it, I turned my phone on silent and chugged a glass of wine. I made Mia promise not to say a word to anyone, because if Wes found out, I honestly think he would've killed him.

Not a minute later, I saw my phone light up as a text came from an unknown number. Opening it, I saw a picture of Wes sitting in what looked to be a hotel saloon area, with not only businessmen but several beautiful women. Though I couldn't tell if they were anything other than business associates, they looked classy. Confused by the number, I thought maybe one of his guards was sending me a picture to ensure he was fine. I decided not to put too much thought into it and finish the movie with Mia.

Once the movie was over, I had ten missed messages, three from Wes.

> HI, SAM. CALLED YOU EARLIER, BUT MUST'VE MISSED YOU. I LOVE YOU AND WILL CALL WHEN I ARRIVE AT MY ROOM LATER. STILL IN MORE MEETINGS FOR A WHILE. TALK TO YOU SOON!

"Of course, business meetings, but who's sending me the picture?" I said to Mia.

I continued to read through Weston's texts:

Meet me in room 258.

Cannot wait to see you again and to make up for lost time.

Remember not to tell your brother or guard where you are.

Lost for words, I closed out of the messages and moved to the unknown-number messages. More pictures. First was a beautiful blonde, fair-skinned woman sitting next to Wes on the couch and looking at paperwork. Next, they were drinking champagne together, followed by him getting up to leave. Then there was a picture of what looked to be her heading in the same direction. And last but not least, a text:

I guess I will win this time.

Why does that female look so familiar?

I threw my phone across the room and cried. Mia picked it up and scrolled back through the messages. "Sam, I . . . There must be a reason behind this. Who sent you these? Are you sure the photos are real?"

"I believe so. Look back at his message from this evening. Coincidence? I've got to leave here, now."

"It's late. Let me call Dylan to come pick us up and take us back to my place. Dad's out of town, so it's fine."

I gathered what little belongings I had with me. Andres's room was right next to the front door, so we had to be extra careful as we snuck out. As we got on the elevator, Andre opened the door and locked his eyes on me. Luckily, the door closed, and we cursed the elevator all the way down to move faster.

Mia and I sprinted to Dylan's car as we heard Andre behind us yelling my name.

"Miss! Miss Sam! Where are you going? Does Sir know? Miss, I have orders to watch over you!"

We heard this on repeat as Dylan drove away.

"What the hell are you girls up to?" Dylan asked.

"I'll explain everything later," Mia said to Dylan. "Just get us to my house, babe."

I hung my head in silence on the way.

Back at the apartment, Andre called Sir, unable to reach him. After multiple tries, he called Carl, who answered.

"Carl, is Sir with you?"

"Yes, he's close by but still in talks with a client. What's going on? Is it not late there?"

"Yes, it's almost two in the morning, but the Miss just ran off."

"What do you mean, just ran off?"

"Exactly what I mean. I could hear a little of her and her friend's conversation, and she was crying. It seems her friend's boyfriend picked them up when they snuck out. I tried to chase her down. Miss looked very upset and wouldn't talk to me."

"That is very strange. Sir's phone is at the bar charging while he's sitting in on the meetings. Let me check it and see if she's messaged him. I'm not sure I can interrupt him, but let me try."

"Okay, Carl. Call me back with orders."

Weston's POV

On the other side of the world, Carl picked up the phone to check Weston's messages. After clicking on Sam's name, he was shocked to find what had taken place. Even more so, he wondered how it could've happened. The stamped times the phone was here, Sir was over there. And he knew his Sir's obsession with his soon-to-be wife. He wouldn't have even looked at another woman. This wasn't good if Sam was imagining the worst.

With phone in hand and head down, he walked over to Weston. "Sir, may I borrow you for a minute?"

"Give me five minutes to finish, Carl, and you can tell me then."

"Yes, sir."

Carl texted Andre.

SIR IS FINISHING UP THE MEETING NOW. I FOUND THAT SOMEONE HACKED INTO HIS PHONE AND SENT INCRIMINATING MESSAGES TO MISS. STAND BY FOR ORDERS.

Andre texted back.

10-4

Weston got up from his meeting, shook the clients' hands, and made his way to Carl. "Carl, what is so important? It's not like you to interrupt a meeting. You better have a great reason, or there will be punishment."

"Yes, sir, and I apologize, but Miss ran off from the apartment just a bit ago." Shaking, Carl handed Weston back his phone with the messages pulled up.

As Weston looked at his phone, his jaw clenched, and Carl could feel his anger fill the room.

"What the hell do you mean, ran off? Where is Andre? How in the hell did these messages get on my phone?"

Carl tried to calm him down and explain the information that he knew.

"Find her, now! No one sleeps until she's found and safe!"

"Yes, sir." Carl immediately got Andre on the phone and delegated orders.

CHAPTER 29:
Someone Needs to be Afraid

"Mia, I want to keep this quiet and deal with it outside of the media and our families. We'll make the announcement when it's been settled. So, no one can know where I am, and no one speaks of this outside of us three, got it?"

Dylan and Mia nodded their heads and looked at each other.

Right then, Weston called my phone, but I quickly declined. Carl's number popped up, then Andres's. Mia's phone started ringing, then Dylan's. Everyone froze listening to the ringing phones, so we turned them off. Once we calmed down, there was knocking at the door.

"Miss, I know you're in there! I need you to come out now and come back with me."

"What am I supposed to do now, Mia? He's literally tracking me down."

"Let me handle this. Go hide in my room."

I went upstairs and looked out the window, only to see several guards surrounding the house. I whispered to myself, "Who in the hell is this man, and what is he doing?"

"Hi, Andre," Mia said. "It's nice seeing you again. Look, Sam is asleep upstairs, and I'm not going to wake her up after what she's been through tonight, thanks to your boss. So, you just go back and tell him whatever you need to tell him."

"Sorry, ma'am, but I have a direct order to watch out for her. I'm unable to leave without her. If you insist she stays, then I stay, too. I'll stay out here tonight to wait for her to come out in the morning."

"Whatever, man. Good luck getting to her, because it will be a cold day in hell that I let her go back to him." Mia tried to slam the door, only to have a big black boot stop it.

"Not that I should discuss Sir's personal matters with you, ma'am, but there has been a misunderstanding with the messages."

"Oh, really? Even the pictures?

"Pictures?" Andre stated with confusion. "Again, all I can state is there has been a misunderstanding. Please relay that to the Miss." Andre then walked away and called Carl.

"Carl, I've located Miss. She's at her friend's house, and I was told that she's sleeping and not to be disturbed. The friend Mia mentioned pictures. Are there pictures from Sir's phone that were sent to Miss?"

"No, not that I found. Sir is with me and heard all you said."

Weston yelled into the phone, "Andre, do not let her leave that house, and find out what these damn pictures are!"

"Yes, Sir."

Back at Mia's, there was a knock at the door.

Mia looked at Dylan. "Ugh, why won't this man go away?"

Dylan walked to the door this time and flung it open.

"Man, go away! Sam is not coming with you tonight. So, go! And tell Weston he's really messed things up this time. What an idiot."

"Sir, again, these are misunderstandings you heard before, and I'm not here to take Sam just yet. I need the pictures, please."

"Mia, he wants the pictures that Sam received."

"I don't know about this, but hell, I guess we're already this involved. Let me grab her phone, and I'll send them to you."

"Thank you, sir and ma'am."

Mia turned on Sam's phone, put in the passcode, and looked at Andre. "There better be one hell of an explanation for all of this. There, I forwarded the pictures to you. Now, if you don't mind, we're going to bed, as well." Mia shut the door and went to check on Sam, only to find that Sam had actually fallen asleep on the bed, curled up with a pillow.

Dylan and Mia headed to the guest room for the night, hoping tomorrow would be better for everyone.

Throughout the night, Andre had sent the pictures to Carl to share with Weston.

Weston left Carl to investigate video footage from the evening and board the plane home. Knowing there was nothing he could do about the nine-hour flight, Weston dozed off.

When I woke up the next morning, I sat up in bed trying to take in everything that happened. I needed to go to work. After leaving a note for Mia and Dylan, I walked out the door. The guards were all still there, and Andre walked towards me.

"Good morning, Miss. Are you heading to work this morning?"

"Yes, but I've already called a car."

"Nonsense, Miss. I'll take you. I'm already here."

"Fine, whatever. Let's go."

Andre quickly texted Carl to let him in on the latest happenings, so he could alert Weston when he landed.

After getting home, I rushed upstairs to change clothes and apply some makeup. Saying good morning to my parents, I grabbed a muffin and went to the barn office. All I wanted was to lie low and throw myself into work. I had already run through the ranch tasks by the time Kiera had arrived. I had her move some meetings around since I wasn't in a place to handle business in person. Next was the Hughes account. High dividends with little losses—that's what they needed by the end of the day..

My phone had been surprisingly quiet. I was torn between wanting Weston to call so I could ignore him, and not wanting him to call at all so I didn't have to listen to the lies. I let Kiera know I was taking a break outside, and I headed back to the house for some lunch. With all the guards around, I felt like a prisoner in my own home.

"Miss, where are you going?"

"Does it really matter at this point, Andre?"

He stared at me like he could take me, tie me up, and hold me hostage himself just so he wouldn't have to bear any wrath from his leaders.

"I'm heading inside to grab some lunch and will be heading back to the office. At this moment, I have no plans to leave." I gave him a wink that left him baffled as I walked off.

Out of the corner of my eye, I saw him frantically sending a text. I was definitely more curious to know what he was more afraid of other than Weston. Then again, I had my own sense of fear those days.

Mama had already packed my lunch to-go, and walking back to the office, I saw Nate waiting at the door.

"Nate, I'm already not in the mood because of your shit from yesterday, let alone last night. Please leave before I call Andre over here."

"Just give me five minutes, please!" Nate pleaded.

"Fine, but please be quick."

Nate went into a long, heartfelt speech about how he was so jetlagged and tired that he wasn't in his right mind and that it was no excuse, but he just felt so much pressure in all aspects of his life. He swore he would never touch me again ad and pleaded for me not to quit. I was a glutton for punishment and quickly threatened his life if he did something stupid again, but I told him we could move past this and continue to work together.

"So, can we now start over? And would it be okay if I took you and Keira out to dinner tonight?"

I could tell he saw hesitation on my face.

"To say, uh . . . to say thank you for all your work with the business. As a business meal, we can even write it off." Nate smirked.

"Well, if it's for business, then why not," I said with a subtle smile as I tried to find normalcy.

I had Kiera give him the full tour of the office and the space for the hedge fund company, then we spent the remaining hours looking at some older accounts and vendors. It was now 4:30. Since Nate was staying in the guesthouse again, we agreed to meet on the front porch of the house at 5:00 p.m. to head to dinner. After going inside, I let my parents know I would be going to dinner with Nate and Kiera for a business meeting.

CHAPTER 30:
Why Not Be Irish

We were met with only stares. Maybe it was the man's charming foreign looks next to me or if everyone knew I was supposed to be with Weston. Luckily, Kiera arrived at the Mexican restaurant we chose shortly after and sat next to me, hopefully helping to deter some of the rumors. Why should I be the one caught and outed for cheating on the front page when Weston was the one who had done wrong. As drinks were poured, the three of us were having a good time getting to know one another. I really did a great job of picking Kiera, and Nate seemed very impressed with her, as well. Maybe it was the drinks, but I was starting to think Kiera was quite smitten with our English boss. Laughing in my head, I thought they would be a cute match. She was slightly shorter than him at 5'4 to his 6'2. She had wavy blonde hair past her shoulders, piercing blue eyes, and a cute button nose on a very charming, slim face.

Nate and I are talked about our favorite places to travel, and Kiera piped in, saying she'd never been out of the country. We then started scheming for future business trips so we could solve this problem for her. Nate seemed excited to show her the world. As they got lost in conversation, I excused myself to the restroom. Stepping into the stall, I heard someone else enter, but the footsteps sounded like they were in front of my stall.

BANG! BANG! BANG!

"Sam, come out right now!"

Shit, it's Weston.

Being my stupid drunk self, in the most Irish voice I could push out, I said, "This isn't Sam but Irene. Please back off of my stall, and step out."

"Sam, you have ten seconds to step out, or I'm breaking this damn door in."

"Feck off," Using the Irish slang I picked up when I visited Ireland for several months.

"1, 2, 3…"

"Ugh!" I got myself together and walked out, pushing right past him to the sink.

His eyes burned holes in my body as I washed my hands. Before I could rush out of the bathroom, he spun me around and pushed me up against the cement wall.

"Let go of me. I'm completely done with you!" I yelled as I tried to free myself.

"Do you really not trust me? You just go against me after a few texts and pictures and don't even reach out to ask what the hell is going on? Let me explain! Dammit, Sam!" He punched the wall next to my head.

I stared, wide-eyed, at the blood trickling down from his knuckles. His mouth quickly covered mine while his tongue desperately pushed past my teeth, pulling me tightly in his embrace and not letting me breathe as his tongue entangled with mine.

He must've gotten a taste of my tears, as he quickly pulled back and looked at me. "Sam," he whispered calmly, wiping my tears away.

"Wes, what explanation can you have when pictures and texts clearly tell the story?"

"This!" He handed me his phone with video footage and time stamps, showing him in his meeting. In the upper right-hand corner, a smaller video played of a woman at the bar with a phone that looked similar to the one I was holding.

"Oh my," I whispered under my breath.

"Miss Dupont? Samantha, are you in there? Are you all right?"

"Oh, no. It's Kiera." I looked at Wes. "You locked the door? I need to finish my dinner meeting. We can discuss this tomorrow."

"No, you're coming with me tonight to the apartment."

"I don't think I will," I said, and walked to the door and opened it.

"Samantha Jane!" he said through gritted teeth as I walked out.

"Hey, Kiera! I'm good! Weston had called, so I wanted to take his call where it was quiet. Let us go back." I hated lying to her.

Once back at the table, we had one more drink before calling it a night.

We walked out to a stellar car revving up its engine, its bright lights in our direction as we tried to load into the Uber.

"Who is that? That's not a car you see every day, especially in a small town like this. That's a McLaren 765LT," Nate stated.

Instantly, I realized exactly who it was, and almost as if on cue, he exited the car and walked over.

"Um, Nate, please see that Kiera gets home safely. I'll see you on Monday."

"Are you sure, Sam? Your face is telling me you'd rather go home."

I knew if I didn't push them to leave soon, there would be a scene. "No, really, I'm good, Nate. Thank you." I hurried over to Weston and pulled him back to the car.

Not a word was said in the car, and at the apartment, neither one of us wanted to cave first, though I did find the first aid kit to clean and wrap his hand until he could be convinced to go to the hospital.

After another twenty more minutes of silence, he looked at me. "You really have nothing to say to me?"

"What do you want me to say? I'm sorry for accusing you of cheating, though it seemed I had all the evidence. Not to mention, I'm tired and stressed from having to dodge reporters for the last seventy-two plus hours because your mom made our announcement to the world.

Or how about the fact that I'm constantly surrounded by the men in black? Please enlighten me . . . What do you want me to say right now?"

He moved closer to me and grabbed my hands. "Sam, we'll figure out who's after you . . . after us. And I understand that you thought you had all the evidence, but you don't get to walk away without talking to me because your feelings are hurt. And you think you'll actually be able to leave me this time around? You are mine. No one or anything will ever come between us, but you have to trust me." He pulled me into his arms and straight into his hard chest, allowing me to inhale his delicious scent.

I was defeated. "Okay, I got it. I trust you. Sorry. This week has been tough. But I will come straight to you next time. Also, please don't be harsh on Andre. I didn't allow him to fulfill his orders properly while you were gone. We tried everything to deter him and the men in black."

Weston laughed. "So, I heard. And about my mom . . . I'll deal with her tomorrow. This is a change for you, Sam, and I want everyone to respect your privacy as much as I do. Unfortunately, that may not always be the case. Just remember I'll protect you from anything."

I kissed him on the cheek and whispered, "Thank you."

"By the way, did you not finish furniture shopping?"

"Why do you ask that? Mia went with me, and we totally did. Everything is being delivered this Sunday."

"Oh." He looked at me sideways.

"What? Say what you have to say, Weston."

"You must've gotten one hell of a deal." He picked up the black card sitting on the table and handed it to me. "I'm sure what you picked is tasteful and fitting. Just hold on to this in case you find something you like more."

Now I was the one looking at him sideways. "Oh! I get it. You checked to see what I spent, but to your surprise, it was way less than expected, right?"

Weston's face twisted up.

I was proud of my own independence and paycheck. "You know I'm not such a boring trophy wife, right? I split the cost with you. And a fly is going to land itself in that mouth of yours if you don't shut it," I said, teasing him.

"Samantha Jane, that was not the deal."

"You seriously can't be mad at me for not putting everything on your fancy card."

"I just want to take care of you in every way that I can and give you the luxury others dream of."

"Just spoil me with yourself, and I'll be happy."

"Well, that's a given. But on a serious note"—he pulled another card out of his wallet—"this one is yours. Keep it on you and spend it at will. What's mine is yours," he said as he picked me up and carried me to the bedroom.

While I was still in shock of having my own black card, he quickly distracted my thoughts, putting me on the bed.

"It's already been too long since I've had you." He quickly took control, and there was no time for me to react. Clothes were ripped off, and my body succumbed to his in every way.

Weston's POV

Lying awake, thinking about those last twenty-four hours had been pure hell. At least my Sam was back in my arms, and we were finally moving in together that weekend. I just had to figure out who was behind all this mess, though I had a good idea who. I just needed proof to deal with her properly. For now, I was going to keep holding my soon to be wife in my arms. The thought of losing her again over something so stupid made me sick, but the thought of losing her at all drove me mad.

I get that I'd hurt her in the past, and she had to learn to trust me all over again with her heart, but damn, she really fell into the flight category. Was it me that had damaged her like this? Anytime something bad or painful happened, she took off. We were going to have to discuss that, and in the meantime, there would be more bodyguards for her and the family. I had too much to lose now.

CHAPTER 31:
Many a New Day

*I*t was finally Sunday, and we were moving into our house. We'd moved what we could, but the furniture had to be delivered. In all the craziness, Weston had talked to his mother, his dad was MIA in China for work, and my daddy was feeling better and even went out roping that morning. Nate had settled into the guesthouse, where he would be staying for the next month. Since Weston had rushed home to deal with the drama, he would be flying back out Monday for the week to finish up his dealings. And then our engagement party was to be on Saturday. There was a lot going on in life, but we were all looking ahead.

Weston was out on the back deck on the phone with an ashen look, so I strolled out there to bring him some fresh lemonade.

"All right, Carl. Keep me posted, and I'll discuss with Sam." He wrapped his arms around me and kissed me on the forehead. "Hey, babe."

"So, what news does Carl bring today?"

"He found who was behind the messages and pictures. Ready for it?"

"Yes, who?"

"Laura Belle." He stepped back to gauge my reaction.

"Your ex? The one I met when I got home? I'm honestly confused."

"Her family has some ranking and quite a bit of money—old and new. Unfortunately, she's using what she can to drive you away, along with bringing her sister down with her. I didn't realize Laura knew my passcode. She was the one who sent you the messages. And the blonde in the photos near me was actually her sister. Though they look similar, there's just enough difference."

"I did think she looked familiar but couldn't figure it out. So, now what?"

"Carl did trace them back Stateside, but then they both sort of disappeared. We've deployed men all around this area—home, the airport—along with some men looking out back in Georgia to see if they pop up there. As much as I hate it, I have to leave tomorrow. It's important you keep Andre nearby and not fall for any traps. Also, I think it's best if you stay back at home with your parents until I am back—just as a precaution."

"I promise, and I'm fine with going back home for the week. You don't think she'll try something this week, do you? Our engagement party is Saturday, and even details of that are as tightly sealed as we could make it."

He held me close. "I promise you, the party will be splendid with no issues. Nothing will stand in the way of celebrating our future."

I stood on my tippy toes and kissed him. "I love you, Weston Lee."

He picked me up, and I wrapped my legs around him. We kissed lustfully as he carried me into the living room. I laid on the couch, with his body hovered close to mine, and not once did his lips leave mine.

The doorbell rang.

I tried to move my mouth from his and gasped for air. "Wes, I think the furniture people are here."

Weston looked behind him to the open window on the door.

"One minute, please! I think we might've made the men out there blush." He smiled coquettishly at me and then got up and answered the door. "Please, follow me this way so I can show you where everything needs to go." I sat on the couch, hiding until they had gone upstairs. After a few hours, all of our furniture was moved in, and the decor was up.

Our sweet home.

We decided to order in for dinner and have a quiet night at home. He set the table with little candles on our twelve-person farm table, and then he even cleaned up dinner while I took a shower. I was in love with our shower, especially the waterfall showerhead.

"Enjoying your first shower in *our* house?" he said as he peeked his head in.

"I am. Care to join me?"

"Thought you might not ever ask."

I suddenly found that I had the best view in the corner of the shower. I could watch him undress in the mirror. Seeing him finish undressing, I quickly turned my back to him.

When I felt his full presence behind me, I just melted. He rested his chin on my shoulder and encircled his arms around my waist.

"Are you happy?" he whispered in my ear.

I turned around to look at him and lifted my hand up to his face. "How can I not be happy right now? I'm over the moon being in our exquisite home together, I'm soon to be Mrs. Lancaster, and we're finally starting our lives together."

He leaned into me while laying a soft kiss on my lips.

"What about you? You're the state's most eligible bachelor, leaving the single life behind."

"Are you teasing me right now?" His stern face was so close to mine, the water ran down his nose, forming droplets on my chin as I stared into his light ocean blue eyes.

"I know *not* what you're referring to . . ."

He grinned. "It seems you're feeling quite impish today."

Now I was in more trouble than I intended. By the time we ended, our voices were hoarse, and I honestly believed every corner to every piece of furniture had been christened with our love.

CHAPTER 32:
Nightmare in Egypt

It was in the middle of the night when I was awakened by Weston yelling and shaking. Quickly, I jumped out of bed to turn on the light before going over to his side of the bed.I tried to coax him awake by first speaking softly and gently touching his face; to then shouting his name when he grabbed my upper arms so tightly. It was if he felt I was the one attacking him at that moment.

Finally, his eyes popped open, but it was still as if he was not all there. Looking quite dazed, I whispered "Weston, its me. It's Samantha." Bravely bending down to kiss his lips. I felt his hands loosen on my arms, and his labored breathing calming down. "Samantha....did I hurt you?" As he took my face into his hands to make sure I was ok. "No, I am fine. Are you okay? What was happening in your sleep?"

"It was just a nightmare, nothing to worry your pretty face about."

"Wes, come on. This is not the first time your nightmares have woken me, but I will say this is the loudest I have heard or seen you. Do they have something to do with what happened to you a few years ago? You were yelling in English and what seemed maybe like Arabic."

+ All he does is look down while he took my hands in his, then holds them close to his lips. "You can tell me Wes. Let me be there for you this time."

"I guess the stress of everything that has gotten to me. Almost like I have that feeling again of uncontrollable panic and fear. A feeling where I can't breathe. I never want to feel that again. That time in my life was dark, Samantha. Though I try not to let it define me, it is always in the back of mind. Especially when I feel threatened, or I sense you might be in danger.

"Baby, what happened to you?" As I took him in my arm, leaning his head against my chest. Gently running my fingers through his dark silked hair. In a cracked voice, "If I tell you, you will never look at me the same. I do not want you to know what I am capable of when I am not with you."

"I promise I just want to love you. To love all of you. There is nothing you can tell me Wes that would change any of that." I could feel his breathing start to pick back up and then he crawled over me to get out of bed. He stands next to the bed, looking at me with the most unlit blue eyes I have seen from him. Almost as if there is an impending storm about to surge through the ocean on a gloomy day.

"It was right after I stepped into the VP position at Lans. I was making and closing deals left and right. But we were struggling on closing the petroleum deal in Egypt that would benefit not only them, but the neighboring countries where we had factories and adding jobs. The government there is not the cleanest due to a certain controlling mafia. So my dealings were with Anhur Maher. His men are thugs and have no qualities other than being killing machines. Anhur Maher was the type of guy you wanted on your side, not the other way around. Carl and I decided to take the chance to meet him in person. To solidify the deal. We took all the safety and security precautions that we could, along with bringing several men with us as we embarked to uncharted territory. Unbeknownst to us at the time, my father had screwed him out of a deal years prior, and that we were lured into a trap. As soon as we began exiting the plane, shots were fired. Several of my men were killed instantly, as the remainder of us rushed back in and demanded the pilot to take off.   They had us surrounded and rushed onto the plane. Taking myself, Carl, and the rest hostage by tying our hands back behind and blindfolding us. They led us down the tarmac, into vehicles and it felt like hours went by until we finally stopped."

Weston stops to take a drink of water from the bedside table, then finally sits down next to me. I am now wide-eyed and enthralled by this story. Getting anxious that he might not continue, but then he took a deep breath. "They dragged us out of the vehicles, throwing us into a dark room. There they chained our arms and legs to the wall, but took our blindfolds off. I counted that there were eight of us left, from the fourteen we had at the beginning. Carl was next to me, trying to tell me it was going to be ok. I knew it wasn't going to be nor has it ever been after….. Time passed slowly, but Anhur Maher makes a visit. Telling me the long story of how my father betrayed him not only with money but slept with one of his women also. That I was going to suffer the consequences for him until he paid up. Anhurs men began stripping us naked while pounding their fists onto us. Pictures were taken for proof to send back to my father so negotiations could begin. I honestly thought to myself, we would not be there long. My father would do whatever it took to bring his son back. Days went by and my hope dwindled. Each day was filled with beatings, starvation and further humiliation. After the fifth day, they started to shoot my men in the head, one by one, for every day my father delayed agreeing to the deal. They just left my men's bodies there to rot next to us." I can tell Weston is struggling with emotions of being alive and guilt over those that were murdered due to the actions of his father. I pulled him closer to me so we could feel each other at that moment. For him to know I am thankful he is still here and he can lean on me. "Everytime I closed my eyes, I would picture your smiling face in our favorite field of bluebonnets. Just us laughing and being happy. All I wanted was to be in your arms and knew somehow I needed to make it through to win you back."

At this point I feel the tears streaming down my cheeks as he continued. My throat was too dry to even speak a word. "Finally on the tenth day, after five of my men have been shot; Anhur states they have finally reached a deal and we would be going home. By nightfall, a group of marines barged into the small building we were in. All we could hear was gunfire throughout and see lights headed in our direction. A huge breath of air was released by all of us, once the marines introduced themselves, called our names out, then surveyed the scene. Two men worked on breaking our chains then handing us blankets to wrap ourselves in. It took another group of men to move and carry the dead bodies and load them up. We were quickly taken to a nearby base to be assessed and answer questions. Within 24 hours of being rescued, the alive and dead headed back to the States.

♦ "As hungry as I was, I couldn't keep food down for weeks. Only causing me to lose more weight. It took even more weeks for my body to heal of all the bruises and gashes. I had plastic surgery to remove all the scars, but if you close enough, you can see some remembrance of them." He stops to show me a few on his scalp as well as his back and abdomen. Honestly if you did not know they were there, you would never do a second glance. I found myself memorizing his body all over again, to ensure I do not forget where they are located and to love them as they are a part of him now. "Several weeks go by and I am pissed as hell. Not just at my father, but for not being able to protect myself or the others. I reached out to a marine that was part of the rescue mission and he got me set up at their recruiting facility in San Diego to train. So I left for several months, trained hard and came back ready to handle shit. While I was gone, I had Carl tracking Anhurs every move, as we plotted our revenge. We caught up with him in South Africa, trying to lie low in a small German town. Needless to say, this time it was us who caught him and men off guard. My men killed all his men right on the spot. Then I shot Anhur Maher straight in the head, between the eyes as he pleaded for his life. In that moment, I swore no one would ever take advantage of me, my family or company ever again."

I bend over placing a kiss on top of his head, holding him tighter than I was before. I don't say I am sorry, as I know that is the last thing he wants to hear. My mind quickly flashes to one of the pictures that Nate shared with me. Weston was standing there with a gun pointed at a man who backed against a wall. That has to be who he just told me about. "How did you not get caught?" I asked softly. Now worried he might be taken from me, especially if someone like Nate could access these types of pictures.

"Money talks, my love. As well as Interpol and the government had been chasing him for years for several crimes and terrorist attacks. He is no one that anyone will ever miss. So there is no need for you to worry." he stated, kissing my forehead.

"Okay.....um, so what the news says is true then? About you being a ruthless and powerful man?" Lifting my chin up to lock his eyes with mine, "Sam, I will not lie to you ever. I do what I feel must be done to maintain leadership and power. I have never done anything that was not warranted. The same goes for my men. If you ever have questions or concerns, please ask and I will be honest. I never want you to fear me or trust me."

"I don't fear you Weston, but I don't want to fear for us either."

"My sweet Samantha as long as we are together, there is nothing to fear." As he pulls me tight into his arms, I realize I have never felt safer.

CHAPTER 33:
Getting Fancy

*L*uckily, it had been a fairly quiet week. Weston got home from his trip at 3:00 a.m., so I let him rest as I finished preparing our gifts. Mama and Mrs. Lancaster only let us have a say in our gifts to our bridesmaids and groomsmen, so I put on the personal touches. My ladies' boxes had only the best: half-carat diamond earrings in a platinum setting, wine tumblers engraved with their names, mini bottles of wine, a black silk robe embroidered with "Bridesmaid—to be worn when we are getting ready on the big day," along with some bath scrubs and a personal note from me. Of course, Mia would be my maid of honor, so her robe reflected that.

Weston didn't have any boundaries with gift-giving. He decided on tailor-made vests and sports jackets that would be worn on the wedding day and a fine bottle of Michter's bourbon.

Mia and Dylan came over to get ready with us and for Mia to help me with my hair and makeup.

"I still can't believe I don't even know where this event is taking place," Mia exclaimed.

"Well, hopefully this method works to keep as much of the press away as possible. Mama wouldn't even tell me, but I do have a slight idea on where. We should be getting our text here in the next thirty minutes, and then we can head on out."

"There is so much suspense around this party. It's been the talk of the town for weeks!"

"I think anything to do with me and Weston is always the talk of the town."

"Very true."

Mrs. Lancaster made this a black-tie affair, which made this party fancier than the actual wedding. Looking into the mirror and channeling my inner Audrey Hepburn, I felt inspired and gorgeous. Mama had a dress made for me that basically mimicked the black Givenchy dress in *Sabrina*. Mia did my hair up in a braided twist, embellished with a golden leaf headpiece. My makeup was on point, and the look was complete with my black and golden heels.

"Mia, I'm ready to go!"

"You look stunning, Sam. Ah, we need a selfie!" She whipped out her phone and took several pictures of us together and a few of me solo.

"With the way you look tonight, Mia, Dylan cannot possibly say no to you about anything." She was in a one-shouldered black dress that not only had flowing layers, but a split up to her high thigh, showing off the length of her legs.

She gave me a hug. "Well, I'm not the bride, and it's your night, so let's head down."

The guys stopped mid-sentence once we walked into the living room.

"Ladies, you both look like perfection," Weston said as they walked over to us. He took my hand and twirled me around. "You, my love, look ravishing tonight."

"Why, I think the grace of eloquence is seated on your lips, sir. I, too, must say how dashing you look tonight, Weston Lancaster."

Before he could kiss me, all our phones started dinging.

"We finally got the location!" Mia shouted.

Weston requested a limo for all of us, and as we piled in, I realized Carl was sitting up front and Andre was driving. I was glad we had Weston's top men with us.

About forty minutes later, we pulled up to the party, and I was in awe. Our parents rented out The Reserve at Dancing Elk. It was every bit as eloquent as it was rustic, and it looked as if the yard and surrounding fields were fluttering with lightning bugs with all the fairy lights laid and strung out.

Weston took my arm in his and led me inside.

The corridor was filled with greenery, candles, and roses with black ribbon embellishments. There was a table that had a large wooden plaque where everyone could sign their names, and the other tables were full of pictures of me and Weston growing up. There were so many memories we'd made.

At once, my mama came out from behind the wooden French doors. "Are you ready, sweetie?"

"Yes! Can we finally go in now?"

"Follow me . . ."

She knocked on the door, and then suddenly both doors swung open. The room was stunning, and it was almost like walking into a woodland fairytale. There were antler chandeliers hanging from the ceiling and willow trees growing in the room with gorgeous moss and vines everywhere. The centerpieces were a mixture of high- and low-cylinder vases filled with water and assorted wildflowers. The place was lit with candles all around. There was an open bar to the left and a large projection of photos to the right on the opposite wall. Under the projection, on a table, was a sign that said "Soon to be Mr. & Mrs.", and it was covered with my favorite flower—bluebonnets. It was breathtaking.

"Mama, this is incredible. It truly portrays a woodland fairytale." The tears started to come. "This truly is too much."

"Oh, look. Here comes Arlene now."

Weston reached out to give her a big hug, and I followed.

We continued to compliment them on how unbelievable the place was and how thankful we were for them.

"This is my only son that you're marrying, my sweet Sam. But I've always thought of you as my second daughter. May this be one of many extraordinary events you are part of together. Now I need to go visit with the other guests. Please excuse me."

"I should, too," Mama said. "Let me go check on your dad before he drinks too much."

"Okay, Mama. See you later."

Wes pulled me into his arms. "Just you and me, kid!"

"Who are you calling kid?"

"Have you seen some of those throwbacks? Look, baby Sam . . . Scrawny Sam . . . Wannabe tomboy Sam . . . Crimped hair Sam . . . Surfing Sam. Ah, and one of my favorites . . . prom Sam."

"Okay, okay, enough. Don't make me start calling out your flaws."

"Flaws? These aren't flaws. They're moments I remember always wanting to be near and protecting you." He had to lift my chin up off the floor and stop me from gawking at him like a teenage girl. "I've always said it, Sam. It's always been you from the beginning."

Enjoying being slightly taller in my heels, I kissed him on the lips and whispered a sweet naughty promise in his ear.

"Well," he said, "let's get this party started so I can hold you to it." With that, he spun me out onto the dance floor.

Even Nate found his way to me and politely asked Weston for a dance with me. Surprisingly, Weston said yes and then started dancing with his sister, Maddie. Out of the corner of his eye, though, he watched Nate's hands and movements.

"You look so beautiful this evening, Sam. To be honest, it's hard to admit, but it seems I must move on from you and admit my defeat to Weston. I've seen how happy you are since my time here, and I think tonight only solidifies it all for me. This won't be easy for my uncle, either."

"Well, thank you, Nate, for the compliment. As for your uncle, whom I do adore, I think we're all best as business partners."

"I agree with your last statement, but if that man of yours ever lets you down, I hope I can be there to help you through it. Even if it's just as a friend."

I hugged him. "You're very kind, Nate, and I truly take your words to heart. It's always great to have a friend in higher places."

Going back to dancing, he said, "I actually have my eyes on that assistant of yours. She's actually here with me tonight."

He turned his head and winked back at her, and I waved to her and smiled.

"Oh, good. She does seem smitten with you, but don't go and steal her from me. Well, I mean, professionally. I still need to ask Weston if I can keep her permanently since she came from Lans Enterprises. I'm too spoiled with her to turn to anyone else."

"I'm sure he won't be able to say no to you. Besides, you have her for now . . . until I decide to whisk her away to England."

"Ha! I think you should just stick around here and learn to become a cowboy."

After the dance ended, I headed to the bar, and he headed back to Kiera.

After the delicious steak and lobster dinner, it was time for more announcements, speeches, and gifts for our favorite people. Weston had gotten our moms beautiful, diamond-studded bracelets with the ranch's emblem as a charm, and of course, some Mitcher's for the dads. Then I asked Mia to be my maid of honor and Dawn and Jenny to be my bridesmaids. I had to say I was more excited for Weston's turn to present his gifts to his friends. Of course, Jackson was asked to be the best man, followed by Dylan as a groomsman. Then he called Carl on stage with us.

"Carl, can you please make your way to the front?"

In true bodyguard fashion, Carl was there in a split second.

"Sir, what can I help you with?"

Weston handed him one of the boxes. "This . . ." Carl looked at him like a deer in headlights, and Weston pushed the box towards him. "Read the name. Open the box."

I was laughing and crying at the same time.

Carl opened the box and was still in a state of shock.

"Many of you have known me for all of my life, or several years, then you have also known, and maybe even dealt with, Carl. He has been by my side since college, has never wavered in standing in for or even in front of me. He's always respected my decision and looked out for me, even when I didn't ask. I cannot fathom standing at the altar without my closest brothers and confidants, and that includes you, man. I trust my life in your hands every day, so it's only fitting you stand with me as I marry the love of my life."

Carl was getting teary-eyed while trying to crack a smile on that serious face of his. "It will be my pleasure and honor, Sir. Thank you!" He nodded to Weston and then hurried back to his post before we could convince him to stay.

Mrs. Lancaster closed the speeches. "Now, there's one last big announcement we know everyone has been waiting for all evening. It's the announcement of the big day! Now for the big reveal!"

Suddenly, the lights went out, and in the middle of the dance floor was a projection of "August 18th" with an "L" through the middle. The same monogram began bouncing on the walls. Everyone was hollering and losing their minds watching as "Love" by Frank Sinatra began to play.

Weston whisked me away to the middle of the dance floor. We glided and twirled, ending with me being dipped and kissed in front of everyone. Between the wine, the room temperature, and this man, I was flushed.

CHAPTER 34:
Respect

The following Monday, we headed to the ranch to work. As soon as we arrived, Jackson took Weston to finalize the paperwork on real estate in Oklahoma and in Kansas. It was unbelievable how much the ranch had expanded over the year. I headed out, and I saw Daddy helping the ranch hands load up a herd of cattle to send over to two ranches in Oklahoma. Jackson would be following them out there to make sure all was settled and to meet with the new ranch hands. Weston and Jackson brought in their good buddy, Riley, to manage the Oklahoma and Kansas ranches, so we had hoped having someone we knew personally would keep order.

Nate and Kiera walked over from the guesthouse. I really didn't want to have to put in dating regulations for work.

"Well, good morning, you two."

Kiera looked away shyly. "You're here early this morning, Miss Dupont."

"Not really. It's a quarter to eight." I smirked. "Y'all go have some breakfast inside, and I'll see the both of you when you come in." I gave Nate the evil eye.

As I walked into the office, Weston handed me all the paperwork with signed checks to transfer. We went over the accounts and contract to make sure Riley was completely processed and could be in the system by the end of the week.

"Thanks," I said. "I'll do all this now so everything is in order before Jackson and Riley head out later."

He kissed me on the head. "Sounds good. My father just summoned me, so if you need me, I'll be at the house."

"Hope it all goes well," I said, trying not to look concerned.

The door opened again, and without even looking up, I knew who it was.

"Kiera, there are some new client files upstairs I need you to run background checks and legitimacy on. Mr. Hughes sent them over, but I still want to do our own validation. Please bring me the final reports when they're complete."

"Yes, Miss Dupont, I'll work on this right away."

"Thank you," she said as she walked up the steps.

"Now you, President Hughes, please take a seat."

"Why do I think I'm about to get reprimanded even though I'm ranked higher than you?"

"I'm not here to reprimand anyone, but I would like to say my peace, if I may."

He nodded. "Go ahead."

"I can't say a word on office romance because I'm getting married to an owner. And whether this is serious between the two of you, or just for fun, is none of my business. But Kiera is my assistant, so she's partially my business. She's smart and level-headed. Don't ruin her!" I pointed my finger at him. "Don't allow her to veer off track with her plans. Also, you're staying at the ranch as a guest. Though you're rich, noble, and my boss, respect this ranch and my parents. Don't go gallivanting women around here like they're objects. And I'll say the same about being around town, as well. This town is small and gossips, a lot! You can refute that as needed."

"Well . . ." Nate cleared his throat. "Thank you for voicing your concern, Miss Dupont. I completely understand your concerns and am aware of Kiera's talents and ambitions. We're at a very young stage in this thing together, but I see the same potential in her. I hope to only help her advance—not divert her direction. Furthermore, no other girls have been on this property other than Kiera. And just so you know, she's been here since Saturday when we arrived back from your engagement party."

My eyes grew large.

"I assure you I've been the utmost gentlemen to her all weekend, and I asked your parents in advance if she was welcomed."

"Okay. It seems we've settled all personal matters and are on the same page." I chuckled. "Now, Nate, can you review the clients Keira is working on? I'm thinking you may know them in some capacity, so I'd like your personal opinion on them. Your uncle wants to grow his company, but we also need to be hesitant on who comes in and not take on more than we can handle right now."

"I don't mind doing so at all. I have some Stateside investor meetings this morning to work through, and then we can review them together this afternoon."

"Sounds good. Thank you"

Nate headed to the conference room, and I threw myself back into the ranch tasks for the remainder of the morning.

Weston's POV

Over at the Lancaster Mansion, I seemed to be in a face-off with my father.

"Did you have you men follow me these last several weeks? I expected more out of you, Weston."

"Have you been trying to demolish all the work and planning I've completed over the past year? Father, I expected more out of you. You are still sitting as president of this company, and it's hard for me to fathom why you're intentionally harming your own company."

"I see, I see. Though it seems you've come out on top, unscathed."

"Well, Father, I learned from you that there is no choice but landing on top, untouched. So, would you care to explain what the hell you've been up to?"

"Certainly, son. I am finally stepping down to just be on the board. So, that means you will then be acting president of Lans Enterprises. The announcement will be made this Thursday to the public, with a ceremony to follow."

"This seems sudden. What's your endgame?"

"I admit, I screwed up. A large investment fell south, and I had to make up the funds for it and do some client pleasing to satisfy the loss. I had faith you would take care of everything on the low without causing more problems. Besides, everyone agrees it's time for you to step in as president. It also means less time at the ranch and more travel. But I'm sure you'll be able to handle it all."

"Are you trying to make me hate you even more? I'm not against becoming president, but with all the shady shit you've done, I should've pushed you out myself a long time ago. This is a billion-dollar company. Are you really trying to screw everyone over on purpose? I literally had to chase you around the globe and clean up all those damn messes. And you purposefully took me away from Sam."

"Son, I've said my piece on everything. I'm no longer in the way of the two of you, as it seems you're determined to be with her, regardless of what I have to say. She softens you in this world, and you need to exude power and demand respect. I do love Samantha, as she is family to us, but you are my son, so I worry for you, first. And that worry is that I fear she will be your demise. With the business, I became greedy, so I strove for more. With that, I made some deplorable decisions with a few sketchy businessmen. But you fixed it all, and now the company is in your hands. I have all the confidence you'll make everyone proud and tons of money."

"Unlike you, Father, I can do and be both. As for you, come between us again, and I will turn the company upside down. Next time, I won't be so nice to come to your aide. Just remember that."

"I hope you can, son, I really do. As for the latter, I understand and will be nothing but supportive. I hope we can now put the past behind us as we move forward in the future. You're getting married and will hopefully soon produce an heir, or heirs, to fall in line with the Lancaster men." as Mr. Lancaster reached out a hand to Weston.

He reached out a hand to me, but I denied it and turned to walk away.

"One more thing . . . I heard from the Williams that guards are near their home, and it seems someone is searching for Laura Belle. Know anything about this?"

"Father, all I will say is you can warn them that if Laura Belle tries to come after Sam again, it will be her last day breathing."

"I see, son, and will pass on the message. Let me get back to business, and I'll visit with you later this week."

I walked out of the study and called Carl from my phone. "Meet me at the downtown office in thirty minutes."

CHAPTER 35:
Let That Pony Run

Wes and I discussed whether I wanted to bring Admiral to the house with his horse, Bella, and deliberating, I decided to leave him at the ranch. He was older, set in his ways, and loved being here. I just needed to make sure to give him extra love and rides when I was at the ranch. I also let him know Maddox was all packed up and ready to go. Weston would be by to pick me up in about an hour. I could either eat dinner with my parents or Andre could drive me home. I decided to stay with Jackson and Lucey.

Over dinner, Lucey told me how she and the baby were doing and asked for help decorating their new house. I was shocked to find out that it was going to be move-in ready in less than two weeks. After dinner, we did some online planning and shopping.

"Just send me the bill, Sam," Jackson said, laughing, before he and Riley set off on their journey.

Mama joined in on the shopping spree while Daddy rocked on the front porch with Mr. Lancaster. It made me wonder what he wanted to talk to Weston about earlier. I guess I would ask when he picked me up. For now, I was just enjoying being around my family after a crazy few weeks. It felt like I had come home from a world tour, only to leave again. On the bright side, I did get to see my parents daily, and we had the weekly "family" dinner, so we all seemed to be adjusting well with the change.

I heard a truck drive up and thought it was Wes, but I walked outside to be greeted by Andre.

"Is everything all right, Andre?"

"Yes, Miss. Sir is running late with a meeting and has asked me to come pick up you and Maddox and bring you home."

"Um, sure . . . Let me grab his things."

"I can retrieve it, Miss, if you just want to load yourselves up."

At this point, everyone was staring.

Daddy asked, "Is this the new normal for you, sweetheart?"

"Oh, no. Wes and I came together this morning, so I don't have my car here. You know me—I'd rather control the reins than be riding rear. But it seems he's running late, so Maddox and I will head home. Love you, Daddy." I gave him, Mama, and Lucey a hug and kiss and said goodbye to Mr. Lancaster.

Maddox and I loaded up to head home.

We pulled into the drive to see that Weston was already home. Maddox jumped out and ran to the backyard. Chasing him, I found Wes hanging out on the back porch, still in his suit, with a bourbon in one hand and looking off to the distance. He seemed so in thought, he didn't even hear me sneak up behind him.

"Hey, babe! Everything okay?" I kissed him on the cheek.

"Hey, Sam. I'm just processing some events that happened today. But we can talk about that later. I have a surprise for you. Follow me." As he walked to the stables, Bella had her head out of the stall and was already situated. Then I saw a big, speckled nose come out from another stall.

"Who's this?" I asked.

"Go and look."

Walking down to the stall, I came across the most beautiful buckskin quarter horse with a mane as dark as midnight.

"He is so handsome! Where did he come from?"

He smiled. "I brought him in from Florida. I've been looking at him for a while. He comes from a winning bloodline with exceptional genes. Only four years old. I had a feeling you wouldn't want to move Admiral, and of course, Bella doesn't like to be alone."

"He's completely mine?" I was in awe of the beauty of this horse. "What's his name?"

"Whatever you want it to be. He's all yours, babe!"

By the way this guy was already nuzzling up to me, I could tell he had a wonderful temperament, and his amber eyes were soulful.

"He already looks so strong and distinguished, like an old soul. I think Mr. Darcy Dupree will do, but we'll call you Teddy for short." I scratched his muzzle as he neighed.

Wes put his arm around me, chuckling. "It seems he likes it."

"Thank you. He's amazing, and you are the absolute best! Let's let them out to graze and run for a bit."

We opened the stalls, and off they went. Bella seemed to enjoy Mr. Darcy's company as they galloped through the fields. I pulled out my phone to snap a picture of the scene. This was a moment in time I would always want to remember. At the same time, I captured a picture of my husband-to-be as he watched the horses with the corner of his lips slightly curled up.

CHAPTER 36:
The Gala

Lans Enterprises just made the public announcement that Weston Lee Lancaster would be stepping into the president role, as Clint Wayne Lancaster stepped down to be on the board while his son took over. I honestly couldn't believe the amount of press that showed up there and at the gala. It was a full red-carpet event.

As we waited to get out of the limo, Wes looked at me. "Are you nervous?"

"A little. There are so many people and cameras here. This really is the first time we're stepping out into the public in person."

"Just stay with me, and you'll be fine. The whole world will be in awe of your beauty and jealous you're on my arm."

"You are so preposterous sometimes."

"All right. It's time. You ready?"

"I'm as ready as I can be, Mr. President." I bit my lower lip.

"Oh, Sam. It's been so hard holding myself back from ravishing you already tonight, and you go and do that, my little minx." He grabbed my chin and looked lustfully into my eyes.

Luckily, the passenger door opened, and we were faced with all the noise and camera flashes from the paparazzi. Weston looked at me with warning eyes, got himself together, then stepped out of the limo. He presented his hand to help guide me out. We stood side by side with camera flashes and questions coming from all directions. With his hand on the small of my back, he led me up the red carpet, and we stopped in the middle for some more pictures and interviews. I was taking it all in and saw that Weston was a natural. He remained unchanged by the fame and craziness.

Though all press was told personal questions were off-limits for all of the family, especially Weston Lancaster, there seemed to be a few that tried to push the envelope.

One interviewer said, "President Lancaster, this must be the infamous Samantha Dupont accompanying you tonight."

Weston nodded.

"Miss Dupont, can you tell me who you're wearing tonight? You look stunning next to the president.

"Oh, it's Zin, my best friend's company. Miss Mia Zinser designed it, as well as the coordinating vest Weston is wearing under his jacket." I was donning a long white dress, adorned with a sparkling silver design, that was low-cut in the front with a slit up the right side. Mia really did a brilliant design and job on this dress for me. It fit all my curves perfectly and seemed to grab Weston's attention.

"Will this same Mia with Zin be designing your wedding dress?"

"Possibly . . . when that time comes." I tried to keep my answers short and not divulge too much information.

"Are we saying that the wedding is not in the near future? Also, President Lancaster, the last time you walked the red carpet for an event in New York, four months ago, you had a beautiful blonde on your arm. Being the most eligible bachelor around, is it that easy to always find a woman to be on your arm?"

Weston's jaw clenched, and he squeezed my hand as Carl began walking over to get ready to punch the guy. Weston gave a look to Carl to hang back. All of a sudden, I was pulled into his arms and then dipped down. Weston he held me under my back and on my right leg that had now been pulled up, while he inhaled my mouth into his. His intimate moves caught everyone's attention, and bringing me back up, he still held me in his arms, glaring at the interviewer.

"Does it look like I'm still an eligible bachelor? Have I ever shown such affection for a woman in the public eye? I suspect you will apologize to my fiancée before I make sure you never report a piece of news again."

Before the reporter could even say another word, we walked into the plaza, where the party had begun.

"Are you fine, Sam?" Weston asked me.

"I'm all right, though I'm still swirling from that unexpected moment out there," I said, smiling.

"Well, to be fair, you had it coming . . . But my apologies for taking full advantage of the situation."

"You're forgiven, Mr. President. Now, let's go mingle and enjoy this night celebrating you."

He kissed me on the cheek, and we walked off hand in hand.

The night went off without a hitch. Weston never left my side. I could tell his employees and colleagues were all shocked to see him in such a kind manner and letting his guard down a little. As the night wound down, he was in a hurry to sneak out, so I followed him out back into the limo.

"Take us home, Andre. Put the window up, and make your radio loud."

"Yes, sir!"

Weston grabbed my body and pulled me on top of him.

"What are you planning to do in this limo, President Lancaster?"

"Anything I want, my dear. I'm the president."

He unzipped my dress down the side, and my breasts were now exposed. He began to caress them, with nibbles and kisses on my lips and down to my chest. I let out soft moans, letting him know I wanted more.

"I want to taste every inch of you, Sam." He gently laid me down on the floor of the limo. Nibbling and sucking at my skin, he worked his way down to my navel. My fingers ran through his dark tresses,

187

slightly tugging at them. He let out a groan and then pressed his hand between my inner thighs. His finger found its way into my panties, and he ripped them off. Then he pulled the remainder of my dress off so I was lying bare under him. I reached up to unbutton his shirt and lifted it over his head, then I started for his belt, slightly grazing his aroused member while doing so.

"You make me want you right now," he whispered, and pulled his pants and briefs off in one motion. His hot bare skin to mine, a slight moan left my lips as I buried my face into the crook of his neck, kissing and sucking his skin so he knew the feeling of what he did to me every time. I gently ran my fingertips up and down the sides of his abdomen, making him shudder as he pulled me towards his mouth to kiss me deeply. He moved his hand down to my core and maneuvered his hand against my folds. I was pooling wet with desire.

He whispered, "I need to taste you. Let me taste you . . ." He made his way between my legs, and my breathing became staggered as I felt his breath on my sensitive skin. With a flick of his tongue, I moaned and arched my back, widening my legs to give him more room. He groaned in desire as he deepened his tongue inside me, swirling and flicking it around. My body felt on fire with tingles, ready to let the waves of pleasure wash over me. Weston must have sensed this and traveled back up right when I was about to have an orgasm. I brought my thighs together to compress the overwhelming, aching, tingling feeling while staring at him as my eyes filled with tears and desire.

"Not yet, my dear. Now that I've tasted you, I am ready to have you around me." Weston made his way back over me, separating my legs again. He placed his hardened member against my thigh, then distracted me by nibbling on my ear as he smoothly slid himself into me. My core clenched around his enlarged member as he began to thrust quickly. We were both sweating and moaning, completely forgetting we were inside a moving vehicle. It was almost as if the vibrations from the road made it more intense. My legs wrapped up around his waist, pulling him closer inside me. I couldn't get enough of him. He began to slow down, pulling himself completely out of me, then slowly guided it back in again, deeper this time as he thrusted slow and hard, rocking my core into a blissful orgasm.

"Oh, hell, Sam! That's right!" He released himself deep inside me, groaning and quivering over me and sending my body back through another orgasm.

Once we finally came out of our state of lust, we realized we were home. As we stepped out of the limo, he carried me into the house and drew a bath for me. During the bath, I was so relaxed that I found myself drifting off. He carried me out of the tub and put me to bed.

CHAPTER 37:
Texas Heat and Gatherings

*J*uly had ended, and we were less than three weeks away from the wedding. Mrs. Lancaster had me meeting with wedding dress designers for several weeks to find the perfect one, followed by many fittings. I decided I wanted Mia to enjoy this time with me as the maid of honor—and best friend—and not stress about creating the perfect dress. Mia designed and created the ladies' dresses and the groomsmen's vests. The dresses were all alike—strapless, short with a layered, ruffled skirt, and in the most beautiful blue-gray material I'd ever seen.

The August heat had approached and was hotter than the July Texas heat. Everyone was working overtime to keep the animals cool. The air even went out in the barn office, so Jackson had to fix it about a week ago, stating I was freezing up the air conditioner. Poor Nate, who had left and come back from England, looked like he could have passed out from heat exhaustion at any moment. Kiera bought him a neck fan that I never saw him without.

Being president hadn't been much of a change for Weston, stepping up from vice president. He'd been working like a madman trying to keep the wolves at bay. Luckily, most had backed off in the last few weeks. I started to turn a blind eye when it came to the news. Some stories seemed quite scandalous or unthinkable. Wes told me he'd be honest and tell me if I asked, but I just didn't care to know. The less I knew, the better. That's what I kept telling myself. Anyways. The whole town ignored it all because the Weston Lancaster they knew could never have been part of something so insane.

It had been weeks, and there had still been no news of Laura Belle and her sister's whereabouts. It made me uneasy not knowing what and where they were scheming. Men in black guarded the house, ranch, and office constantly. Andre was my faithful travel companion I couldn't seem to leave home without.

Mr. Lancaster had "retired," and my dad was feeling really good, so they made a few trips to Oklahoma and Kansas to check in on Riley and the ranches down there. After the wedding, they planned on taking the wives on a trip to Hawaii for two weeks, which would be well deserved for all of them. Most of our Wednesday family dinners consisted of Hawaii planning, wedding planning, and baby talk with Jackson and Lucey.

Speaking of Jackson and Lucey, they were settled into the new house. As a gift to them for the wedding and baby showers, Mama and I decorated the whole thing. All that was left for them to do was pick a theme for the nursery and decorate. Lucey was pushing five months and barely looked like she was carrying a basketball around. Pregnancy looked splendid on her, as she was always glowing and had hardly been sick. That made me hopeful that mine would be easy when the time came.

We were two weeks out from the wedding, and family was already starting to trickle in. Mama, Mrs. Lancaster, and Lucey's mom were trying to coordinate with family and friends for all the upcoming big happenings. Mama decided to bring our family and friends into town for the bridal shower, bachelorette and bachelor parties, and a baby shower for Jackson and Lucey. Mrs. Lancaster and her family and friends came the following weekend. Mama wanted to kick Nate out of the guesthouse. She rented out a few bed-and-breakfasts nearby and hired a few college guys we knew to drive everyone back and forth.

Friday night was the baby shower for Lucey and Jackson. Mama had gone all out in the backyard. It was decorated in all cowboy hats and ropes with lanterns swinging from them since we found out they were having a boy. I was glad Mama's hunch was right or we would've flipped from cowboy hats to princess tiaras. Tables were all decorated in a red and blue bandana pattern, topped with little glass boxes of flowers, and she had our favorite local BBQ catered. Everything matched to a T when Mama planned. Nothing went untouched. Even the cookies were Texas-shaped with cowboy hat–topped cupcakes. Between family and friends, about fifty people showed up. Lucey cried as she opened her gifts, and Jackson shook his head, wondering where they were going to put everything.

Seeing I was barely staying awake, Weston excused us and carried me into the house and up to my room. Even half asleep, I could hear laughing and all the oohs and woos from everyone.

***

The next morning, I walked out into the front yard, where Mama had a large, beautiful, white canopy tent in the middle of her garden, adorned by an elaborate flower entryway. It looked like a tea party for a queen. Tables were set up in fine white and rose gold overlay with decadent flower bouquets. Since the shower was early, we decided on a brunch menu of warm pastries, egg and bacon taquitos, and kolaches.

"Mama, you've outdone yourself again! I'm blown away. How did you find the time to host both showers and family this weekend?"

"Oh, sweetie, you're my only daughter. Why would I not make time for this extra special occasion?" She put her hands around my face. "My beautiful daughter is finally marrying the love of her life. We've all waited for this day to come. This is a time to celebrate so many things. Don't worry about your dear ol' mama. Just enjoy it, okay?"

I gave her a big hug. "Yes, Mama. I will, and thank you again."

She walked off, yelling at the guy who stepped on her rose bushes, and all I could do was laugh because he was in for it.

Weston soon found me. "Wow, your mom went all out. I can't imagine what the wedding will look like."

"Between our parents, it might be the wedding of the century—even though I told them not to go crazy."

The wedding shower flew by, but everyone had a great time telling embarrassing stories about Weston and me growing up. There was practically no food or mimosas left, which was a good sign. In lieu of presents, we asked for donations for our favorite rescue and conservation charities. The amount raised was over $5,000. Some of our older family friends still gave us gifts like new china, embroidered bath towels and robes, a blender, glass vases, and picture frames. Weston and I made the rounds, giving each person a hug. My great granny and aunties swooned over him like he was John Wayne. He obliged them, and secretly, I think he loved it. After everyone left, it was almost 1:00 pm and time for us to get ready to leave for our night out.

Since everyone went against my joint bachelor and bachelorette party idea, Wes and I would be going our separate ways for the next twenty-four hours. They all schemed to separate so we could have true bro and girl time.

We jumped in our designated vehicles and headed in separate directions once we hit the interstate. The girls were heading to South Padre and the boys to San Antonio.

CHAPTER 38:
An Old Flame

*I*n under three hours, we arrived at our beach resort. The game plan was to party all night and then chill at the beach the next day before heading home. I was allowed to text Wes on the way down, but my phone had been confiscated for the evening. Andre, along with a few of the men in black, were not keen on that idea, so I was ordered to wear a pair of earrings that had a tracker. I told them they were lucky the earrings went with my outfit. The girls thought it was absurd for me to have to wear a tracking device.

After all of us finished getting ready in our swanky club attire, we headed out to dinner at the Sea Ranch Bar. We were a sight to see, everyone in a black dress or romper, and me with my low-cut white romper. Not one to usually care for attention, there was no hiding in the crowd.

Once guests in the restaurant figured out it was a bachelorette party, drinks and shots began flowing at our table. A few upscale people noticed who I was, asked to take pictures while congratulating me and speaking highly of Lans Enterprises. I, of course, smiled and was cordial to all, but I was thankful to get out of there and move on with our night.

The next stop was Tequila Sunset Bar, which always had an awesome DJ on Saturday night. Half of my group was single, so they pleaded with me to ditch the men in black.

"Y'all, I will try, but there are no promises." I walked over to Andre. "Hey, you are frightening off the guys for my single friends? Can you please make yourself more hidden in the corners and not like you're actually with us? I'm already wearing a tracker."

He phoned Carl, who was with Weston. "Miss is asking if we would back away from the group. We're apparently scaring the locals away from the singles. Yes, she's standing right in front of me, glaring . . . Okay. Ten-four." Andre hung up ordered his men over intercoms to blend in and hide themselves better but still keep an eye on me.

"Thank you, Andre. We appreciate it." I strutted back to the group.

Mia and I stayed back at the bar while the rest went to the dance floor. We took Jell-O shots and caught up on Dylan and her fashion boutique.

"I'm so happy for you, Mia! It seems like everything is progressing with your business, and fingers crossed you're the next in line to tie the knot." We both squealed and took another shot.

"Sam, this is our year to conquer it all. We always planned it this way. I'm just glad you finally came home because a lot of things would be completely different right now. Do you think if you hadn't come home, Weston would've gone to find you again? I totally think he would, but I'm not sure how much time it would add to the timeline."

"Eventually, I think. I definitely think our paths would've crossed, sooner than later. I'm not sure if it would have the same impact as love at first sight again and fast-tracking to this point, but I like to believe we are meant to be together in some lifetime."

"You both totally are meant to be, now, and every lifetime before and after this one." Picking up another shot, Mia shouted, "Cheers to Sam and Weston!"

The whole bar repeated her cheer and drank. I tried to hide behind my drink umbrella.

A guy from behind me said, "Samantha? Samantha Dupont?"

Mia and I turned around.

Holy shit.

"Noah!" I shouted. "Oh, my gosh. What are you doing Stateside, let alone in Texas?"

"Samantha, I can't believe it's actually you." He hugged me. "I'm here for a surfing convention before heading over to California and then Maui. What are you doing this way? Last you told me, you were in Montana."

"Yeah, a lot has happened, Noah. I'm actually down here for my bachelorette party. I'm getting married in a couple of weeks."

Noah gawked at me. "No shit? Well, congrats to you, Samantha."

I felt a tapping on my shoulder, and I turned to see not just Mia, but all the girls staring at us.

I laughed. "Noah, you remember Mia, right?"

He came in for a hug with her. "Yes, I totally do. How's it going, Mia?"

"Going good, Noah." She looked sideways at me.

I introduced him to the rest of the girls with me, pointing out the taken versus the single ones.

"Well, hell . . . My sponsors are here. Let me buy a few rounds of drinks."

"Oh, you do not have to do that," I said.

"Please, Sam, it's the least I can do. I wouldn't be where I am today if it wasn't for you pushing me. You also might be the first girl who truly broke my heart."

"Aw, Noah, thank you. The girls will go crazy for some drinks. And I'm truly sorry if I broke your heart. No ill feelings between us, I hope."

"Of course not. I'm truly happy for you." He shouted, "Now, who wants some drinks?"

After several rounds, everyone was feeling pretty buzzed, dancing and having a blast. I headed off the dance floor and sat back down at the bar to rest. Noah joined and ordered another round. We began catching up on his family, events back in Australia, and I learned that he still donated his time to the wildlife conservation out there. Mia, Dawn, and Jenny were checking up on us every so often. I laughed as I looked out on the dance floor because all the "in-relationship" ladies had formed a circle around each other, while my single friends had men surrounding them.

We started talking about my life back in Texas and the ranch. I let him know that anytime he was free, he could come by to check it out. My family would be happy to host him.

After another round came out, I realized I wasn't feeling great. As soon as I stood up, I looked at Noah, who quickly became a blur, and then everything went black.

CHAPTER 39:

Track (Her)

Mia went to check on Sam, but she was no longer where she'd left her.

"Excuse me, bartender," Mia said. "Have you seen my friend who was sitting here with the tall blond Australian?"

"Yes, she actually passed out, and he carried her out of here—I'm guessing to get away from the crowd and for some fresh air."

"Shit!" She ran over to Jenny and Dawn. "Hey, we have a problem. Sam went missing with Noah. The bartender says she passed out and he carried her outside. We need to go look for her."

The girls looked frantic.

Jenny said, "We have to keep this on the down low so Andre and the men don't find out."

They walked around the outside of the bar and down by the water. After several loops around, they realized she was nowhere around.

Mia sighed. "I'll go tell Andre. She does have a tracker on, so hopefully she's nearby and he can help us find her. I really don't think Noah would do anything, but I just don't like not knowing where she is."

Mia searched the crowd until she found Andre and waved him over.

"Yes, Miss Mia?"

"Andre, do you know where Sam is?"

"Why are you asking me? She was sitting at the bar five minutes ago when I made my rounds."

Mia explained what the bartender said and that they'd searched everywhere.

Reeling all the men in, Andrea asked if anyone had seen her leave. One saw her go into the bathroom but never saw her come out. Andre went to inspect the restroom and found a window opened that a person could have easily climbed out of. He pulled out a device from his pocket. It showed her moving slowly at first, but all of a sudden, she moved quickly. Andre realized she must've been in a car, but at least she was still on the island. He called Carl.

Everyone saw Andre hold his phone away from his ear as Carl yelled, "Sir has been drinking heavily with the guys and having a great time, and now you have to call me with this? Damn it, Andre! Let me discuss this with Sir. Be on standby!"

Within two minutes, Mia's phone rang, and she put it on speaker. "Dylan!" she cried.

"Mia, are you okay? What's going on? Weston is losing his damn mind. He just had Carl order a private jet to fly down there. We should be there in about forty-five minutes or so, and we're boarding now."

"Wow! He must have something on standby. Things don't move that quickly, but I guess he is the president *and* a billionaire. I just know I'm scared right now not knowing where my best friend is, if she's all right, and what Weston is going to do to all of us if we can't find her."

"Just breathe, Mia. We'll find her. I love you, and I'll see you soon. Just stay where you are."

"I love you, Dylan. Be safe."

Mia saw that Andre must've been on the phone with Carl, getting the next orders while looking at the tracker. She saw that the tracker had finally stopped moving. He deployed his team to the area where the tracker icon stopped to set up a parameter. They were not to do anything but keep watch, check in, and await orders.

~✧~

Weston's POV

My head had been spinning since I received the news that Sam was missing. My Sam, gone? It would be my last breath before anything happened to her. As the guys and I boarded the plane to head to the island, I received a text message from an unknown number.

> NOT SURE YOU WILL MAKE IT TIME. I PLAN TO RUIN HER SO NO ONE WANTS HER EVER AGAIN . . . INCLUDING YOU. ENJOY THE LIVE VIDEO FOOTAGE.

Then a link popped up. My jaw clenched, and I turned ashen as I opened the link. My Sam was handcuffed to a bed with her head hanging down. She looked to be unconscious.

"Carl, track this damn number and live feed, now!" I yelled while punching the seat in front of me. "Shit! Someone's been watching all of us this entire time." I slammed my phone down, and the whole plane went quiet. I could sense all eyes on me, so I picked up my phone and played the live feed to the TV.

Everyone watched in horror. None of us knew what was to come.

CHAPTER 40:
Awaken

I woke up to a stabbing pain in my arm. My head was killing me, and as my eyes fluttered open, and with slightly blurred vision, I saw someone in front of me, holding my arm.

"Ouch!" I yelped.

I closed my eyes for a second and reopened them with clearer vision. Startled, I said, "What the hell are you doing to me?" I started kicking and screaming, only to realize my other hand and feet were tied up. I was unable to escape. I stared at the masked stranger. "Who the hell are you, and where am I?"

"Oh, Samantha, do you really want to know?" she stated.

That was one voice that I couldn't forget. "Why are you doing this to me, Laura Belle?"

She took off her mask. "You catch on quicker than I thought. Or maybe not if you are asking me why."

My body began to tingle. "What did you do to me?"

"Oh, this is going to be more fun than I could've imagined. Let's just say you were given a high dose of a powerful mixture of drugs. Don't worry, it won't kill you." She smirked. "But you might want to kill yourself before the night is over."

"You can't do this! He would be with you if he wanted to be with you. Why are you torturing me?... My body is on fire!"

"Why you? Poor you! You should have just stayed gone, sweet Samantha. Another few months away, I would've had him locked down for good. All mine!"

My whole body was having an uncontrollable sensual sensation, tingling through my core and making me lightheaded.

"Well, I think it's time to start the show, don't you?"

"What does that mean?" I asked faintly, trying to control all urges.

"Guards, come in," she stated over the intercom.

As they came in, they surrounded me. "Now, Samantha, we're going to play a little game of cat and mouse. As I walk out of here, the guards will untie you so you can roam freely in the room. But then we're going to let someone else in here who has had just as many drugs as you and is having the same type of 'feelings.' Good luck!" She walked out laughing.

I tried to fight off the guards. "What do you mean, the same feelings? Who's coming in here? I want answers!" I screamed frantically as they held me down and released my ropes.

One lit some incense off to the side, and another pointed a gun at me. They all walked out, and I was left curled up in a ball crying, praying Weston would come save me. That *somebody* would come save me soon.

Another heat wave rushed over me, and I felt like I was on fire, so I ripped my romper off. Thankfully, I had a bandeau top and underwear on underneath it. It still didn't conceal much, but I also knew I wasn't in my right mind and needed to overcome these urges and hot flashes

All of a sudden, the door opened, and the guards tossed someone on the ground, then slammed the door shut. I slowly walked over and tapped the guy with my foot. Still no movement. I bent down a little to roll him over.

"Noah!" I started tapping the side of his face, and he finally groaned and opened his eyes.

"Sam . . . Oh, shit. I'm so sorry. Are you okay?"

"No, I'm not, but what do you have to be sorry for?"

Looking down at the floor and away, Noah mumbled, "I gave you those drinks and dragged you out of there."

Stunned and still itching my skin that seemed to be getting worse by the minute, I slapped Noah across the face. "You did what? How could you?"

"I am being blackmailed by some stupid shit I did in Germany during the off-season that could ruin my surf career. The woman said she didn't want to kill you, nor would she physically harm you, but that she just wanted to teach you a small lesson. I was an idiot, Sam. If I'd known her grand scheme . . . I just figured you'd be fine. I am so sorry. Shit! Sam, I need you to stay on the other side of the room . . . now!"

I slowly started backing up to the other side, wafted by the strong incense that made me want to lose my mind. I tried to blow it out, but it only got stronger. I started wondering if it was also coming through the vents.

"Sam, try to breathe as little as possible. The incense is said to be an aphrodisiac. It looks to have a strong effect on you, along with the drugs she put in your body. Just stay as calm as you can."

"What did she give me, Noah? What's her plan? Please tell me!"

"She wants to ruin you by catching you having sex with someone other than Weston—to catch you cheating, so everyone will then see you as the woman who is a spoiled narcissistic slut that not even a billionaire like Weston can please. Those were her words, not mine."

"This is unimaginable. How can she make that happen?" I felt my own core yearning, and I squeezed my legs together and sat in the corner on the floor.

"Looks like you already know how, Sam. It reaches its peak at about thirty minutes, with no tapering off for a while on its own unless you fulfill your body's needs. My symptoms are just beginning." He took off his shirt and shorts, standing only in his briefs.

I'd been with this body before and knew what it could do. Though it held no comparison to Weston, my body wanted to betray me as I steered my mind elsewhere while looking at the floor. Trying not to claw my skin off, I started to bite my own hand to relieve some of the pressure. Several times after doing so, I began to taste the sweet iron bitterness of my own blood.

"Fuck!" I yelled. Maybe moving around would help, so I started pacing back and forth. Noah was now rolling on the ground, groaning and trying to suppress his own urges as they heated up. I silently prayed that someone would find me soon.

~✧~

Weston's POV

Back on the jet, the whole flight was silent, gawking as we watched the scene unfold. Carl had asked me several times if I wanted to take it off the big screen, but with my jaw clenched, I just shook my head no.

The flight finally landed, and Andre met me and Carl as we got off the plane.

Before he could even speak, I plummeted my fist into Andre's jaw, about knocking him over. "Don't think I won't kill you once this is all over with!"

"Uh, yes, sir!" He tried to regain his composure. "Here are the coordinates of the Miss's current location. As you wished, we've been watching the live feed to ensure nothing worsens so we can intervene, if necessary. No one has come in or out of the building, but we do now know it's completely surrounded by guards. Backup is another fifteen minutes out from the location, and we're five minutes away. How would you like to proceed, Sir?"

I looked down at my phone to the live feed. It had been about ten minutes since I checked, and I could already tell things were getting tense in the room. Sam had reached her peak, and it looked like Noah had, too. He was inching towards Sam, and she was trying to talk him back. The screen cracked in my hand from squeezing it so tightly.

I demanded, "We need to make a move, now, with or without backup."

Carl stepped in." Sir, we're outnumbered right now. If we try, you won't even make it to her. We just need to keep a close eye on what's going on with her, as well as over there." He pointed in the direction of the building. "I think we're going to be very last minute with this, and we have to make it count."

A text appeared on my phone.

> ARE YOU ENJOYING THIS YET? HER EX-BOYFRIEND IS ABOUT TO HAVE HIS WAY WITH HER, AND THERE IS NOT A DAMN THING YOU CAN DO!

I texted back.

> WHAT DO YOU WANT, LAURA BELLE? LET HER GO! TORTURE ME INSTEAD!

She texted.

> OH, BABY, IF ONLY YOU WERE ENOUGH NOW. SORRY, BUT YOU ARE TOO LATE!

One of Weston's men came running up. "Sir, we found the power source to the building. If we can have our men lined up to go, we can turn the power off at the right time to throw them off."

All the men circled up, even the bachelor party who was sacrificing themselves for the cause spent the next several minutes working out their strategy of attack. I still stared at my phone, feeling that every second that passed meant Sam would be more unsafe.

CHAPTER 41:

Ruined

"**N**oah, stay back. I'm warning you. Please control your urges, and don't come any closer."

"I'm trying to, Sam, but it hurts so badly, and my body is on fire. I need you to make me better, and I can make you better. You are so tempting in front of me. How could I not want you right now?"

"It's just the drugs, Noah. Please!"

"Just let me hold you, Sam. I won't do anything but hold you."

"I seriously doubt that. I know damn well what will happen if our bodies touch right now" Trying to calm my own urges, sweating and extremely dizzy, I fell off the bed trying to jump away from Noah. I could feel a sting in my ankle, and I wasn't sure I could put weight on it. Before I could roll away, Noah jumped on the bed and pulled me up on it. As hard as I tried, I was no match for his strength—drugged or not—so I just started crying as he crawled on top of me.

"I'm sorry, Sam. My conscience is telling me not to, but my body is urging me to do so. It's too painful not to relieve myself. Just let me relish in you again." He pressed his member to my inner thigh.

I screamed, "Noah, stop it!"

He ripped my bandeau top off and moved his hands around my breasts and stomach, then worked his way to my panties. "I want you so bad, and I can tell you want me, as well."

Suddenly, it went dark in the room. I sensed that Noah had sat up, so using all my might, I kicked him off the bed, swung myself off, then rolled under the bed to hide.

"Fuck, Samantha! Why did you have to go and do that?"

I could feel his body weight back on the bed, and he realized I was no longer there. He got off and shuffled around the room, trying to figure out where I was. I held my breath, not moving my body that was wet and in need of intense pleasure. The feeling of my body being on fire in a blanket of snow began to uncontrollably twitch the more I tried to suppress it. My foot knocked against the bedpost.

"Sam, are you hiding from me under the bed?"

Unable to sense what direction he was coming from, I realized how dizzy I'd become. Suddenly, he pulled me out from under the bed by my foot. The floor scratched my bare stomach and chest raw as he pulled me across it. I dug my nails into the floor, to no avail, and screamed at the top of my lungs.

Noah quickly flipped me over on my back and ripped my panties off. All I could do was close my eyes, awaiting the worst as he hovered over me with his hard erection at the entrance to my core. Unable to hold on anymore, I blacked out.

I woke up to dim lighting and tried to figure out my surroundings. It was a hospital room. The door opened, and I saw Weston and my parents walk in. Seeing that I was awake, Weston walked back out to grab the attending physician. Mama gave me a hug, and I could tell she and Daddy had both been crying.

Confused, I asked, "Mama, why is Weston here?"

"Oh, honey, why would he *not* be here? He rescued you from the incident yesterday. He's been so worried about you, he barely left your side."

"What incident, and where am I? Also, when did he start worrying so much about me? He's the one who left! Please send him away!"

"Samantha, are you confused? Weston is your fiancé. Sweetie, you two are getting married in less than two weeks."

I gawked at her when Weston and the physician came in.

Weston took my hand in his as I struggled against him.

"Sam, you're safe. I'm here and never leaving your side again until I die." As he bent down to kiss me on the forehead, I stared at my parents to help me.

Mama looked worried and turned to the physician. "Um, Dr. Adelle . . . It seems Samantha doesn't remember what happened to her. She also doesn't remember that she's engaged to Weston."

I could feel his eyes glaring at me as if I'd just broken his heart into a million little pieces.

"Sam, are you joking right now? Because this is not the time to prank me."

"Weston, I'm not being funny. The last I recall is never hearing from you again, graduating, and getting ready to head abroad."

Everyone gasped and stared at Dr. Adelle.

He ran through tests with me and asked me a series of questions. Judging by the faces of others in the room, I guess I got most of them wrong.

"We did discuss slight amnesia when discussing her case because her body was in such shock from being under a heavy influence of drugs. Though we're still figuring out everything that was in her system, she was also unconscious by her own means because her mind and body were under such stress. I was hoping it wouldn't be a symptom for her since she's healthy, but we did warn you it could happen. The good news is, her amnesia won't last. The bad news is, we don't know for how long it will last. This will be up to Samantha and her brain. What you all can do to support her is keep her in familiar settings and talk about recent things to help trigger her mind. But don't overwhelm her. As she begins to regain memories, she could have severe attacking migraines. This is not only frustrating for you, but for her as well. Now that she's awake and alert, I'd like to keep her for one more night for observation, but if all goes well, she can go home in the morning and just follow up with her primary care in a few days."

"Thank you, doctor," my parents said, then followed him out.

Confused and speechless, I turned to face Weston. "Weston, I don't understand what happened to me. How could I have forgotten the last several years of my life?" I cried. "All I know is my heart is breaking being this close to you, and I'm aware of all the sadness and anger I apparently had years ago."

He wiped my tears away and sat next to me on the hospital bed.

"Sam, you'll remember everything, including our life together. I understand you're hurting right now, but you can't push me away. Not after everything. We're a piece of each other, and I know your heart knows it. If I must win you back all over again, I will." He kissed the top of my head. "As far as what happened to you, the doctor said it would be best for you to remember on your own. But please remember this . . ." He held my hands, gazing at me with those crystal blue eyes. "I will never forgive myself for what happened to you, but I hope one day you'll forgive me and not try to leave me. Because you can never leave me Sam . . . never!"

Where did this possessiveness come from? Is the more recent Sam aware of this?

"Um, Weston, can you loosen your grip on my hands?"

"Oh, sorry," he said as he released them. "I'm going to grab you some dinner. I'll be back shortly."

"Okay, thank you."

Looking down at my arms and legs, I saw bruises and scrapes all over. What the hell happened to me?

Weston's POV

I couldn't shake what I saw that night. Every night I woke up in a sweat, feeling like I couldn't breathe. The whole scene replayed in my head.

Once the team disabled the power to the building and backup had arrived, we all rushed in. Mission one was to rescue Sam. Mission two was to find Laura Belle. We had our teams split up once we entered the building. Hitting each floor and busting every door open, by the time we got to the fifth floor, the team was becoming ragged, but we kept pushing through. Finally, on the tenth floor, we heard screaming. Breaking down every door, we finally found her halfway down the hall, with him hovering over her on the bed. The guy saw us, jumped up quickly, and cowered in the corner.

Running to the bed while my men pointed their guns at him, I froze. Her naked body was covered in blood and abrasions. Finally shaking myself out of shock, I yelled, "It's Sam! It's her! Call an ambulance!"

Dropping down quickly, I took her pulse. "Oh, thank God, she has a heartbeat."

Pulling a blanket out of my backpack, I quickly but carefully wrapped her up and carried her down the stairs and out of the building, crying and praying that she would wake up. But she didn't wake up until three days later.

Without sleep or a shower, I refused to leave her side. Family and friends had come and gone, offering to look after her so I could take care of myself. But no one seemed to understand that there was no me without her. On the fourth day, she finally woke up but couldn't remember we were back together, about to marry, and what she'd been doing in Texas all this time.

When we'd left the hospital and were back at our house, I'd offered to sleep in the guest room. My heart and body ached having to leave her in our master alone, especially when I heard her screaming from nightmares. Some were about me, but I had a sense she was starting to remember things and just couldn't decipher between reality and illusion.

On the fourth day after leaving the hospital, I could tell she was starting to feel more comfortable around me. It helped that when she was decorating the house, she put pictures of us, family, and friends everywhere. Her mom brought over her traveling scrapbook, so she had started to look through that. Maddox hadn't left her side since she came home, and she found comfort with him. I just wished it was me she was finding comfort with instead of the distant stares I'd catch her in occasionally.

She came downstairs while I was cooking breakfast.

"Oh, when did you start cooking?" she asked shyly.

"When you requested that on Sunday mornings we eat breakfast in bed. So, we switch off every Sunday Cooking and have "us" time–but you always find a way to coax me into cooking every Sunday." I walked over to her and kissed her on the cheek while bringing her coffee. Realizing what I just did, I apologized. She faced me. We were so close I could smell her sweet honeysuckle scent. Her deep hazel eyes gazed into mine like she wanted me—like she needed me. Trying to restrain myself those last few days from touching her had been nearly impossible, and now that I was tempted, I was unsure if I could turn back.

I slowly lifted my hand to her face, and she actually leaned into it. My body began to shake with excitement and fear. "Sam, may I kiss you?"

She nodded, so I leaned in and gently pressed my lips against hers. It was like a shock of electricity just went through me. She was pressing back, and her hand slipped behind my neck, almost pulling me towards her more. Using my tongue to lick her lips, I asked her to open her mouth a little, and I finally felt our tongues entwine. I picked her up off the kitchen stool, wrapped her legs around me, and carried her to the sofa. Both of us barely found a second to breathe as we were deep in the moment together.

The phone started ringing, and I begged it to stop so our moment wasn't ruined.

"Hey, you might want to answer that, Weston."

"No, it can wait. I have the most important person in front of me right now." I smiled and leaned back in to kiss her.

Her hands quickly went up to my chest, stopping me. "I'm so sorry. I don't know what just came over me, but I can't do this right now." She pushed past me and ran upstairs.

Before I could even call out to her, my cell rang again.

"Dammit!" I yelled, and kicked the sofa. "Hello! This better be important!"

"Yes, sir, it is. Laura Belle has come forward after we dealt with her parents and siblings. She's requesting a meeting with you to negotiate."

"To negotiate? What, with her life? Because I'm going to strangle her with my bare hands if I see her in person. Carl, you tell her to either turn herself in or jump off a bridge."

CHAPTER 42:

Kissing You
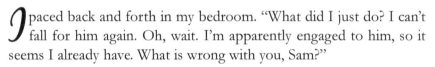

I paced back and forth in my bedroom. "What did I just do? I can't fall for him again. Oh, wait. I'm apparently engaged to him, so it seems I already have. What is wrong with you, Sam?"

My head was spinning, but my heart was yearning, and it seemed my body was, as well. This was such a complete mess, and I wished I could remember everything.

Knock, knock.

"Sam, can we talk?"

Why is his voice so sexy?

Slowly making my way to the door, I tried to get myself together. I placed my hand on the doorknob and realized I was shaking as I turned it. "Hey," I managed to squeak out.

"Hey, I wanted to come check on you and talk. Have a moment?"

"Uh, yeah, sure. Come in."

We took a seat on the chaise near the large back window I'd apparently bought and put there, which made perfect sense to me because I loved it in that spot of the room.

About to speak over each other, I let him go first.

"Sam, I hope you're not scared away from me after what just happened. To you, it must've seemed we were moving fast, but that's a typical moment for us. Sometimes, numerous times a day. I must've become lost in the moment because I've been missing you so much these last several days. I'm so thankful you're here, but it's like watching you through a lens. My Sam isn't here right now. I'm trying to be patient and give you space, but I also think it would be great for you to spend more time with me. Your heart is broken from the past, but now, it's mended. So, I'd really like to take you out on a date today and relive some experiences we recently shared. What do you say?"

"Well, I think that would be great, actually. I really would love to gain my memory back and recover what this is between us. Yes, my heart is broken, but to be honest, that moment we just had felt right. My heart aches for you, Wes. I don't think it ever stopped after all these years. My mind has put a wall up, and they're both battling it out when it comes to you." I looked down at my hands in my lap.

He reached out and softly touched my cheek. "Oh, Sam. I love you so much, and it's breaking me that you're reliving all the heartache I caused you. Just know you're mine and I am yours for the rest of our lives . . . and after."

Nodding, I allowed him to pull me into his chest. Surrounded by his incredible spice and luring aroma, I took a deep inhale and relaxed in his arms, closing my eyes. While he ran his fingers through my hair, flashes surged through my mind, but they were too quick to recall.

I snapped my head back and held my head.

"Sam, what's wrong? What happened?"

"Just give me a minute . . ." I bent down, holding my head tightly in pain. Taking deep breaths, it seemed to ease after a bit, and I could lift my head back up.

Fear was written all over this man's face, and it even frightened me.

"I'm good. I'm not sure what really happened. My eyes were closed, but all of a sudden, pictures, like moments, quickly flashed through. It doesn't seem I can recall any of them, though."

Weston took a sigh of relief and wrapped his arms around me. "Well, that's good, right? Maybe your memory is starting to come back. Do you want me to call the doctor for a follow-up?"

"No, I'm fine now. Let's just continue on with our plans for the day."

"Only if you're sure," he said, looking into my eyes and once over my body.

"I'm fine, Weston. I promise."

"Okay, then. Finish getting ready, and I'll meet you and Maddox downstairs. Dress to stay cool. It's hot today."

One last kiss on the forehead, then he strolled out, leaving me to get ready.

I was quickly interrupted by my phone ringing. Nate's name was on the screen, so I hesitantly answered. I met him at my parents' house a couple of days before. Though I knew I should've known him, I had no recollection of him. Luckily, my parents and Weston filled me in, so I was informed he was my boss at the company we run together. Also, luckily, as it must come naturally to me, I could still do my jobs at the company and ranch, but it seemed everyone had been covering for me since I came back.

"Hi, Nate. How can I help you?"

"Hey, Sam. How are you feeling? Any changes?"

"I'm good. Still no memory gain yet, but I keep hoping it'll happen soon."

"Well, I'm sure glad to hear you're doing well. I hated to call and check in like this, but I'm about to fly back to England for a business meeting, but then I'll be flying back next Thursday with my uncle and family for the wedding and festivities. Also, I want to let you know that Kiera is coming with me to England."

I remembered Kiera was my assistant. "Oh, that sounds like a good time. Nate, you said you were coming here for a wedding?"

"Um . . . yes, Samantha." There was a long pause on the line. "Well, thank you for accepting Kiera coming with me. I have to go now. We'll talk later. Goodbye."

I stared at the phone in confusion. Who's wedding, and why was he so short with me? Letting it go, I headed downstairs with Maddox to meet up with Weston.

We loaded up and headed out. I was excited for the day.

Weston planned the perfect day. We first stopped by Nik's Pizzeria for my favorite pizza, then we headed to the ranch. We tacked up Admiral and another one of our horses, Cisco, to then head down the trails by the river. He even brought a blanket with wine and fruit to snack on. Weston let me ask a million questions about everything, hoping answers would trigger my memory. It felt like I was getting to know him all over again, though I could tell there was something dark and distant about him. I noticed how composed he was now, along with being very articulate when he spoke to others. With me, he definitely seemed more relaxed and not so on-guard, which was more like the Weston I used to know. I had taken in the sight of his muscles that had grown and were defined. And his dark features and chiseled jawline had some serious roughness to it. He still looked hot as hell—the perfection of a cowboy angel.

We sat out there for hours until the sun began to sink behind the rolling pastures and my favorite hill covered in bluebonnets. The sky turned into an artistic painting of pinks and oranges that gently brushed across the sky as the sun burned a burnt orange, almost red. We knew then it was time to head back to the house before it grew darker.

We were back at my parents' house for dinner. We had been there every night for dinner since I was released from the hospital. It was nice being surrounded by my family and having some normalcy as my body fixed itself. Mama told me that Nate left earlier that evening with Kiera.

"Speaking of Nate," I said, "he mentioned he would be back for a wedding next weekend but didn't tell me who. Is it someone we know?"

Everyone looked at each in confusion, then back at me.

Mama was the first one to speak up. "Well, sweetie, we mentioned this to you in the hospital right when you woke up and were upset with Weston being there. But do you remember how we told you that you are engaged to Weston?"

I nodded my head and then took a quick glance at Weston, who then took my hand.

"The wedding next weekend is yours, sweetie." She paused, giving me time to absorb what she'd just said.

Weston wrapped his arm around my waist and clenched tighter, as if I might run away. It seemed everyone at the table was holding their breath. I was thinking I needed to handle this delicately, but I was also not feeling very rational at the moment.

"Is this wedding still supposed to be happening with everything going on?" I asked.

Dad chimed in. "Darlin', we're all convinced you'll be fine before your big day, so we haven't begun canceling or rescheduling anything. Everyone has been prayin' for you to get better and regain your memory, so there's no reason we should lose hope and change our plans."

"Yes, Daddy, but what if? What if I don't get better before Saturday? At what point is the plug pulled on all of this? Or am I going to be forced to marry him anyway?" I cried out, using all my strength to escape his arms.

Rushing out of the house, I didn't look back. I headed to the large pond and found myself sitting on the tree swing, catching my breath. Could I really just marry this man after everything? I get that I was "supposed" to be in love with him and that we'd begun building our lives together, but that was all with the part of the Samantha that is missing. Not the one sitting there, confused.

Someone stepped on a stick, giving themselves away that they were nearby.

"Please, just go away," I pleaded.

"It's just me. I come in peace."

"Hey, Jackson. I guess you're fine to stay," I said, trying to smile.

"Thanks, sis. Just wanted to come check on you. Everyone is pretty shook up back there, and it took everything to hold Wes back from running after you. I figured you could use some space."

"Much appreciated. How is he? It must've sounded awful coming out the way it did, but I don't know how I'm supposed to marry him when I'm not the Sam he fell in love with and loves. My mind keeps throwing red alerts every time he's around."

"Sam, you've always been the same Sam to him. Whether it was twenty years ago, the five years ago you left, or when you came back. His heart beats only for you, and right now, I can tell you he's not doing so well. I'm honestly not trying to guilt you into marrying the guy, but just know his love and feelings for you have never wavered. If anything, he's fallen more in love with you since your return home this summer."

"Really? I just wish my memory would hurry up and come back to me. The funny thing is, my heart wants him near. It seems right to be with him when he's around. But I feel like I'm stuck five years ago, ending my senior year brokenhearted and ready to escape."

"No, I totally get that, Sam. Maybe right now you need to let your guard down and see how things progress."

"Maybe you're right. I'll try."

"Good. Now that that's settled, let's head back. Lucey was already falling asleep when I headed out here, so I need to take her home and to bed."

"Okay, let's go then. And as always, thank you for being such a great brother."

After we headed home, I apologized to Mama and Daddy. Of course, they told me it was all good and that we would all rally through this together. Speaking of together, where was Weston? I hadn't seen him since we'd come back. Mama must have noticed me scanning the room for him, and she told me he was up in my room with Maddox. I took a deep breath and headed up.

Opening the door, I saw the two of them on my bed, cuddled up and flipping through the TV channels. As soon as he heard the door creak, they both jumped up.

Weston jumped off the bed and rushed over to me to pull me in his arms. "Are you okay?"

I pulled back a little bit so I could look up at him. "Yes, I'm fine. I actually came up here to check on you, but here you are, worried about me." I put my head down.

He then grabbed my chin to tilt my head up and planted a sweet, soft kiss on my lips. "You always come first to me, so, naturally, I would feel worry for you over my own self."

"Wes, I'm sorry about my outburst earlier. I didn't mean to say 'forced.' My mind is swirling right now, and—"

He stopped me with another kiss. This one was more passionate than the last—more pressure from his lips against mine. I thought about what Jackson said about letting my guard down, so I decided to do just that. My hands quickly found his head so my fingers could rummage through his dark hair. He began pulling away, so I let my hands glide down to his neck.

He stared at me. "Samantha Jane, you never have to apologize to me for anything. You can never do wrong in my eyes. If you're upset with me, there must be a reason. If you have an outburst over a situation, I know there's a reason. I will always be by your side. Do you understand?"

Speechless, I could only nod my head in understanding. Then he led me back to my bed.

"Would you like to stay here tonight?" he asked.

"That would actually be really nice. I can tell a headache is coming on, and it's pretty late."

"Okay. I'll be downstairs on the couch if you need me."

As he was about to walk away, I grabbed his hand. "Actually, would you mind staying with me tonight? I've been having nightmares lately, and it would be nice not to wake up alone again."

With a shocked look on his face, he agreed.

CHAPTE 43:
Felt Too Real

Punching and screaming at the top of my lungs for help, I found myself in a small room with wooden walls and a bed in the middle. A man was chasing me in the room, and I couldn't seem to escape him. My clothes seemed to have been ripped off, and what was that smell? It was familiar. Hiding under the bed, I was trembling and holding my breath. The man pulled me out from under the bed, and I started to scream again, trying to fight this giant guy hovering over me.

"Sam! Sam! Wake up! I need you to wake up!"

I could feel weight on top of me, and my arms were pinned down next to me.

"Sam!"

Where was this voice coming from? It sounded like Weston. I started yelling out for him, but I just kept hearing him from afar, as if he couldn't find me.

A sharp pain in my side made my eyes open in an instant. My eyes grew wider as I glared at Weston sitting on top of me, holding my arms down. I started to panic more.

"Samantha, calm down. I had to hold you down because you were stuck in your nightmare and throwing punches."

Breathing heavily, I saw red marks on his chest, where it looked as if someone had hit him. He crawled off me and loosened his grip on my arms so I could sit up. Sitting next to me, he put his hand on my back and rubbed it gently to help me calm down.

"What happened?" I asked.

"You were having a nightmare, and I had to pinch you hard to wake you up. Do you remember anything from it?"

I proceeded to tell him what I remembered, and the whole time his jaw flinched as I saw his hands were now balled into fists.

"It felt so real, smelled so real, and the guy looked so familiar." I trembled, and he pulled me into his arms and held me close, rocking me back and forth.

"I'm so sorry. I will never forgive myself for any of this."

"What does this have to do with you?" I said, still snuggled into his chest.

He pushed me away from him slightly so he could stare at me.

"Sam, that wasn't a nightmare. You're replaying the events of that night."

I could only blink at him, as I was taken back.

"Here, let me see your phone."

Handing it over, I was more puzzled as he searched through my pictures. He finally stopped and showed me a picture of me and some guy together.

"Do you recognize him?"

Taking the phone from his hand, I stared at the picture, then began scrolling to look at surrounding photos. I quickly realized they were taken in Australia, and my mind started racing and flashing with moments of conversation. I whispered his name, "Noah."

Our whole time together came flooding back to me, with a snapshot back to that night with him on top of me. My head began to throb painfully, so I did what I did earlier to help ease the pain. After several minutes, I came to, and Weston was holding me in his arms, so I looked back up to him.

"Weston, I remember the guy, Noah. I remember everything about him, even when we were in Australia. But I can't remember after he was hovering over me in the room."

Weston's skin had turned cold, and he shuddered as he looked back at me. "It's because you blacked out, Sam. By the time I got there to rescue you, you had already blacked out."

A loud gasp left my lips. The first thing I could think of was Weston walking into the room and another man being intimate with my naked body. Crying, I said, "I'm so sorry, Weston. How could I let this happen? I've betrayed your trust."

Then it all hit me at once. Laura Belle flashed into my mind.

"Wait, it was her. Where's Laura Belle? Her men? Where's Noah? We were both drugged, and neither of us was in our right minds, Weston. Oh, my gosh. Was the video released? Did I shame your whole family and life? Did I—"

"Slow down there, and breathe, babe. Noah was taken care of and shipped back to Australia. He is alive, though he looked pretty rough. My men didn't hold back on him. LB has been captured, and we're dealing with her right now. Most of her men didn't survive that night. If they did, they were taken to prison with maximum punishment. No video was ever released. We were able to destroy the video footage and the room where she was recording. By some miracle, my men were able to catch her off guard, though she was still able to flee. I won't lie to you, though . . . She did have a live feed broadcasting out of the room. She sent me the link, and my eyes didn't move off of you for a moment."

"You . . . you mean, you saw everything happen? Who else has seen this?"

"Outside of my men, and the bachelor group on the plane, I'm not sure. I couldn't tell if anyone else was logged in. But Carl and my men are watching closely to make sure nothing falls in the cracks and gets out. I promise you, I will protect you from this!" He gripped my shoulders tightly with daggers in his eyes.

"Weston, I hate to ask you, but did he touch me? Did Noah have his way with me after I blacked out? I can't imagine what your mind must have been going through."

"No, he didn't. I made it there in time, but a few more seconds, none of us would've been so lucky. But you can check your medical exam record as well. There was no contact. And even if there was, I never would've blamed you, ever. I watched you being drugged, fighting him off, and being scared. And you're right—seeing you the way I did will never leave my mind. But that is my punishment for not being with you and protecting you."

"Weston, don't blame yourself. That woman is crazy, and though I would appreciate not being attacked by any of your exes again, I cannot and will not blame you for any of it."

"I totally get that, and whether you blame me or not, I'll spend the rest of our lives making it up to you." He kissed me on the cheek. "Enough about all the bad stuff right now. So, with you remembering Noah and the events of that night, can you recall all your lost memories?"

"No," I said, disheartened.

He grabbed my face with both of his big hands. "This is a positive and a step in the right direction. You've now faced your assault and understand what happened to you. How's your head?"

"It's okay. Still hurts a little, but nothing some sleep can't fix." I looked at the clock. "Wow, it's three a.m."

"Yes. Let me get you tucked back in so you can go to sleep. Can I hold you tonight?"

I grinned. "I would like that very much."

Weston tucked both of us under the covers and wrapped his strong arms around me. Feeling his body next to mine felt like home.

CHAPTER 44:
To Do or Not to Do

*I*t was now Wednesday, and a few things had changed since Sunday night. Weston was now back in the master bedroom with me, as we both had found we slept much better in the comfort of each other's arms. Since I had faced my nightmare, they were less frequent or intense. I had also gained several more memories, but they had been very sporadic. Mama gave me until this afternoon to make a decision about marrying Weston now or postponing. My family was still in town since the showers, and the Lancaster families would start rolling in on Friday morning. Basically, if we were canceling, it needed to be then. Weston had to go to the office for several meetings, so Mia had come over to hang out and to help with this dilemma I was in.

"Mia, what should I do?"

"My honest opinion?"

"Yes!"

"You just need to go ahead and marry him. Whether it's now or a month from now, does it really matter? You two belong together. And regardless of whether your memory is fully intact or not, your heart knows what it wants. Are you really going to deny it?"

"This is so frustrating! You do have a point, but I want so badly to have my memories of us when I marry him. Mama told me we'd planned on writing our own vows. How am I supposed to do that now when these last several months currently don't exist to me?"

"I can help you if you want. I might not have been there for everything, but you also never held back from details, either." She gave me a wink and laughed.

"If I recall, through our whole friendship, you've *never* let me skim on details."

"True!"

"In all seriousness, Sam, just marry the guy. You'll have your memories back soon enough, and you don't want to regret missing out on this day you've waited for all your life. Every detail is in place. It just needs the bride and groom."

"Thank you, Mia. Well, let's head to Mabel's so I can stuff my face before calling Mama with a decision."

After our yummy lunch break of cheesy fries and double fudge chocolate shakes, we called Mama to let her know my decision about the wedding. Then Mia dropped me off at home.

I didn't see Weston's truck, but I did catch several guards surrounding the property. I wondered what was up with all these men in black.

A jolt of pain hit me just then, and a memory flashed of Andre, Carl, and multiple bodyguards surrounding myself, the family, and the houses. Okay, then. These men in black had been around. Where was Andre? Quickly pulling out my phone, I called Weston, who didn't answer. I felt as I was walked up the steps to the home. As soon as I turned the knob and opened the door, I was greeted by a very rambunctious Maddox. Bending down to pet him, I started to sway, and then my vision blurred to black.

Weston's POV

As I sat in a meeting, my phone rang for five minutes straight, but I was unable to answer it. One was a missed call from Sam, as well as her new bodyguard, Declan. Showing my phone to Carl, I pointed out his name, and he left and made a call while I continued the meeting. Not even two minutes later, he walked back into the boardroom looking stiff and solemn.

"Meeting adjourned," I stated.

Carl filled me in. "Sir, Declan found Miss unconscious in the house with the front door open. It seemed she had just gotten home. They rushed her to the ER, and she's now being evaluated."

All the blood rushed from my face, but without hesitation, I grabbed my jacket. "Let's go!"

Before Carl could even park the car at the hospital, I was flying out of the car and through the door. I ran up to the front desk. "Hi. Samantha Dupont's room, please."

The nurse asked, "What relation are you to her, sir?"

"I am her damn fiancé! Do you seriously not know who the hell I am? I need her room, now!"

"My apologies, sir, and yes, I do know," she stated, avoiding eye contact. "Room 202, sir."

Running down the hallway, I filed past all the rooms until I reached hers. Taking a deep breath, I walked in. My Sam looked so peaceful, like an angel. She was hooked up to some monitors and had an IV going.

Behind me, Carl said, "Find me the physician! I want an update."

Dr. Taylor quickly walked in to provide an update. It seemed she was awake when she arrived, but she seemed very groggy and said her head hurt. So, my nurse gave her some pain medicine to relax after they performed a head scan, which came back clear. That we were just waiting on some pending lab results. He said that her brain was overloaded with the stress of trying to recall her lost memories. Trying to reassure me that all this was pretty common when a patient starts to remember things at a fast pace, among other stresses.

I knew she had been remembering quite a bit lately but had been upset that she hadn't recalled us reuniting, on top of the wedding that was supposed to happen Saturday. I wondered what her decision was, as I knew she had until this afternoon to let her mom know. I would marry her right then just to have made her mine already.

I thanked the provider for his swiftness in attending to her, along with the updates. I called her dad to inform him of what happened and that as soon as she woke up and they did another check-up, she would be discharged home. The thought of them coming all the way over seemed moot, so I told them I'd call them when we headed home so they could meet us there if they wanted.

I turned back to Sam, who was still in a deep but restless sleep. I crawled into the hospital bed with her and wrapped her in my arms, then whispered in her ear, "I love you."

CHAPTER 44:
Seriously, Again?

My eyelids fluttered open, and I realized I wasn't at home but back in the hospital. This was seriously getting old. Trying to push myself up, I felt weight on my chest. Looking down, I was taken back by Weston's head of midnight black hair and dreamy, handsome, sleeping face. Poor guy. I knew he must've been exhausted with all of the events, including work and taking care of me. I ran my fingers through his hair, and tears started to form in my eyes with the realization that I really loved him. This man was a part of me. He was my home.

He started to stir, so I quickly wiped my tears and stopped sniffling. He quickly sat up to face me. "Why are you crying?" He caressed my cheek with his hand.

"I'm not crying. It's just allergies," I said, trying not to look directly into his gaze.

He quickly wiped away a lonely tear under my eye. "Well, you missed one, darlin'."

I had a frustrating memory of never being able to hide anything from him, so I just gave him a smirk.

"You can tell me about it later. How about I spring you from the joint?"

"Really! Yes, please! And Wes, I'm sorry if I scared you."

"No need to apologize. You're dealing with a lot right now. Just lean on me. I'm working from home for the rest of the week so I can be right there with you."

I looked down at my hands twisting. "You don't have to do that. I'll be fine."

"No, I want to, and I can. So, it's settled, okay?" he said more sternly than I was used to.

All I could do was nod my head in submission as his dark glare washed over me.

He must've noticed my eyes widening when he spoke, so he kissed me on the forehead. "Let me retrieve your papers so we can head home." Then he walked out of the room.

What in the world was that?

His eyes even darkened when he spoke to me. Even my inner "I am woman" recoiled not to say another word. Before I could put my thoughts in order, he strolled back in so we could go. Even while protesting, he helped me out of my hospital gown and into my clothes. Not that I was shy—because he *had* seen me before—but my chest and stomach still had a few bruises and wounds that were still healing, and I really wanted to take a shower.

Upon walking out of my room, a nurse quickly caught up to me and handed me a piece of paper.

"My apologies, Miss Dupont. I forgot to add these to your discharge papers, as we just your lab results in. It has your follow-up appointment on it as well as some helpful suggestions."

"Oh, thank you so much." Not thinking too much, I folded it up and placed it in the pocket of my sweatshirt.

Finally home, I headed upstairs to take a shower. Being nice and relaxed, I didn't notice until the water started to turn cold. I must've been in the shower much longer than I thought. As I walked out of the shower to grab my towel, the door opened.

"Hey, Sam."

"Ah!" I rushed to wrap the towel around me.

"Sorry . . . I didn't mean to frighten you, but I'm kind of glad I did," Weston stated, grinning.

I felt like I knew that grin all too well now, and I needed to brace myself for something to come after. His eyes gleamed at me as he strutted over. I tried to avoid his gaze, but he quickly put his hands on my waist and pulled me towards him.

"I'm going to kiss you now," he said. "Please don't try to stop me."

Before I could process what he'd just said, he had me in a deep kiss. His tongue soon became entangled with mine, and I wrapped my hands around his neck. My towel fell to the floor, and Weston pulled away from kissing me, taking a step back to take me all in.

"Damn, Sam, you are absolutely breathtaking," he panted.

I bit my lower lip and looked back up at him slowly.

"You're a bad girl. Do you want to be punished?"

"Punished?" I squeaked out.

Almost with a devilish laugh, he picked me up and put me on the marble counter-top in the bathroom.

Pulling my chin up to him, he quickly devoured my mouth again before making his way to the nape of my neck with his soft, full lips as his hands caressed my breasts. Little moans found a way of escaping my mouth as he explored my body with his mouth and hands. Weston found his way between my legs, taunting me with his tongue. My fingers gripped and ruffled his hair as he glided his tongue in and out of me.

"I just want to savor you. I've been missing this . . . missing you." He continued sending my body into a spiraling orgasm while I screamed his name and arched my back.

Cupping my face in his hands and in between sweet pecks on my face, he said, "I want you, Sam. No, I need you! Honestly, I don't think I can hold myself back any longer." He gazed into my eyes, melting my heart.

Pulling him toward me by his collar, it was me who kissed him. Not even bothering to unbutton his shirt, I ripped it open, causing the buttons to fly across the bathroom. I unbuckled his belt and pants so he could slide them off. I was filled with desire, and my body yearned for him so much, it hurt.

Bringing his forehead to mine, we both gasped for air.

"Weston, please take me." I grasped onto his bulging, curved biceps.

"As you wish, my Sam," he whispered in my ear.

I wrapped my legs around his waist, and he carried me to the bed. He gently laid me on the bed, and his member had sprung free as he hovered over me. Holding my arms above my head with one hand, he took the other to position himself into me. I let out a loud moan as he drove deeper into my core. He knew it drove me insane not being able to wrap my arms around him, as he was in control and continuously thrusting into me while caressing my body with his other hand.

"Weston!" I called out.

With lustful eyes looking back into mine, he released my arms. In one swoop of a motion, he was now under me. I took the initiative to taunt him. Circling my hips around on top of him, I kissed around his neck and chest and finally sat up on top of him. Placing my hands on his tan, toned abs, I slightly lifted my lower half up, then slowly glided back down his shaft.

His eyes rolled back in his head. "Oh, shit, Sam. That feels incredible. Don't stop! Please!"

After a few more times, I could feel my own body getting restless with the tease, so I circled my hips on him before I came back down to kiss him.

Our hips rocked together as I pushed myself back on him to deepen the impact with every motion. We both moaned loudly, and saying each other's names intensified the atmosphere, but soon we found our sweet release together. Sweating and hot, we curled up together, breathing heavily.

"Wow," was all I could say.

He let out a slight chuckle. "You can definitely say that."

After a few minutes, I looked over at him. "What did you want to tell me earlier when you walked in on me?"

His eyes went wide, then he placed his hand over his face before glancing at me.

"What?" I said.

"Well, I came to tell you that dinner was ready and that your family was downstairs waiting on you." He looked at me like a sad puppy waiting to be scolded.

My face turned crimson. "Oh, shit, Weston! Do you think they're still here? Do you think they heard anything?"

"There's one way to find out. Let's dress and head down."

As we walked downstairs, we realized it was pretty quiet. Thinking we got away with the deed, we strolled into the kitchen as the aroma of food took over our senses.

Hearing the sliding door open and "Are you finally ready for dinner?" had me jumping out of my skin and clinging to Weston, who looked completely unfazed by it all.

"Oh, hi, Mama. It smells wonderful."

She tried to conceal her giggles. "Of course it is, sweetie. You must be famished." She winked at Wes, who smiled back.

I punched him in the chest, then my whole body turned red.

Mama called everyone into the kitchen from the patio area. I saw that not only my family was there, but also the Lancasters, Mia, Dylan, and a few aunties who wanted to come by.

I shook my head, looking at Weston with daggers. "This all would've been good information to have a while ago."

Laughing, he kissed my head, then ruffled my hair. As he walked over to the liquor cabinet, he gave me a wink.

This damn man! All too embarrassed, I tried my best not to make eye contact with anyone at dinner and kept the conversation short.

Finally, after everyone left, I chased Weston around the house and told him I could literally kill him. I finally jumped on his back to try and take him down but soon realized my petite self—compared to this giant—was no match. Before I knew it, we were in round two of love-making in the living room.

Weston's POV

Dressed in my tailored suit and looking over our pictures on the fire-place, I ran through my week while waiting for Sam to get ready. Those last few days with my Sam had been incredible. She'd finally started to warm up to me, even though not all her memories were intact. But she seemed to regain more every day. I'd been able to kiss her, hold her, and make love to her, almost as if the incident had never occurred, but I could still sense some emotional distance. I made sure I held her tight at night to keep her nightmares away. It seemed for both of us, they hadn't come back since we started sharing the same bed again.

On the business front, I'd have had to deal with shameless enemies and put them in their places. You would've thought they wouldn't have come after me, but I guess some like a challenge they know they'll fail. I was just thankful Sam didn't pay much attention to the news. My money and status typically kept me untouchable, but the new and upcoming reporters didn't know how to stay quiet. Her thinking that I was a murderer or a sinister man wouldn't be good for her mind. She told me she believed I couldn't have done such horrific things to people who didn't deserve it. All she had to do was ask, and I would be a hundred percent honest with her. Whether someone was dealt with personally by me or my men, that was still their blood and tears on my hands.

After torturing Laura Belle's parents and younger siblings by cut-ting them off from their financials, guarding them at the house so they were unable to leave, having her father beaten, and messing with her family's businesses and namesake in the public, Laura Belle finally turned herself in to the police. She confessed to everything, even the

233

threatening letters and pictures I was receiving at work about Sam. I was still contemplating killing her myself for what she did to Sam. Her parents had now disowned her completely, so she would be in a living hell until her last breath. My people on the inside would ensure it.

It was now Friday, and our rehearsal dinner was later in the evening at the ranch. I would take that as a sign she was still willing to marry me the following day, but I was going to tell the moms that, even if she had said not to cancel anything. This had been the one thing Sam refused to discuss with me, no matter how hard I pressed. I did tell her that if she wasn't willing to walk down the aisle, I would carry her down it myself and that the wedding would be happening as planned. She looked slightly frightened when I growled those words, so I tried to play it off as a joke. She told me the previous night that she wasn't ready to tell me she loved me, as I had asked why she only smiled when I told her I loved her. I had longed to hear those words escape her lips since that awful night—to hear and know that her mind and heart were still in line with mine.

I sent my men to help the moms and wedding planner with the finishing touches for the night, as I wanted the atmosphere to blow Sam away and make it exude so much romance, she would have no choice but to tell me she loved me. I even had a special present tucked away in my pocket for later that evening at dinner.

Hearing a rustling sound, I turned around to find her elegantly gliding down the stairs. Quickly taking a picture of her with my phone, I moved to greet her at the bottom.

"Samantha Jane, there are no words to describe how beautiful and exquisite you look right now." I bent down and placed a kiss on her cheek.

"Thank you, kind sir. You're looking pretty dashing yourself," she said, blushing.

"Only the best for my Sam." I took her arm and walked her out of the house, then placed her in the limo, keeping my eyes on her and arm around her during the ride.

CHAPTER 46:
Rehearsal Dinner

The car turned up the driveway to the ranch, and Weston thought it would be best to blindfold me halfway there. My nerves were shot, and a million butterflies fluttered in my stomach. The decision to go through with this wedding had taken a toll on me. Even he and my parents mentioned the weight I'd lost in a short amount of time, but they didn't pry too hard, knowing everything I'd gone through recently. This decision, though, continuously weighed on my mind and heart. My love for him wasn't a question, but these missing months, only allowing me to dwell on the past, had been painful. Luckily, most of my memory over the last five years had come back, but my wishful thinking of having the last several months remembered before I said "I do" was about to timeout.

Everyone had reassured me that I was doing the right thing—that I just needed to relax and quit stressing over it.

Weston parking the car brought me out of my thoughts. "Stay here. Let me guide you," he said.

Soon enough, the door opened, and he took my hand. His usual calm, cool hand was now hot and clammy. I wondered if he was nervous about everything as well. As a million things ran through my mind and I tried to grasp a hold of my breathing, I heard gasps.

"Weston! What's going on? Can I take this off now?" No longer feeling his presence next to me, and frustrated I hadn't received an answer, I untied the bandanna to pull it down.

I walked into a woodland fairytale with fairy lights everywhere—in the trees and grass—and floating lanterns in the pond. This view brought a strange, yet familiar feeling to me, as if I had seen it all before.

As I turned my head side to side, trying to take it all in, I realized all our family and friends were smiling at me and standing around, and the moms looked like they'd been crying.

What on earth is going on?

As if someone had heard me, I heard, "Ruff, ruff!"

Maddox was next to Weston, who was kneeling down on one knee, with a giant rock in his hand.

I gasped and brought my hands up to my face.

"Samantha Jane Dupont, I love you. I understand this isn't the ideal situation, so I wanted to give you a memory you can hold on to at this moment. I'm not a capable man without you. All my decisions have always been about or for you, and that, I promise, that will never change. My heart will only ever love you, my eyes will only ever see you, these lips will ever only kiss you, and these hands will only ever hold and caress you. You and I are linked together forever, as if written in the stars. And I know you feel the same in your heart." He seemed to pause to read my face as I cried and rubbed Maddox's ears out of nervousness.

"Please marry me, Sam. Marry me tomorrow so we can always be tied together."

Still stunned from everything, I stepped forward to be closer to him, grasping the ring that had been hanging from my neck since my first hospital visit after the incident. But outside, I felt the tense atmosphere, as if all the air had been sucked away.

"Weston, I . . ." I looked at everyone around us, and then back to Weston.

Even Maddox looked nervous as he stared at me with his paw on Weston's knee. Suddenly, several flashes streamed through my mind, causing me to quickly lean over and hold my head. Weston came to my aid quickly and held me and asked if I was all right. He sounded so far away, but he was right next to me.

Keeping my eyes closed tightly, I saw him and me in the water, then all dressed up at dinner somewhere, then us rolling in the sheets in a hotel room, and then his first proposal. A smile grew across my face because I knew these were real memories, not just dreams.

The flashes stopped, and I looked up at Weston. Gaining my balance and placing my hand in his, I said, "Weston, I will marry you tomorrow."

Looking pale and shocked, he said, "Can you repeat that louder, Sam? I'm not sure everyone heard you, and I need witnesses."

I laughed. "Yes! Yes, Weston! I will marry you!"

Everyone cheered as he picked me up and swung me around, then slowly lowered me down his body and cupped my face in his hands to kiss me.

"I am truly the luckiest man in the world. Now, let's go celebrate with everyone," he said as he placed the new engagement ring on my finger.

We partied and celebrated the night away with our friends and family.

In order to keep everything "wedding" a surprise, but also sticking to traditions, Mia whisked me away to her house for the remaining hours so I could hopefully catch some sleep before the wedding. Weston stayed at Jackson's house for the night so he could help set up in the morning before getting ready.

"Girl, this is going to be the wedding of the century," Mia said, with a lot of excitement at two in the morning.

I laughed. "We're not royalty, Mia. Surely, it won't be that big of a deal."

"Did you forget that your engagement made worldwide news?"

"Oh, shit. I did! But now that you mention it, I do recall the craziness of it. Wow, how am I marrying this man again?"

"Um, maybe because he only wants you. Were you completely surprised tonight?"

"Yes! Where was my warning . . . best friend? You're supposed to have my back!"

"I do, and that's why I didn't tell you anything. Let me see that new rock of yours."

While sliding it off my finger, I took a minute to admire it. The center, princess-cut diamond had to be at least eight to ten carats, surrounded by gorgeous, deep-green diamonds along a platinum band.

"Wow," escaped my lips.

"That must've cost a fortune, Sam. You know, the green diamonds represent a fresh start to your new life together."

I passed my ring off to her so she could take a closer look.

I decided to text Weston:

> WITH ALL THE CHAOS TONIGHT, I REALLY DIDN'T HAVE MUCH TIME TO ADMIRE MY NEW RING. IT'S DAZZLING AND BREATHTAKING. THANK YOU. I CAN'T GET OVER THE INTRIGUING GREEN DIAMONDS ON IT, ESPECIALLY WHEN THE LIGHT HITS THEM JUST RIGHT.

He wrote back:

> YOU DON'T HAVE TO THANK ME. THE WORLD IS YOURS, SAM. OTHER THAN THE MEANING OF A FRESH START, GREEN DIAMONDS ARE FAIRLY RARE. BUT YOUR GREEN DIAMONDS ARE THE RAREST OF THEM ALL. AFTER SEARCHING FOR THE RIGHT GREEN DIAMOND AND COLOR, THIS ONE STOOD OUT ABOVE ALL THE REST IN THE WORLD. IT'S THE COLOR OF YOUR EYES WHEN YOU'RE HAPPY AND IN LOVE. THIS IS THE COLOR I DREAMED OF YOUR EYES BEING FOR SO LONG, AND THESE LAST SEVERAL MONTHS, I'VE BEEN GRACED WITH THEM.

I replied:

Aren't you a man of many words with an exquisite tongue? I will cherish this ring always. Know my eyes have only ever shined this color for you.

CHAPTER 47:
The Dress

Mia and I rolled out of bed around nine a.m. The wedding wasn't until five that evening, but there was still lots to do. She was not only helping me and the bridesmaids get ready, but she had to be at the ranch early to check on the guys.

I woke up quite dizzy but pushed it off from the long, overwhelming night. Mia's dad made us breakfast and seemed to be slightly teary eyed about me getting married. He'd always treated me like his other daughter since Mia and I had been inseparable since forever.

After breakfast, Dawn and Jenny arrived to start getting ready. The moms had arranged a full spa service to come to us. First, we had massages and got our nails done. We were all in heaven. We had some downtime before hair and makeup, so I was binge-eating chips and salsa on the couch while curled up in my favorite sweatshirt and pants. Mia was hollering at me to put my undergarments on because she was about to start my hair and makeup.

"What time is it?" I asked while throwing chips at her.

"It's already two, Samantha Jane! Let's get going . . . Chop, chop!" she said, chasing me with a pillow to go upstairs.

Both screaming and laughing, we made it upstairs, and I started to undress. Pulling off my sweatshirt, Mia saw a piece of paper fall out.

"What's this?" she asked.

"O, just part of my discharge papers from the other day. The nurse forgot it in my papers and brought it out when we were leaving, so I just stuck it in my pocket."

"I love how you live in this sweatshirt, even in hundred-degree weather, and forget about stuff inside of it."

"Well, this is the best coziest sweatshirt, ever!" I grabbed the paper and threw it on the bed. Mia helped me with my white corset that had silk ribbon running through it in the back. And then I put on a matching slip that hung on my hips and would give my dress some fluff.

"Okay, now that that's done, let's go check on the girls and start getting you ready."

Right before we headed downstairs, I grabbed the paper from the bed, to place back my bag. Remembering it is supposed to have a follow-up appointment on it, I decide to open it to make sure it is nothing I need to reschedule since I will be on my honeymoon for the next week or so. As soon as I open it, I am surprised to see my followup is with my OB Gyn doctor, Dr. Holly. Followed by a list of pre-natal care items. In the corner of the page, I see where the nurse drew a heart with "Congratulations" in it.

Oh, my . . .

I quickly hid the sheet in my overnight bag.

It's your wedding day, Sam. Focus on what's important at this moment.

When I walked into the living room, Dawn was the first to see me and make eye contact. "You look like you've seen a ghost, Sam."

Everyone turned their attention to me. "Um, yeah . . . I just had some flashes with a sudden headache. Hey, Mia, can you loosen this up a bit?" I struggled to untie the ribbon to the corset and steady my breathing.

Mia loosened the ribbon and got me situated for my hair and make-up to start. "Sure you're okay, Sam?"

"Yep, I'm good. It happens fast, but I'm getting used to it."

There was no way I was about to share what I'd just read when I hadn't even dealt with it myself. And how was I going to tell Weston? Let alone, before I even confirmed this was legit. *Why was I not informed before I was discharged?* "Um, just give me about 5 minutes." I grabbed my phone and walked out on the back porch to call the hospital. Luckily the nurse I needed was on call. She confirms that I am pregnant and apologies for not getting the information to me sooner. There was a delay in getting the lab work back along with Wes being very adamant about no one bothering me. Then he quickly took charge of getting me discharged to go home as rapidly as possible. The nurse said she was elated to catch me as I was leaving to pass on the information, but did not want to be in my fiance's wrath for keeping me. I profusely apologized to her and thanked her for being honest and forthcoming. *I swear this man of mine can be so infuriating.*

All right, Sam, it's your wedding day. Let's just make it through these next several hours.

Mia went to work on my hair, putting it into a vintage look, with braids along the sides that met into a fancy bun—like something from The Great Gatsby era—and it was topped off with two small leaf hairpins in the back. My makeup was subtle but flawless, with just enough blush and lipstick to pop color against my white dress.

The girls were ready, so now it was time to put me in my dress. Not having been able to recall it, my eyes watered when I saw it. The simple elegance of it made it stunning. The girls helped me step into it, then pulled it up. It was a sleeveless, open-back, A-line dress with a floral lace bodice that went into an illusion neckline and over my shoulders. It fit all my curves perfectly until it flared slightly at the bottom and finished with a chapel train. The lace and beading were beyond intricate as they flew over the tulle.

Mia added my full-length, scallop-edged veil with the same beading of the dress. "Final touch!" she said.

"You look like the perfect bride, Samantha. I think I'm going to cry!" Jenny said.

"No tears until after pictures, the ceremony, and more pictures," Mia said. "Keep it together, girls!"

I saluted her. "Got it, Mia!"

I looked in the full-length mirror, and all my worries drifted away. The realization set in that I was about to walk down the aisle to be with the love of my life.

CHAPTER 48:

It Is Time

*I*t was time to make my way down the aisle. The family and bridal party pictures had all been taken, but my favorite would be Weston and me back to back, unable to see each other but surrounded by the bridal party. My ladies said he looked phenomenal—like a Greek-God-turned-cowboy, and by all the hootin' and hollerin' from the boys, it took all of them to keep Wes from turning around to catch a glimpse of me.

I stood next to my daddy, getting ready for him to walk me to Weston. Luckily, the path to the aisle curved as it made its way to the altar, so I was able to step out and take in the breathtaking site without being seen. The groomsmen walked arm in arm with my bridesmaids. They all looked perfect together, thanks to Mia. Then Maddox headed down as the ring bearer. I can't say I'd seen a more handsome ring bearer than that big ol' guy.

"You ready, baby girl?"

"I am, Daddy. I really am." I gave him a kiss on the cheek.

"All right, then. Let's do this."

Clenching my perfect bouquet of sunflowers and bluebonnets in my hands, while my arm was intertwined with Daddy's, we began the walk. As we came to the curve in the path, I took a deep breath, knowing that as soon as we turned the corner, he would be there at the end of the aisle, on the edge of our bluebonnet field.

My breath hitched as his eyes locked with mine, pulling me towards him as if he were some kind of force field. It felt like an eternity until I made it to the altar and stood next to him. As soon as I did, he had me in his arms and whispered, "You are the angel of my dreams, Sam. You are breathtaking."

I had no words and could only look in his eyes and smile until my thoughts were interrupted by the pastor.

"Who gives this lovely lady, Samantha Jane Dupont, to be married to Weston Lee Lancaster?"

"My wife and I do," my Daddy said. He kissed me on the cheek and then shook Weston's hand before sitting down next to Mama.

The pastor started into the ceremony with a prayer and expectation of marriage.

"As I hand it over to Weston and Samantha to state their vows, I first want to start them off with this . . . *Love is patient, love is kind. It does not envy, it does not boast, it is not proud. It is not rude, it is not self-seeking, it is not easily angered. It keeps no record of wrongs. Love does not delight in evil but rejoices with the truth. It always protects, always trusts, always hopes, always perseveres.* Corinthians, Thirteen. Now, Weston, you may begin."

"Samantha Jane Dupont, my Sam . . . There are not enough words to express my love and affection for you, so I will spend our lifetime together showing you how in love I am with you. I will spend our lifetime proving to you how wonderful and special you are to me. How without you, I am not whole. My heart is offbeat when it's away from yours. You being with me is everything, and I cannot wait to spend forever and beyond with you. I love you, Sam." He held my hands, and his eyes teared up.

As I was lost in thought and trying not to bust into full waterworks, the pastor patted me on the arm to let me know it was my turn.

"I'm not sure how I'm supposed to follow that, but I'll give it a try," I said, laughing as I tried not to cry anymore Along with the loft of laughter from the audience. "Wow. Here we are. A dream that had once turned into a fairytale, you have now made my reality. I must've been blessed by the stars above to have had you by my side all these years—and now—because I truly believe I'm the luckiest girl alive. You have my heart, my body, and my soul. You also encompass my best memories—old or new and in between—because I remember it all now."

Weston looked like he was in shock, and I heard the crowd gasp and then cheer.

I placed my hand against his cheek. "It has always, and will only, ever be you in my heart, Weston Lee Lancaster. I love you."

Weston pulled me towards him and kissed me subtly on the lips, then looked down at me. "You don't know how happy you just made me with those three words and that you have your memories back."

The pastor said, "Whoa, cowboy . . . I haven't even announced you husband and wife yet, so settle down."

Once the crowd calmed down from laughing, we moved on to the ring portion and I do's.

As if he couldn't announce it fast enough, the pastor said, "By the power invested in me, through God and this grand state of Texas, I now pronounce you husband and wife. You may now kiss your bride, Mr. Lancaster."

In one smooth motion, I was in his arms, dipped down, and kissed passionately. Grabbing my bouquet from Mia, Weston swooped me up in his arms and carried me off.

"Where are we going?" I said, laughing, but I soon realized we couldn't leave yet because we had more pictures to take. "Wes, we need to turn around . . . We have pictures and family back there."

"Don't worry. I'll have you back in a few. Jackson and Mia know how to handle it."

He finally stopped at my favorite giant black willow tree—the one that had been part of the land for centuries, and the one our initials were carved into. Weston quickly brought out his phone and snapped a selfie of us in front of our initials on the tree.

"This will be my favorite wedding picture of all," he said, grinning from ear to ear. "There's just one more thing to do before heading back."

"What's that?"

"Give my wife a proper kiss." He grabbed my chin to tilt it up, and as his tongue maneuvered through my lips to intertwine with my tongue. Only the need for oxygen seemed to pull us apart.

"I'll have you all to myself later, so I guess I have to share you for now. Let's head back."

"Okay, husband," I said with a smirk and a wink.

"Oh, wife of mine . . . The words sound like a sweet melody escaping from your lips. Let me bring you back before I can no longer control myself."

CHAPTER 49:
The Reception

*E*veryone was famished from picture-taking, and we couldn't wait to dig into some food. The area where we'd had the rehearsal dinner the previous night had been turned into the reception area. There was a large, white circus tent filled with tables covered in exquisite decorations, a large dance floor, and a stage. Beautiful log tables were outside and blended in with the scenery decorated in wildflowers and lights.

Soon, the bridal party was announced, and then we heard, "Now, please stand up and welcome Mr. and Mrs. Lancaster!"

Everyone was up on their feet, clapping and cheering as Weston guided me out onto the dance floor. Our song, "Can't Help Falling in Love," started playing, and I just sobbed into his chest. As he kissed my tears away, we swayed together to the music, separated only long enough to twirl me and then dip me at the end of the song.

"Can we stay like this all night?" I asked.

"As you wish, my wife, but first, let me make sure you're fed."

I followed him to the bridal party table as everyone gazed at us and clapped. We smiled and took our seats next to our friends. Food had been served, and I noticed our families spared no expense on the meal, as everyone had been served tender filet mignon or chicken with grilled shrimp and garlic potatoes—meals fit for a king and his nobles.

As dinner was finishing up and before the cutting of the cake, our family and friends made their way to the stage, one by one, to share their moments of us and speeches. For half an hour, we all laughed and cried.

Afterwards, Weston and I made our rounds to the guest tables to say hello and thank everyone for coming to share this day with us. We arrived at the table where the Hughes were, and I was elated to see them.

Nate had brought Kiera as his plus one, and they looked adorable together. We hugged and ran through some quick logistics since I would be taking off for a week or so.

Then I turned my attention to my England family and hugged them. "Mr. and Mrs. Hughes, I'm so happy you both made it. I really didn't want to wait another six months to visit with you."

"Oh, Samantha, you know we wouldn't miss this for anything. Though you're not with Nate and won't become a true family member, you will always be a second daughter to me."

"You are so kind, Clara. Oh, and speaking of . . . Let me introduce you to my husband, Weston Lancaster. Weston, this is Mr. and Mrs. Hughes, who I always talk about and work for. And this is Nate's uncle and aunt."

He shook hands and greeted both of them pleasantly.

Mr. Hughes said, "I believe some rumors may be true of you, Mr. Lancaster."

"Is that so, sir? Like what?" His lips went flat, and he put on his alluring poker face.

"That you really are tall, dark, and handsome. And that you have exquisite taste and are a fine businessman."

Weston nodded with a slight smile, as I gently squeezed his hand, warning him to be nice.

"Maybe, in the near future, if our paths cross in the business realm, we can treat each other with respect. We both seem to hold the same special lady in our heart—and to high standards."

"Of course, Mr. Hughes. Your family members are great friends of Sam's, so they will be of mine, as well."

"Good to hear, Mr. Lancaster. Now, Samantha, since you're missing our August family vacation, my wife has already planned out April for us. Here's the itinerary and all the travel arrangements you need for the both of you. This is our treat . . . as your wedding gift. Of course, these are also selfish reasons to have you around. Sophie will be joining us, also. She was heartbroken about missing the wedding but couldn't miss her courses right now." Mr. Hughes handed me an envelope.

I opened it up, revealing a week-long getaway to the St. Regis Bora Bora Resort in Tahiti.

"Oh my! Mr. and Mrs. Hughes, this sounds incredible, and we cannot wait. We both thank you so much for everything!"

"You deserve to be pampered and treated well, Samantha. And we look forward to getting to know your husband more, too," Mrs. Hughes said, sending me a wink.

I giggled.

"Well," Mr. Hughes said, "we have a flight to catch in a few hours, but we'll be in touch soon. Both of you enjoy your honeymoon and time off." In Mr. Hughes fashion, he kissed both of my cheeks before leaving.

Weston had tightened his grip on my hand, and we continued to make our way around the tables.

The wedding cake had now been brought out, and I was overwhelmed at how gorgeous it was. It was five tiers high with the boho-chic theme of partially frosted, ombré-style, with vanilla bean frosting that turned to a gold dusting. The top layer had a gold Mr. and Mrs. cake topper. The tiers were adorned with a few bluebonnets and sunflowers to match the wedding flowers. Wes and I cut into the cake together to find it was white cake filled with chocolate ganache. I was truly in Heaven as Weston fed me a piece. He then left a little icing on the side of my mouth, but before I could use my own tongue to lick it, he used his in a very sensual manner. I was truly a blushing bride in front of everyone.

We headed to the dance floor for our dances with my daddy and his mom, then we switched to him dancing with my mom and me with his dad. Dancing with Mr. Lancaster was slightly awkward, but I kept a smile on my face through the conversation. Regardless, he was my father-in-law and a powerful man. He did seem to be asking me a lot of questions about the honeymoon and upcoming future plans, but he became frustrated when I wasn't able to give him any answers. Before we parted, he told me to watch my back now that I was a Lancaster—that it would be upsetting to have anything else happen to me. Looking at him oddly, I told him thank you and walked back to Weston. Since it was our wedding day, I elected to share this information with him later on so it didn't leave me unsettled.

Mia walked over with Dylan carrying glasses of wine, as the night was finally coming to an end. It was about time for us to embark on our honeymoon, even though I had no idea where we were going.

They passed the glasses to us, and Mia said, "I wanted to make sure I sent you off before you're ambushed by the crowd out there."

"I love you," I said, giving her a big hug. "I promise to check in daily."

Weston cleared his throat. "Okay, maybe every other day."

Mia raised her glass, and we followed. "Cheers to friends that are family. Cheers to true love and meant-to-be's. May you two be blessed with love and happiness in every lifetime." We all clanked our glasses together then brought them to our lips.

I stopped abruptly, remembering what I read earlier.

"Sam, what's wrong?" Weston asked, noticing I didn't drink.

"Um, it's just that . . ." I looked around to find my parents, who I spotted and waved over. I did the same with the Lancasters and a few others. Our small circle grew with our main circle of friends and family, as others had been ushered outside for the sendoff.

Looking around, I knew this was news that should be shared with everyone, and I wasn't sure how Weston was going to react. This wasn't something we'd even addressed since getting back together.

"Sam, honey, what's going on?" Mama asked, petting my arm.

"I think . . . It's just that . . . I'm not able to drink this because"—I locked eyes with Weston"—because I'm pregnant."

Everyone screamed and cheered around me, then smothered me with hugs and kisses. I looked back up to Weston, who looked to be frozen in fear.

I took his hands. "Weston . . . Can you say something? This is nothing we planned for right now, but . . ."

Before I could even finish, he covered my mouth with his. Pulling back, he picked me and spun me around in his arms. "Are you kidding, Sam? This is incredible news!" Carefully putting me back down, he held me close. "I didn't think this day could surpass my expectations any more than it already has, but I'm overjoyed."

"Really?" I asked, crying.

"Of course, babe. There's no better time than now to start our family. Let's head out before we're off schedule, and we'll have you checked out once we're settled in tomorrow."

"Sounds like a good plan."

We said bye to our friends, family, and Maddox, of course. And we thanked our parents again, especially our moms, for everything they had done, only for them to find they were now planning for little Lancaster.

We gave them a few minutes to situate everyone outside, and then we ran out through the aisle of sparkles. Quickly waving goodbye, we slid into the limo, and not long after, we were on the Lancasters' private jet.

Weston's POV

My Sam was officially my wife. I never knew I could feel so complete and so in love with one person. Now she was carrying our child. I'd already messaged Carl to send over the best of the best OB to our villa tomorrow, no matter what it cost. There would only be the best for my Sam and our child.

She was all cuddled up in the seat with her head in my lap, and I let out a slight chuckle when I saw what she was wearing. She still had my sweatshirt from high school football that she deemed her favorite sweatshirt and wore constantly. It was our wedding night, but I wouldn't trade that view for anything. Besides, I'd let her sleep now so I could keep her up the rest of the morning once we arrived.

We were going to do a sailing tour of Greece, but now that she was pregnant, I didn't think that would be the best idea, so we'd be island-hopping by car or ferry. We'd start in Crete in a villa at the Creta Maris Resort for two nights, then I had Carl rent us a house in Mykonos for several days. I figured I'd let her choose the rest, as unbeknownst to her, we'd be traveling for the next two and half weeks. Wherever in the world my Sam wanted to go, I would make it happen for her.

CHAPTER 50:

A Perfect Day

This man was too much. After ravishing my body for hours after we arrived at the villa, I was finally able to catch the light of day while enjoying the spectacular view of the island by our own private pool. I was finally relaxed, only to find Carl and Declan hovering over me.

"You're both blocking my sun. Can I help you?"

"Sir would like to see you in the living room," Carl said. "He's arranged a physician to check on you."

"Right now?"

They nodded their heads in unison.

I got up, threw my cover-up on, and walked inside.

Weston came over to kiss me on the cheek and wrap his arm around my waist.

"Dr. Wells, this is my wife, Samantha."

We shook hands. "Nice to meet you, Samantha."

"You too, Dr. Wells."

Dr. Wells took out her pen and notepad. "I have a few questions to ask you, Samantha, and then I'll perform an ultrasound. Do you prefer to have your husband with you or not? Some women are nervous or embarrassed discussing such private matters in front of their spouses."

Before I could even speak my own mind, Weston looked at me with a hint of anger. "You're fine with me staying with you, right, darling?" He squeezed my waist tighter.

All I could do was look away, then back to Dr. Wells. "It's fine."

We went through her questionnaire fairly quickly, as I was absolutely embarrassed having Weston next to me. I let her know that the results showed I was about two months pregnant. She took my vitals and said everything looked good with my blood pressure and pulse. She then had me lie on the couch for the ultrasound. She squirted the gel on my stomach, then began rubbing the wand on it. It didn't take her long to find our baby so we could hear the little heartbeat.

Squeezing Weston's hand, I began to cry. "That's our baby!"

"That's incredible," he said.

Dr. Wells flipped on a screen. "Look right here. This is your little peanut. After I gather some measurements, I'll print copies out for you both."

"Thank you." I cried as Weston kissed me and wiped my tears away.

After several minutes, Dr. Wells handed us our copies.

"Samantha, by my measurements, you are looking to be two and a half months along. You're almost at that three-month mark, so I recommend not participating in anything extreme or rough for the next couple of weeks, just as a precaution."

"Yes, doctor."

Weston piped in. "What about sexual activity during this time and her pregnancy?"

Only if looks could paralyze his mouth sometimes.

"Well, intimacy is fine as long as it's on the gentle side. I'll be honest . . . Seeing the hickeys and bruising on Samantha's body leads me to believe you're on the rougher side of play, Mr. Lancaster."

His poker face didn't even flinch, but I turned bright red, wondering about the marks he'd left that I couldn't see.

Weston didn't answer, and Dr. Wells just looked at both of us. "Just be slow and gentle. Also, the bigger she gets, the more uncomfortable she's going to feel, so again, mind your manners during this time, Mr. Lancaster."

All I could do was giggle at him as his eyes turned a darker shade of blue. "Thank you, Dr. Wells, for the advice. We have taken note and will follow."

After I saw her out, I burst out laughing, looking at my stone-cold husband.

"What are you more worried about? Me getting bigger or the no sex if you can't be gentle with me?"

Weston stared down at me with that damn look and grin. "Oh my, wife . . . There are many ways I'll be able to tease you and have my way with you. I think it'll be you begging me for it—begging me to be harder and faster." He devoured my mouth, and in an instant, I'm undressed in the living room and sitting on the couch as his mouth and tongue ignited my core. In the middle of it all, I could finally take his shirt off and feel his skin under my hands as I anticipated my body's release.

"You always taste so sweet, Sam. I'll never be tired of tasting you. Just relax, and let yourself go." He spread my legs farther apart, his tongue performing acrobatic tricks inside my folds. I was panting and wanting him even more. Without a word, I slid off the couch to un-buckle his belt and shorts, pushing all his clothing off of him so he had to stand up to step out. Before he made another move, I pushed him down onto the couch and then straddled him. He caressed my breasts as I paced myself before the urge of wanting him harder and deeper inside me hit me. Moving his hands from being tangled in my hair and his mouth from my neck, he grabbed my hips so I could ride him into our perfect storm, where we found pleasure together.

After falling asleep on the couch, we woke up just in time to doll up for dinner in the village. We met so many friendly people along the way to dinner, and the scenery was stunning. The locals stared at Weston as if he were a Greek god. I honestly couldn't blame them or be mad.

After dinner, we found a little chocolate dessert shop and had our fill of delicious, fresh local desserts. I told Weston he'd be carrying me back if he let me eat any more. I lucked out anyhow, as I rode piggy-back on the way to the villa. I'm sure we were a show to watch, with us laughing and goofing around, not to mention the men in black not trailing far behind.

CHAPTER 51:
Sunrise to Sunset

It had been a few days into our honeymoon, and we were staying in a house in Mykonos. The surrealism of it all had been overwhelming, as I fell more in love with the house and the city every day.

There was a little village within walking distance from our house that we visited daily to grab breakfast. I couldn't sleep one morning, so while Weston was still sleeping, I decided to head out and grab breakfast for us so I could surprise him in bed. As I walked down the hill, I grabbed some pictures of the stunning orange sunrise that blended into the blue color of the island. I captured pictures of a few locals fishing and putting flower carts out. It was a scene that happened every morning, but it brought me a sense of calm and peace.

Once in the bakery, the pleasant aroma of freshly baked bread and cinnamon filled my nostrils. After grabbing my order, I stepped out to see Declan nearby as I scanned the crowd. We nodded to acknowledge each other and began our way back. I thought maybe I'd escaped him that morning, but I'd forgotten he was a silent, stealthy one.

Almost back to the villa, I heard and felt an explosion that made my ears ring, and I must've been pushed onto the ground by the force. Then I noticed I was on top of Declan, who broke the fall for me. Standing up, trying to regain our senses, we looked in the direction of the house, and panic took over me. I started running towards the chaos. As soon as I reached the home, I dropped to my knees, screaming and crying. Our house, along with a few villas next to it, were part of the explosion. As the smoke and dust started to settle, the buildings were in shambles. I screamed Weston's name over and over again but didn't get an answer back.

Declan hollered, "I need to send you away from here, right now!"

I shook my head. "I can't! I can't leave! Where's Weston? I left him in the house this morning. Where is he?" I tried running to the home. I needed proof he was okay and that he wasn't in there. "Declan, where's Weston? Where's Carl and the other men?"

"I'm trying to find out, Miss, but my first priority is your safety. It's not safe for you to be this close. Please!"

Firetrucks and ambulances began arriving and taking over the scene. I rushed to the men, asking for them to check for my husband. Their only response was that it would take time for them to clear the rubble and find any and all missing persons. With that, I just fell to the ground, curled up in a ball, and cried, refusing to move until I knew something more. I vaguely heard Declan talking in the background on his phone, but I was too numb to listen in. Shortly after, he picked me up and carried me to a nearby car.

"Please don't fight me, Miss. I have orders to send you somewhere safe, immediately. Once I do that, I'll be able to update you."

"Just tell me he's alive!"

He went mute on me, so I slammed my fist on the dashboard and stared out the window.

Along the slender, pebble roads, we drove through the town. Staring out my window, I watched all the beauty pass by, only to be jealous of all of it. If Weston would've been there with me, everything would be fine.

Out of nowhere, a car raced towards us, and I began yelling out to Declan. Our car took a sharp turn, but we ended up flipping through the air before I felt a hard impact. The last thing I remembered was wrapping my arms around my stomach for protection before it went dark.

~✧~

"Sam! Samantha! Open your eyes! It's me!" Someone was holding me tightly. "Open your eyes! Please!"

I felt I was hallucinating. It sounded like Weston, and when I opened my eyes, it also looked like him. I slowly lifted my hand up to his face. "I love you," I said, and then I closed my eyes again, thinking I was truly dead.

My top half shook violently, causing my mind to stir, and my eyes opened back up.

"I'm here to take you home. We're both alive, Samantha. We are both alive." He rocked me back and forth in his arms.

My eyes blinked as his tears fell on my face. I realized he was really there with me, so I sprung up, wrapping my arms around his neck and kissing him on the lips, then all over his face. "It's you! You really are alive!"

"I'll never leave you, Sam. Nothing will ever take me away from you. I will be by your side at your last breath, and then after." He pulled me into a hug.

I'm not sure how long we stayed in each other's arms, but I remembered him carrying me out of the car and to the ambulance to get checked out. Outside from some bruises and a large gash on my forehead, both the baby and I made it out okay.

Declan had two broken ribs and a broken cheekbone, but for how bad the wreck looked, we were both very lucky. As far as the other guy, we were shocked to find out it was Blake Sircy.

I was confused about why he was there and after us, but Wes had his men on it. Eventually, Weston put me into a car and didn't let go for several hours. We made our way out of Mykonos, then into Santorini as the pink sunset graced the sky.

Weston's POV

We were still in Greece on our honeymoon, and Samantha didn't want to head home yet, as we knew there would be a lot to deal with once we hit American soil. Ironically enough, we needed to host a press conference that morning to update the media and world on recent events and address concerns for Lans Enterprises. We knew this would cause a shock wave, as we'd been up all night piecing the information together and calling out those who were responsible.

I began. "Good morning, everyone. I'd like to first extend my gratitude to the people of Greece. You are a country of love and support, even to those who do not reside here. We're thankful no lives were lost during the explosion in Mykonos, but some injuries were unavoidable. My wife and I will cover all medical expenses, along with damages to any property caused by the explosion. I have men out there now, so please speak with them. I will personally be there at the end of the week to meet with each of you, as well.

"Now, for the facts. The facts are, the man behind the explosion and kidnapping of my wife is Blake Sircy, the owner of SIR enterprises. He and his counterparts are now dead. Also, my own father was arrested for conspiracy to kidnap, as he played a role in leading Blake to where we were. Though my father is the reason I'm still standing here alive, he's also the reason my wife and unborn child were put in danger. For this, I will have no mercy on him, or to any person who comes after my family. Take this as a warning . . . Do not come for me or any of our family unless you want to see your own tortured and buried in a deep grave.

"I am still the active president of Lans Enterprises and will be cleaning house in the company over the next couple of weeks. This is to be a respected family business—an empire not to be trifled with. Those involved in any scandals with my father, or elsewhere, will be dealt with swiftly. You do not have time to hide or ask forgiveness. Those who thought I was ruthless before, you have now awakened the devil himself. Now, if you will please excuse me, I would like to accompany my beautiful wife to breakfast. For further questions, you can ask my assistant, Carl. Thank you."

Stepping off, I wrapped my arm around Sam's waist, and we both waved goodbye to the crowd. Everyone looked stunned and in fear of moving. I wasn't such a heartless person, and I didn't want to put fear in the locals, so, as we made our way up the street to a local café, we greeted everyone with a smile and had small conversations with several people. My Sam pulled people in by her smile and own beauty. I loved that she was laughing as people approached us for her autograph after seeing our wedding photos that had graced magazines around the world. Though others tried not to make eye contact with me, Samantha always passed them to me to sign, as well, which left the locals in disbelief.

Sitting at breakfast with her, I gazed across the table, and the last forty-eight hours ran through my head.

"We are both very lucky," I said, taking her hand and kissing the top of it.

"We are." She smiled and rubbed her stomach.

To think something could've happened to her or our baby made me shudder.

"This baby is a true survivor after all it's endured," she said. "Even Dr. Wells is shocked."

I looked back at her. "Have you ever thought not being with me would keep you alive and safe? You've been in so much danger since coming back to me."

She slapped me. "Weston Lee Lancaster, if you ever say something like that again, I will jump off a bridge, leaving you alone. Do you understand me? I'm in danger when I'm not with you. Have you not realized this yet? We're in this together—thick and thin, bad and good, life and death. Now, this is not to be spoken about again, got it?"

She looked at me sternly, and I was taken aback by her rigor. Standing up, I moved next to her and pulled her into my arms, reassuring her.

"I'd be lifeless without you. It was an ignorant statement." I devoured her mouth into mine. "Let's head back so I can treat you to some pampering, then we'll spend the remainder of the day at the beach."

CHAPTER 52:
A Piece of Me

*L*ying out on the beach and listening to the waves crash on the shore brought a calming that I had needed. Even after the massages, Weston arranged the morning at the villa, followed by a long, warm bubble bath.

Weston sat next to me under the umbrella with his laptop, trying to take care of a few things since chaos had risen back at the office. He had several men there assisting and taking care of items so we could stay longer. I could tell the chaos and concerns about his mom and sister were troubling him. I was able to put two and two together with what Mr. Lancaster had said to me during our dance and the events that happened. Weston also connected the puzzle pieces . . .

Mr. Lancaster had called Carl early that morning to check on Weston and me, which turned into a warning that something was going to happen where we were staying and that the house needed to be evacuated swiftly and quietly. He said he heard this through one of his sketchy businessmen, but it was to be taken very seriously. Carl took no time in getting Weston and the other guards out, as well as getting nearby residents removed. Within ten minutes of that phone call, the explosion took place, affecting several people nearby.

I turned to smile at him as I sensed his gaze on me.

"Come here," he said in a sensual, husky voice. He put his laptop down, picked me up bridal style, then ran into the water with me.

"Weston! You are so crazy."

He really was lucky I loved him and that he was so attractive he could get away with anything.

"I'm just crazy about you, Sam." He flashed me the smile that made me melt, and I punched him in the arm then took a dive underwater. When I came up, I couldn't find him anywhere. Before I knew it, he pulled my feet out from under me, pulling me under and causing sand and dust to stir up. He turned me around under the water and then put his mouth over mine, breathing air into mine. As we swam up and reached the surface, he was laughing.

"You owe me for saving your life."

I glared at him. "I wouldn't have needed saving if you didn't pull me under."

"Have I ever told you how cute your mad face is?"

"Ugh, whatever," I said as I dodged his kisses.

He then said my name in a sexy tone, causing goosebumps to spread across my body. We ended up in a full make-out session in front of the Perissa Beach.

Later in the evening, Weston hired a chef to cook for us. We ate outside on the balcony overlooking the Caldera.

"I just love this place. I know it might sound silly, but it's like the island is calling to me—like I'm supposed to be here. In all the places I've visited around the world, this right here is my calmness, my peace. I'm sure it has a lot to do with you being here—as you are my home—but it's going to be hard to leave in a couple of days."

Weston gazed at me across the table and pushed over a small box with a glittering gold bow on top.

"Did you even listen to me? And what is this?"

He grinned at me. "Yes, I always listen to you. Just open it, and you'll find out."

I gently pulled the lid off and pulled back the tissue paper. I lifted up a beautiful bronze chain linked to a unique-looking key. I looked at Weston in confusion.

"It's yours . . . This villa is all yours to come and go as you please. I hope you don't leave me behind and stay here forever, but it is yours."

I gasped. "How did you even know?"

"Sam, it'll be a hard day for me when I don't know what's going on in that mind of yours—even on your most stubborn days. It's the same for the house we live in now. I saw your green eyes taking in every millimeter of detail in this place—in this town, even. You float room to room with the amount of poise you've possessed since coming here. I would like to take all the credit for that smile of yours when you wake up in the morning, and all day, and I know this place now has a piece of you."

"You are incredible, Weston." I sat in his lap and kissed him, then finished off the last bite of his Mosaiko.

"That's okay . . . You're eating for two now. Besides, I have something in mind that is even yummier for dessert." With a quick wink, I knew exactly where this night was headed.

CHAPTER 53:
Catching Up

Some time had passed, and we all seemed to have fallen into a new normal, but soon enough, our lives would be tipped upside again.

I was nine months pregnant, feeling like a beached whale as I worked from the couch. Since getting back from our honeymoon, Weston did a lot of travel to assure clients about settled accounts, as well as put others in their place. I traveled with him a little in the beginning, but then I just wanted to be a homebody with my dog and family. Mr. Hughes had Nate and me expand his lucrative business across the globe, so we'd opened up six firms globally, with Nate and me heading all of them.

Nate was now engaged to Kiera. I joked with Mr. Hughes that he just needed me to introduce those two. Everyone loved her, and she was such a smart whip that we gave her control over the three state firms under us. I loved seeing that it was developing into a family empire for them. I was thankful the Lancasters and the Hughes ran different lines of business.

Weston's mom and sister were still living on the property, with Weston taking care of them and with my parents. They were family, regardless of what Mr. Lancaster did. Even though it did take a while for Arlene to come to terms with everything, she seemed to be doing much better and had started dating a guy from the local country club. We were all really impressed with Clark, and he had quickly been integrated into our family.

Mr. Lancaster, on the other hand, was sentenced to twenty years with no parole. Weston said if he didn't die in prison by then, he would file for an appeal to extend the sentence. Other than that, no one really spoke of him anymore. It was as if a generation of Lancasters had been lost at sea and forgotten.

The first week of December, Jackson and Lucey had their baby, a precious little boy named Colton Jackson Dupont. He possessed Lucey's hair and eyes but had Jackson's face and other features. I was so ecstatic for our kids to grow up together, knowing they were going to be so blessed and loved.

A picture of Weston holding Colton flashed through my mind, and my lady parts burned for him. The image of that man, holding a baby in those arms of his and looking so calm, was like priceless art to me. Any day now we would be holding our little bundle of joy—though I wished it was sooner rather than later. I could no longer see my feet, and I was tired of almost peeing on myself rushing to the bathroom. Not the mention the sexual urges I was having that were out of control. Of course, Weston didn't seem to mind. Dr. Wells did say having sex was a way to send me into labor.

The front door opened, and Maddox barked.

"Hey, husband."

"Hello, wife of mine. How are you today?"

"Um, other than tired, big, and swollen? I can tell the baby definitely dropped more, and my blood pressure has been elevated on and off, so I've been drinking water and taking it easy."

"Okay, well, let me call Dr. Wells to check with her." I swear he had her on speed dial because he called her at least ten times a day. That poor woman.

His voice pulled me from my thoughts. "Babe, she wants you to come in now."

"Seriously? Right now?"

"Yes, Sam, right now. Come on, babe, or I'll carry you to the car myself."

"Ha! Good luck with that!" Smirking, I tried to push myself off the couch. As if I'd dared him, he picked me up, then carried me out to his truck.

Weston drove like a madman to the hospital. You would've thought I was already in labor. Before I could roll out of the truck, he was by my side, carrying me into the hospital. His handsome, panic-stricken face had every nurse rushing to him.

"Wes, I can walk by myself." The nurses glared at me as if I'd ruined their chances with him. "What a loving husband you have!" a nurse said. "One should be so lucky to have a doting guy like this."

I said, "Nurse, please send me Dr. Wells and a wheelchair, please."

"You heard her! Go!" Weston snapped.

They scrambled, and we were soon met with Dr. Wells in a room. Weston finally put me down on the bed to be examined.

"Well, Samantha, your blood pressure is quite high, and your water hasn't broken." She pressed her hands around my stomach to get an idea of what position the baby was in, as it was head down the prior week. She wore a strange look. "Let me do a quick ultrasound. I think your baby flipped on us."

The ultrasound confirmed her suspicion. "This isn't ideal, but we need to do an emergency C-section, Samantha."

Weston, who was about to come unglued, yelled, "What do you mean, emergency surgery? Have you not been monitoring her this whole time?"

"Weston, calm down. Things happen . . . Besides, I'm the one going under the knife, not you, so please, calm down." I reached out for him, persuading him to calm down.

"Yes, Mr. Lancaster, we're dealing with a baby, and sometimes things happen. This isn't unusual. I'd typically take the time to try to turn the baby around myself, but Samantha's blood pressure is too high to put her body and the baby under any more stress. This is the best solution for both your wife and baby. Now, if you'll please excuse me, I'm going to call anesthesia and prep the operating room. The nurse will grab you a pair of scrubs to wear in there with your wife so you can stay by her side."

Dr. Wells walked out, and Weston tried to keep his poker face on, but that was one thing that never worked on me.

"Weston, can you do me a favor?"

"Anything," he said.

"Can you call our parents and let them know what's going on so they can be here after the baby is born? On our rush over here, I forgot to call them."

"Yes, let me do that now." He took out his phone and FaceTimed my mama and then his own. They said they would spread the word and that they would be at the hospital soon.

A nurse walked in and gave Weston some scrubs, then she started unplugging all the wires.

"Mr. Lancaster, we are first going to take your wife to the OR and prep her. After you put your scrubs on and go through the sterile room to wash up, and when Dr. Wells is ready to start, they'll let you in."

"Understood." He held my hand and kissed me one time before I was wheeled to the OR. With his forehead up against mine, he said, "I'll see you in just a few minutes, okay?"

I nodded my head.

"I love you, Samantha Jane. Nurse, please remind Dr. Wells who pays her current salary. Nothing is to happen to my wife or child, and most importantly, my wife."

The nurse, who looked scared to death, said, "Yes, sir," and quickly wheeled me away.

CHAPTER 54:
Welcome Home

Forty-five minutes later, we welcomed our baby girl into the world. Weston was the first one to hold her, as I was still lying on the table, but he brought her face to mine so I could see how perfect and beautiful she was. I could tell she already had her daddy wrapped around her little finger and looked just like him. I was hoping since she had Weston's extraordinary looks that she would have my temperament and zest for life. Or she would be just like Weston, through and through.

Oh, our sweet little Amelia Jane. I can already see the fun and trouble we're going to have with you.

Not long after, we were wheeled back to our own room and greeted by family and friends. Weston was enjoying this, as all attention was on Amelia, and he had me all to himself. After he passed Amelia off to his mom, he carefully crawled into bed with me, making sure I was getting plenty of attention and care. Mama even brought the photographer with her so no one had to worry about any precious moments not being captured. I loved how that woman always thought ahead.

I leaned my head up against Weston's chest as he held me, and we were enthralled with the scene before us.

"We truly are blessed, Weston. And so is that little girl right there."

He smiled. "That, indeed. She is a princess and will be treated as such."

"Oh, jeez. Don't go spoiling her already. I have a feeling I'm going to be the bad cop in this parent scenario." I started laughing but knew in my heart it was true.

It was now eight p.m., everyone had left, and we were exhausted. The three of us cuddled in the bed together, and we continued to admire Amelia's beauty and temperament, along with her big, blue baby-doll eyes and long eyelashes.

The nurse came in to check Amelia and my incision. Our nurse had been wonderful and even changed her dirty diapers for us. Maybe it was because I currently couldn't stand up myself, and Weston looked far from being able to change a diaper.

Soon after, Dr. Wells came in. "How's everyone doing?"

"I feel good, and the IV is great!" I pressed the button again."

She smiled. "Well, everything went beautifully today, and you have a perfect little girl. Mr. Lancaster, I've met with your assistant, and everything is arranged for you three to head home in the morning. Nurse Shay will be your home-nursery nurse to help with Samantha and Amelia as needed. And I'll be coming by for daily checkups, as well."

"Oh!" I looked at Weston.

"I figured you—well, we—would be more comfortable at home while you heal, and Amelia can start getting used to her new room and surroundings. Besides, you know Maddox is missing you."

"No argument from me. Thank you for everything, Dr. Wells. We truly appreciate everything you've done for me and Amelia, and acting so swiftly yesterday."

"It's been my pleasure, Samantha. Now, I'll leave you three to rest, and I'll drop by in the morning for discharge."

Nurse Shay handed Amelia back to me so I could feed her. We did learn earlier that she didn't want to latch on to me, but she enjoyed the bottle, so we decided to stick with it, as it made her happy. Wes could now feed her, too, which he loved.

Once she sucked her bottle down, Weston put her on his shoulder backwards and began to walk around, gently patting her back to burp her. She finally let out a big one. We then all three cuddled back in bed and fell asleep.

Morning came sooner than I expected after a long night of pressing the pain-med button with Weston and Amelia on top of me, but soon, we were sent on our way. My mama called to tell me they would be over later so we had time to get situated at home and let them know if we needed anything.

Carl carried Amelia in by her car seat while Weston carried me inside the house, then set me down on the couch. Carefully taking Amelia out, I had Maddox come by to meet her. He laid across my stomach for months, through all her kicks and punches, so I knew he was excited to meet whoever it was that had been making all that fuss.

"Maddox, meet your little sister, Amelia." He licked her gently on the face, making her face twist in confusion . . . or disgust. But her little hand reached out and touched his nose. Maddox then laid down next to me with his head on her legs.

"Good boy, Maddox. You are her protector." He gave me a little whine like he was answering me back. Weston snapped a picture of the three of us and then brought himself in to complete the family portrait. Welcome home, sweet Amelia.

~✧~

Weston's POV

Another crazy twenty-four hours in the books . . .

There were so many highs and lows, I felt emotionally and mentally exhausted. One minute, they were rushing my Sam to the operating room, and the next, our baby girl was born. Dr. Wells should've prided herself on how successful she was during the operation. She told me that it went so well that there should barely be a visible scar once Sam completely healed. Not that it would've bothered me anyway. In my eyes, Sam's beauty would always shine.

I helped Sam upstairs to the nursery so we could put Amelia in her crib. Walking in, it truly felt like a forest with all the woodland creatures around us. Sam wanted something neutral since we didn't want to find out the sex of the baby until she was delivered. I gave her full reign to decorate and hire whomever, and she did just that. Even Carl had let out a few laughs when he helped me put the crib and changing table together.

"Sir, if others could see you now . . . No one would believe what my eyes have seen."

Samantha and I put our sweet girl to bed in her own little forest. After we made sure she was asleep and the baby monitor was working, we snuck out, and I carried Sam to our bedroom. I couldn't help but keep my hands on her, pulling her close to me and kissing her.

"Take it easy there, cowboy. I'm still sutured up. Don't forget what Dr. Wells said."

"You're going to enjoy these next several days, aren't you?"

She bit her lip. "Um, maybe just a little."

"Samantha Jane, you are asking for it."

"Am I?" She shot me a wink and then tried to escape.

I forgot for a split second that she was sutured up. "You are such a little minx, and you about ripped your stomach open."

In all her stubbornness, she said, "It was worth it to see the look on your face!"

I chuckled. "Keep it up, Samantha Jane. I'm keeping track for when it's time I can punish you."

CHAPTER 55:

Growing Pains

"Mommy, Leo and Luke tracked dirt in the house again," Amelia yelled.

"Okay, give me one minute to put Adriana in her high chair," I shouted back. "It's always something with those two boys!"

"Samantha, let me go grab the boys . . . You have enough going on right now," Mrs. Betty said.

We were four kids in, with one more on the way. Three more months to go. We loved our kids, but they were all under the age of six, and two of them were five-year-old twin boys who were the epitome of double-trouble. If it wasn't for Mrs. Betty, Weston's housekeeper, moving in with us to help us while Weston ran his billion-dollar empire and I spearheaded the Hughes' million-dollar empire, along with the ranch work and trying to raise our kids in as much of normalcy we could, I would've lost it already. I thought Weston was trying to build his own personal empire of kids. We'd grown so much personally and together over the years, but we still couldn't keep our hands off of each other.

Weston had truly been the best throughout everything and had never faltered from the promises he'd made me years before. He made it a point to whisk me away to our villa in Greece at least twice a year and countless date nights in between. His obsessive possessiveness over me hadn't changed, and we even had little battles with the kids when he demanded my attention on him. He still managed to have good one-on-one time with each kid on the weekends and on vacations, which, in my eyes, made him even more of an amazing father.

We tried not to make it obvious to the kids that they were surrounded by the men in black all the time, but they had already befriended our two main guys, Carl and Declan. To them, they were extended family. I still abided by my own rule of not asking questions when I heard Weston's name in the news. My awareness was high when it came to knowing what he and his men were capable of. If need be, he would move mountains to ensure his family's safety against the public eye and any enemy. It astonished me how much time had already passed, but it seemed like yesterday that we'd gotten married and officially started our lives together.

Having been pregnant constantly, this little guy would be the last one. We couldn't be more excited to meet him, and he would be named after my daddy, Rhett Sterling. Jackson's middle name is also Sterling to match Daddy's, so he used it as a first name on his second son, who was born a year before. It seemed right to use his name in each of our families.

Mama moved into a cozy house up on the hill, and Jackson and Lucey moved into our childhood home with their family of five. They had two boys, Colton and Sterling, and one little girl named Willow. Mia, the kids' godmother, was happily married to Dylan. Her second baby was due two months after mine, so of course we decided our two youngest would be engaged already. Her oldest daughter, Ada, was four, though she looked six and was gorgeous like a prized doll. My twins already doted on her and protected her, so maybe there would be a marriage there, also. We made sure to have weekly date nights with Mia and Dylan, as well as getting the families together on the weekends.

The past year had been the hardest since Daddy left us to be with the Lord. Weston used all of his connections to make sure he had the best care in the world. The Alzheimer's and severe heart problems became too much on his body, and after two years of worsening, he was ready to leave us and be pain free. I held onto memories of the times he had with his grandkids, and I was glad my oldest would be able to remember him. To the others, he would be the handsome man in photos and the great man we would speak about.

Mama was doing okay. She told me she suspected he would always go first and that she'd prepared herself for it. In the end, I wasn't sure who took it harder—myself or Amelia. She was granddaddy's little girl who'd hung the moon for her. In her short six years, she had spent more time with him than at home, learning the ropes of the business at an early age. Right before daddy passed, we lost his horse, Chance, to old age. I liked to believe he knew daddy was going to be leaving soon and wanted to be ready to carry him across the bridge.

Earlier in the year, we lost Admiral to bone cancer. That horse was the absolute best horse a girl could ask for. We'd been together since Daddy gave him to me when I was eight years old. For weeks I cried every time I went to the stable to visit with Mr. Darcy.

Oh, and let's not forget Maddox, who wasn't getting any younger, either. He was turning twelve in November, and he was still my best friend, but I found it amusing that he'd bonded with our youngest, Adriana. She was two, but Weston thought it was because she looked and acted like me the most. I agreed . . . My other three were spitting images of their father. Even Luke, who had my dark, caramel hair, still resembled his dad the most. Needless to say, the year had been one for the books with losses, growth, and change.

CHAPTER 56:
Graduation

I was beside myself that my baby boy was graduating high school and heading off to Yale, like his father. Amelia had taken a gap year to travel, completed her studies in London for medicine, and was a cardiology physician in Houston. The twins couldn't have been more opposite. Luke studied agriculture at UT, like his Uncle Jackson, since his passion was the ranch and being part of the Dupont family business. Though Leo attended UT also, he studied business and communications and had been selected to take over Lans Enterprises one day. My baby girl, Adriana, was in England for her studies and worked as an apprentice under the Hughes company. She was a numbers genius and had an eye for predicting highs and lows. Nate had been gracious enough to take her under his wing, but I had a feeling it also had to do with Nate's son, Benedict. They'd known each other for years, and she would follow him to the ends of the Earth. Nate assured me they were keeping it professional, but he sensed Ben had feelings for her. Speaking of Nate, he and Kiera didn't last for more than two years. She finished her master's in upstate New York and decided to never return, which worked out because Nate met Lily while handling one of the firms located in Seattle. They have been married for twenty years with their one son, Benedict Nathaniel Hughes.

Tonight was Rhetts' graduation party, and all the family had come back home. We hadn't had everyone home since Christmas, so I was beyond excited. Trying to get everything ready, I was distracted by this handsome, salt-and-pepper-haired man, who couldn't seem to stop staring at me.

"Weston, can you not come over here to help me?" I threw an iced cupcake at him.

"Sorry. You look so beautiful when you're focused on something. It's one of my favorite faces you make." He snaked his arms around me and kissed me on the cheek, then turned me to face him and quickly devoured my mouth with his.

Amelia huffed. "Ugh . . . Can you two just *not* while we're home this weekend?"

"Amelia, don't hate that Mom and Dad still have passionate love for each other, even at their old age," Leo voiced back.

Amelia threw a pillow at his face.

"Who are you calling old?" Wes asked. "I'm still youthful, in every way, at my age. Your mom isn't complaining."

That prompted eye rolls from everyone.

The doorbell rang, and Amelia ran to the door. "Adriana! You're finally here!" Amelia gave her sister a big hug. "Oh, and Ben, you're here, also. Welcome!"

We all lined up at the door to welcome them home.

"Hey, Mama. Hey, Daddy," Adriana said.

"Hey, baby girl," Weston said. "How was the flight?"

"It was good, Daddy. Just long. Where's the graduate?"

"He's at Natalie's house eating lunch with her family," I said. "They'll be joining us for the party later."

"Well, I have some news I want to share, but I can wait until he gets home."

"Everything all right, sweetie?" I asked. "Is it something we need to discuss now?"

"No, I'm great . . . It can wait until later. Come on, Ben, I'll show you to the guest room so you can get settled in."

They walked off hand in hand, glowing.

It was seven, and the party had started. Many of Rhett's friends had joined us to celebrate. It really was such a special day for all of them. Our family was here, including friends that we'd stayed close to through the years. Our kids had the pleasure of growing up together and sharing many of the same pastimes we did back in the day. Weston had his arms around me as we took in the sight of the backyard that had come to life with lights, decor, and people we admired, loved, and adored.

"We did good, honey. Last kid leaving the nest and on his way to greatness."

"I know, but I'll never stop worrying about any of them, no matter how grown they are."

"I know, darling. I know."

About midnight, the party died down. All the parents and siblings had left, but several of Rhett's friends had stuck around to keep swimming and would sleep over. They were enjoying this newfound freedom. Adriana all of a sudden showed up in front of Wes and me in the kitchen as we were cleaning.

"Can we help you, baby girl?" Wes asked.

"We need to have a family executive meeting, now. I have news I need to share."

"Okay, go round up the board members," he said, then looked at me. "She gets her impatience from you."

I laughed. "You realize I can still ignore you, just like she did back in her teen years."

"You wouldn't dare!" He picked me up and set me on the counter, then stood in front of me between my legs. I quickly turned my face to the side to dodge his kiss, only for him to start nibbling at my neck. I accidentally let out a soft moan that triggered him to keep coming for me until I finally caved, meeting his lips with mine.

Soon we heard, "Gross!"

I whispered to Weston, "The Lancaster entourage is here."

He laughed and whispered back, "I'll punish you later."

Amelia groaned. "Y'all do know that it is *not* normal for parents to act this way?"

I shrugged. "It's normal for us!"

"One day, Amelia, you'll find your someone, and you'll understand."

"Okay, everyone . . . I need you all to be quiet!" Adriana said. "While I make an announcement."

We stared at her, waiting to hear what she had to say.

She held her hand up. "I'm getting married!" She pulled Ben to stand next to her. "And I was hired to work for the Hughes Corporation in England and then expand into London."

Everyone shouted and cheered for her and them. I looked back at Weston and could tell his wheels were turning. I figured I'd better intervene first.

"Congratulations, sweetie," I said. "Not to rain on anyone's parade, but this seems sudden."

"Mama, Daddy . . . We've known each other for years and love each other. There is nothing we want more than to be bonded together in marriage. I only have one more year of classes to finish, then I'll take my place at the table at Hughes, alongside Ben and his dad. We're truly keeping this a family business. We want a winter-themed wedding, so we were thinking this December, near the pond where you and Daddy said your vows."

"Oh, sweetie. I can't say no to that. It sounds like you both are well on your way and happy. That's all we want for you." I pulled Weston in to be part of the hug.

The kids knew their father would follow my lead and wouldn't have to worry about a thing when I was involved. There had been plenty of times I didn't involve myself in their arguments, but that was to make them stronger and self-thinkers. If they proved a point to their father, they were doing better than most people in the business. With that, we sent Rhett to Yale in the fall and began wedding planning.

Epilogue:

All I Want Is Time

Looking around my bedroom, surrounded by my family, I take in everyone's faces one last time. My body and age can no longer fight the battle of cancer. Not long after Adriana was married, I noticed some lumps. I should've been better about checkups, knowing it was hereditary after it took my mama from me about fifteen years before. After multiple treatments, surgeries, and eight years of remission, it crept back into our lives, stronger than before. I fought like hell. We all did. Weston called in all his favors to save me, but per the prognosis, we could only prolong it as it quickly started spreading through my lymph nodes. I'd told all the kids to take care of their father because my heart honestly broke for him. Here we are, holding on to our final moments before my last breath would come along.

It had been a few weeks leading up to this point, getting last-minute lists in order, writing letters for my kids and grandkids, and having long talks with Weston. I let him know he couldn't go with me yet—that I need him to stay behind to make sure our kids, our family, and our legacy were all going to be fine, but that I would be waiting for him with open arms on the other side.

I have tried so hard to be a strong pillar for him, knowing that my leaving would break him. We had spent the majority of our lives together, in love, inseparable, and as best friends. It was why we wrote our story. All the guts and glory encompassed it. It is the story of us, to not be forgotten, but to be cherished by our family for generations. To show that love is worth fighting for.

All my kids and grandbabies have come to hold my hand and kiss my head, saying their final goodbyes as my breathing became more rattled and frequent. I can feel Weston's hand in mine, squeezing, and turning my head to face him. I manage to breathe out "I love you" as he kisses me on my lips, stealing my last breath.

~✧~

Weston's POV

My Sam had been gone for three months, and life without her is unbearable. I cry myself to sleep most nights and try to push through the days. I constantly ask out loud, "When will I see her again? When is it my turn?"

I have done what she asked of me: I made sure the kids are all okay. They are a product of her and me, and they couldn't be any stronger or better than that. I passed her letters out to everyone, and upon her demand, I wrote mine out as well to put them with the will. As she asked me to do, I made sure there were to be no loose ends with anything after my departure from this world. All our kids were married and had lives of their own, whether it was running the ranch, Lans Enterprises, or following their own paths. Our grandkids were growing up so fast, and I knew they'd all be fine because of who their parents and grandparents were. We had a great life together, and we were able to raise an impeccable family.

The kids and grandkids come by daily to check on me, but my heart is broken, and I am tired.

"Daddy, Mama would not want you to be like this," my baby girl said while hugging me.

"I know . . . I'll do better." I try not to worry her or the others, but ever since I awoke this morning, my heart had been aching more than it ever had before since she left me. But I also feel a sense of calmness.

As we all gather around the big farm table at the house for the traditional Sunday dinner, the house is filled with laughter and love—just the way my Sam loved it.

For a second, I saw a young Samantha when Amelia's little girl held my hand. She was the spitting image of her grandmother at her age. All I can do is bend over to hug her and kiss her forehead. After dinner, the grandkids start cleaning the kitchen as the parents sit on the back patio sipping wine and reminiscing about their younger years and family memories. I chuckle to myself, as those were definitely some great times. Together, we created this legacy filled with love, ambition, values, and respect. I firmly believe all the Lancasters and Duponts looking down could not be prouder of all the accomplishments on both sides.

It has been another long, exhausting day, and with everyone engrossed in their own conversations, I decide to go lie down in our bed, but something drew me to lie on her side.

Staring at our wedding photo on her nightstand, I closed my eyes, wishing to go back to that day. I soon found myself in a deep sleep, dreaming about her. I caught a glimpse of her off in a field of bluebonnets, with the sky turning red, orange and pink as the sun set. She is in a white cotton dress as her dark brown hair hangs down her back. I catch her honeysuckle scent blowing in the wind. She soon notices me and comes running, jumping in my arms. It feels amazing and real as I held her close, stealing a kiss.

"Welcome home, Weston," she says, placing her hand on the side of my face.

I lean into it. "I've missed you so much, but this dream won't last like the others."

"Wes, you're not dreaming. You're finally here with me."

She squeezes my hand, and when I look past her, I see all of our lost loved ones together. Even Maddox is by her side, wagging his tail.

Looking back at her, I pull her into my arms and realize I am finally home with my Sam again.

The End

Keep up with the author on her Instagram:

@alimarie_writelife

Printed in the USA
CPSIA information can be obtained
at www.ICGtesting.com
JSHW021540030923
47753JS00003B/22